DISCARD

THE MISER

As Lesley Egan:

THE MISER
A CHOICE OF CRIMES
MOTIVE IN SHADOW
THE HUNTERS AND THE HUNTED
LOOK BACK ON DEATH
A DREAM APART
THE BLIND SEARCH
SCENES OF CRIME
PAPER CHASE
MALICIOUS MISCHIEF
IN THE DEATH OF A MAN
THE WINE OF VIOLENCE
A SERIOUS INVESTIGATION
THE NAMELESS ONES
SOME AVENGER, ARISE
DETECTIVE'S DUE
MY NAME IS DEATH
RUN TO EVIL
AGAINST THE EVIDENCE
THE BORROWED ALIBI
A CASE FOR APPEAL

As Elizabeth Linington:

CONSEQUENCE OF CRIME
NO VILLAIN NEED BE
PERCHANCE OF DEATH
CRIME BY CHANCE
PRACTISE TO DECEIVE
POLICEMAN'S LOT
SOMETHING WRONG
DATE WITH DEATH
NO EVIL ANGEL
GREENMASK!
THE PROUD MAN
THE LONG WATCH
MONSIEUR JANVIER
THE KINGBREAKER
ELIZABETH I (Ency. Brit.)

As Egan O'Neill:

THE ANGLOPHILE

As Dell Shannon:

CASE PENDING
THE ACE OF SPADES
EXTRA KILL
KNAVE OF HEARTS
DEATH OF A BUSYBODY
DOUBLE BLUFF
ROOT OF ALL EVIL
MARK OF MURDER
THE DEATH-BRINGERS
DEATH BY INCHES
COFFIN CORNER
WITH A VENGEANCE
CHANCE TO KILL
RAIN WITH VIOLENCE
KILL WITH KINDNESS
SCHOOLED TO KILL
CRIME ON THEIR HANDS
UNEXPECTED DEATH
WHIM TO KILL
THE RINGER
MURDER WITH LOVE
WITH INTENT TO KILL
NO HOLIDAY FOR CRIME
SPRING OF VIOLENCE
CRIME FILE
DEUCES WILD
STREETS OF DEATH
APPEARANCES OF DEATH
COLD TRAIL
FELONY AT RANDOM
FELONY FILE

THE MISER

LESLEY EGAN

PUBLISHED FOR THE CRIME CLUB BY
DOUBLEDAY & COMPANY, INC.
GARDEN CITY, NEW YORK
1981

First Edition

Library of Congress Catalog Card Number 80-2993
Copyright © 1981 by Doubleday & Company, Inc.
All Rights Reserved
Printed in the United States of America

This one is for
Elaine Bechtel
because she likes Jesse best

Perverse disputings of men of corrupt minds,
and destitute of the truth, supposing that
gain is godliness: from such withdraw thyself . . .
For we brought nothing into this world, and it
is certain we can carry nothing out.
And having food and raiment let us be therewith content.
But they that will be rich fall into temptation
and a snare, and into many foolish and hurtful
lusts, which drown men in destruction and perdition.
For the love of money is the root of all evil:
which while some coveted after, they have erred
from the faith, and pierced themselves through
with many sorrows.

                                    I Timothy 5–10

THE MISER

CHAPTER 1

Jesse had seen the old man only once, and that had been six and a half years ago. That had been in the rather dingy old office out on Vine Street, with Miss Williams ineffectually pottering around pretending to be a legal secretary; and in those days he had sometimes taken Saturday morning appointments, still building a practice. It had been a Saturday morning he had seen Jan Vanderveer.

When Miss Williams had peered into his office and said, "The eleven o'clock appointment's here, Mr. Falkenstein," he had gotten up automatically to welcome the new client. In the little anteroom was a tall old man and a youngish woman.

The old man stood up promptly; the woman half-rose and he turned on her peremptorily. "You just wait, Dulcie."

"Yes, Papa." She was perhaps in her early thirties, a plumpish brown-haired young woman, round-faced, nondescript.

The old man came into the office and sat down abruptly in the client's chair. He was tall and gaunt, once a powerful man but stooped a little with age; he had a keen hawk-nosed face, and his voice was sharp and sure. He was shabbily dressed in an old-fashioned gray suit with a vest, his shirt collar frayed. He regarded Jesse sardonically and said, "I'll bet you'll never guess why I picked you. Haven't had any dealings with a lawyer in years. Tried nine of 'em, see? Your gal quoted me the lowest price—thirty-five dollars to make a will."

Jesse returned the sardonic grin. "That's for a simple straightforward will, Mr. Vanderveer. Anything complicated, it might be more."

"Better not be—I got the firm quote. It'll be simple, all right." Vanderveer scowled and passed a hand over his largely bald head. "Howie said I ought to have a will, and he's right, but dammit, it's hell to know what to do. It is hell to get old, and nobody sensible to leave it to. If the wife had ever had a boy—but she never, just the two girls, and women are all fools about money. Hen-brained, the lot of them. I want it all left in trust, only thing to do, dammit."

Jesse prepared to take notes. "Damn it," said Vanderveer, interrupting his first question querulously, "it wouldn't make sense, appoint Howie—partners for thirty-seven years we were, but he's only five years younger than me. If he and Flo had ever had a boy—but they never had any at all. I don't trust banks more than halfway, but I know Semons at Security, he's an honest man and only forty-odd. Thought about it, and I guess that's the only thing to do. Everything in trust, that branch of Security-Pacific— Hollywood Boulevard." He sounded dissatisfied. He told Jesse the names of the legatees absently: his wife, Myra, his daughter Dulcie.

"You mentioned another daughter, Mr. Vanderveer?"

"Marcia. Hah. She needn't expect anything, running off with that damn lah-de-dah college professor. She's provided for—made her own bed."

Jesse regarded him soberly. "I'd advise you to leave her a token legacy at least," he said. "If you pass her over entirely, it could be grounds to contest the will—a direct blood heir." People did come all sorts.

"Hah!" said Vanderveer with a rather wolfish grin. "Marcia'd know better than that. But come to think"—he gnawed at a thumbnail thoughtfully—"could be that damn prissy professor might not. You think so, hah? Leave her a hundred dollars and it'd have to stand? All right, make it like that."

Jesse got the name, Mrs. Marcia Coleman, an address in Claremont. The Vanderveer address was on Kingsley in Hollywood. "And a list of the property—exactly what does it consist of?"

"None of your damned business," said Vanderveer testily. "You just put down, 'everything of which I die possessed'—that's the legal phrase, isn't it? Good enough?" Jesse admitted it would be legal, if not altogether desirable. "All right, you put it down like that. And that's all." His thin lips worked a little. "Hell to get old," he muttered. "Never made a will before, but Howie said I ought not to leave it. Otherwise the state taking a piece—damn government."

It would be a very simple will. Jesse told him it would be ready to sign on Monday. Vanderveer was annoyed at the delay, and had it pointed out to him that it was noon on Saturday and Jesse's secretary had other work to do. He got up stiffly and Jesse escorted him out. In the front office he said, "Say, one o'clock on Monday, we'll have it ready for you to sign."

"If that's the best you can do," said Vanderveer sourly.

The young woman spoke up placatingly. "I can't take a day off to drive you, Papa. Mr. Klein's expecting some important calls on Monday—you could take the bus."

Vanderveer said grudgingly, "Will say you're a conscientious gal—'s right, when you're working for a man, got to give full value." He gave Jesse a rather baleful stare. "The damn D.M.V. took away my license last month—said I couldn't pass the eye test. Damn nuisance—been driving sixty years without any trouble. All right. Monday." He stalked out, the young woman pattering after him, and Jesse went back to his desk to start drafting the simple will. People did come all sorts; but Mr. Vanderveer struck him as the prototype of the fellow of whom it was said, if he couldn't take it with him he wasn't going. Except that that was beyond the control of a mere mortal.

Vanderveer came in that Monday, read over the formal phrases carefully, and carefully signed the will in the large childish scrawl of the uneducated men unaccustomed to penmanship—Jan Willem Vanderveer. Jesse said routinely, "It ought to go in your safe-deposit box, if you have one—or if you prefer you can leave it with me."

Vanderveer ruminated. "I suppose you might as well keep it," he said. "Less trouble. All right." He handed the pages back and stood up.

Jesse had never seen the man again after he shuffled out of the office that day. And a good deal of water had flowed under the bridge since then. He and Nell had been married, and eighteen months ago David Andrew had been born. They had met that old reprobate Edgar Walters, who had died last year and left Jesse quite a respectable amount of money. And Nell had found the sprawling old house on an acre of ground up Coldwater Canyon Drive, and had been amusing herself remodeling and redecorating. These days Jesse was established in the new, larger office in the new building on Wilshire Boulevard, and pampered by his extremely efficient twin secretaries, Jean and Jimmy (Jamesina) Gordon. Clients and cases had come and gone, some dull and some interesting, and in his office safe reposed the wills of a few other clients who preferred the lawyer to have custody; and the name of Jan Vanderveer had faded from his mind.

Until last Monday when Jean had briefed him on the various appointments for the coming week and mentioned it. "The earliest I could fit him in was at three on Friday, there's that divorce hearing, and the Saunders' damage suit—you'll probably be in court on that up to Thursday."

"Vanderveer," said Jesse reflectively.

"He wouldn't say what it was about."

Jesse vaguely remembered the old fellow, wondering if it was the same one, and forgot about it. As he had expected, they had to postpone the court date on the Lenhoff divorce—Lenhoff's attorney was being sticky about the settlement. He was pleasantly surprised when the damage suit went to the jury early on Thursday afternoon—he had rather expected it to trail over into Friday.

As it was, he found himself at loose ends after lunch on Friday, with only one appointment—another client who wanted a divorce—at four-thirty, after Vanderveer. He was studying the latest counteroffer of Lenhoff's attorney—dammit, the man was worth five or six million, and Rose Lenhoff had put up with his drinking, womanizing, and physical abuse for twenty years, he wasn't going to fob her off with token alimony if Jesse could help it—when William DeWitt came in. He looked wet and annoyed. Southern California was evidently going to have another early wet year; at the end of October the second rainstorm had arrived yesterday, and it was drizzling again today. DeWitt, as tall and dark and lean as Jesse, divested himself of his raincoat and dumped an account book on Jesse's desk.

"Go through the motions," said Jesse, eying it. "There's never anything in it, William. Very modest little operation, yours is."

"Have to abide by the law," said DeWitt grumpily. He had finally severed professional connections with the Parapsychology Foundation and formed his own psychic research association; with some personal wealth and a few solid backers, he was happily engaged in, as he put it, redoing the basic research of a hundred years ago, with a couple of fairly gifted psychics; and Jesse had taken on the official job of treasurer. To maintain nonprofit status, the financial reports had to be made, but there was little work to it, the sums involved minuscule. Jesse shoved the account book to one side of his desk, and DeWitt sat down and lit a cigarette.

"People," he said. "People! I have had it with this Finch woman. Dammit, I'm sorry for her, but why do these people have to come wasting our time? Well, I can't say that exactly—"

"What about her?" asked Jesse. "You haven't mentioned that one before."

"That's right, she only showed up about three weeks back. Yesterday was her third session with Cora—no, fourth." Cora Delaney was one of the psychics working with him. "And an intelligent woman, too—she's a lawyer in Santa Monica—but the absolute materialist. She's lost a daughter—only child, girl in the teens, hit-run by a drunk driver—and she's divorced, alone, it hit her hard. She—"

"Wants some communication, proof the daughter's still there somewhere. Haven't any of your tame psychics brought anything through?"

"Dammit, it's never one hundred percent evidential—or seldom, as we both know. But both Cora and Wanda have given her some good solid stuff, better than you often get. An unusual pet name, childhood memories, a couple of dogs they'd had—what I'd call pretty evidential. And the damn woman—first she's in floods of tears, darling Lottie, and next minute it's no, I can't believe it, it's just telepathy, she's reading my mind—"

"People," said Jesse. "As if telepathy was all that common or easy. Makes you tired."

"At least we've got the records for the files," said DeWitt. "But it's annoying. Puts the medium off some. I brought along the transcript of yesterday's session, in case you're interested—really quite evidential when you analyze it—" He brought out an untidy bundle of typescript. Miss Duffy's copy from the tapes was impeccable, but DeWitt would cram it into his pockets instead of a briefcase. Jesse eyed it dubiously and said he'd look it over when he had time.

After half an hour or so DeWitt said he had an appointment with a psychologist at UCLA, and reluctantly took himself off into the rain. Jesse looked over those figures again, told Jean to get him Lenhoff's attorney, and spent forty minutes arguing with him, getting a few grudging concessions. When he put the phone down he glanced at the clock; it was twenty past three. He got up and looked out into the front office.

"Didn't we have somebody coming in at three?"

"Mr. Vanderveer," said Jimmy. "I wish people would be punctual—it throws all the routine out."

Jesse sat thinking about the Lenhoff settlement, and an unspecified time later Jean looked in and said, "He hasn't shown up yet. Should I call to remind him?"

"Who?" asked Jesse.

"Mr. Vanderveer," said Jean patiently. "It's a quarter of four, and sometimes people do forget appointments."

"Oh—yes, you'd better, I suppose," said Jesse absently.

She went away, and past the open door he heard her on the phone. Presently her voice went up in excitement. "Oh, yes, sir. Yes, sir, I see. . . . It's Mr. J. D. Falkenstein, Wilshire Boulevard, and of course— Oh, yes, sir, I'll tell him. . . . Jimmy! You'll never guess—" They both appeared at the office door, and Jean said, "Oh, Mr. Falkenstein—he's been murdered! That Mr. Vanderveer. That was a police officer answered the phone, and he said Mr. Vanderveer had been killed yesterday, and the police will want to talk to you. Of all things!"

"Well, I'll be damned," said Jesse mildly. But of course the crime rate was up, and a lot of innocent citizens were getting killed these days, with the violent ones running around loose. At that moment he wasn't greatly concerned over the murder; what entered his mind was that will. "It was Jan Vanderveer? Jan Willem?"

"Yes, that was the name—"

"And when he made the appointment, he didn't say why he wanted to see me? Well, I don't suppose it matters now. But dammit, it'll be some more paper work. We've got his will on file. I'll have to see the family, set up a date with the IRS and so forth, get the thing into probate." He felt the first stirrings of curiosity as to how the old man had gotten himself killed. "Murder?"

"That's what the officer said."

"Be damned," said Jesse again.

There wasn't anything more he could do on the Lenhoff thing today; he'd have to talk to Rose Lenhoff tomorrow, or, no, Monday, see how she felt about the latest offer. He had three divorce hearings set for next week, and there should be a court date set for that other damage suit, the Osborne thing, any day—that was going to occupy some time. It couldn't be helped. He could probably get some information about Vanderveer from Clock. He looked at his watch and decided he might as well go home, and left the Gordons chattering about the murder.

The new house was on a street called Paradise Lane, up Coldwater Canyon, and it was farther to drive from his office. The street was isolated, with only two other houses on it a distance away from the big old two-story house at the dead end. The house was on an acre of ground, with a chain-link fence all around it; Nell, expecting him home, had left the gate open, which meant that Athelstane was in. Jesse drove through the gate, got out and shut it, parked the Mercedes in the garage next to Nell's, and went in the back door to the generous old-fashioned service porch.

David Andrew, having mastered the art of walking six months ago, these days usually proceeded at a run; he came pounding across the kitchen excitedly. "Daddy! Kitten!" He hurled himself at Jesse. "Kitten!"

"Oh, my Lord, not now, Davy. Later." Of all the nursery rhymes Nell recited and sang to him, David Andrew had seized upon the three little kittens and their mittens as his all-time favorite and demanded repetition endlessly.

Nell straightened from the kitchen table and came to kiss him, his lovely Nell with her bright brown hair in its usual fat chignon on her neck, her cheeks a little flushed from the oven heat. "For once," she said, "he's not talking about those kittens. You'll never believe it, Jesse, but I've discovered Athelstane's secret."

They had moved in a month ago, and it was only last weekend that Jesse had finished shelving all the books and stereo records. Gradually they were settling in, and Nell had nearly stopped changing furniture around in the living room.

At first, when Athelstane, the mastiff, had taken to vanishing for hours at a time, they had supposed he was simply investigating his new domain. There was lawn and shrubbery at the front of the house, a good-sized covered patio, and a little more lawn at the back; but a good half acre there had been left wild, with a tall old stand of eucalyptus trees, a place any dog might spend time investigating. But Athelstane was a people-oriented dog, and when he continued to disappear for most of every afternoon, they had begun to be curious.

This afternoon it hadn't started raining until about one-thirty, and Nell had gone out after lunch, while Davy napped, to plant some bulbs she'd brought home yesterday. She was on her knees, working assiduously with a trowel, at the edge of the eucalyptus grove, when in the silence up here on the hill away from the city she heard Athelstane grunting. When Athelstane was feeling particularly happy and contented, he emitted soft little whuffles; and somewhere there in among the trees he was telling the world he was happy. Amused, Nell got up stealthily and began tracking him. Stepping softly, she followed the whuffles in the tall underbrush; and when she spotted him, for a moment she didn't believe what she saw.

Athelstane, for all his huge size and heft, was something of a retiring personality. He was scared to death of the Clocks' black Peke, Sally; he had never been on terms of friendship with another dog. But here he was now—Nell peered incredulously—uttering little pleased rumblings, and lovingly licking something between his enormous front paws. The brush was thick; Nell stepped closer, wondering if he could have caught and killed something—there'd be gophers up here, mice—and then suddenly she burst out laughing.

Athelstane had evidently made a friend. The object between his paws was, incredibly, a cat—by the glimpse she had, a Siamese cat, blissfully snuggled up against the great brindle chest. At her burst of laughter, the cat leaped convulsively and shot away under the trees, and Athelstane looked aggrieved.

"The big baby," said Nell now, telling Jesse about it. "You can't imagine how funny it looked. Quite a handsome Siamese from the little look I had, it must belong to someone around, one of the houses down the hill." Athelstane had pressed up to welcome Jesse, who pulled his ears fondly.

"Never know what the monster'll think of next. Queer, all right."

"Kittens!" said Davy insistently. "Fee kittens." He tugged at Jesse's trousers.

"Later on, Davy. Before bed."

"We've got time for a leisurely drink before dinner, after I get him to bed," said Nell. "Come on, big boy."

They had the leisurely drink, and dinner, and it was eight-thirty when Jesse settled at the desk in his study and picked up the phone. Just as he'd promised himself, in this house there was a comfortable chair beside every phone. He leaned back comfortably in the high-backed desk chair and dialed, and in a moment his little sister Fran answered.

"So you're feeling better?" asked Jesse.

"I'm always all right by evening," said Fran crossly. "It's the damned morning sickness—everybody says I should have been over it months ago, but the doctor says it's just my metabolism or something and not to worry. So easy for him to say. The longer this goes on, the more I'm thinking this is going to be an only child."

Jesse laughed. "Wait till it's here."

"I can hardly wait. Two more months to go! And I look worse than I feel." Of course Fran was normally svelte and slim and fashionable, and she didn't appreciate maternity clothes.

"Is Andrew home?"

"I'll get him." And a minute later the deep rough voice of Sergeant Clock, LAPD, Hollywood Precinct, replaced hers.

"That damn doctor," it said. "I'm worried about Fran, Jesse. She's feeling like hell, this damned morning sickness or whatever, and that doctor—"

"Now, Andrew. He's supposed to be one of the best around, I suppose he knows what he's doing. Preserve patience and keep the fingers firmly crossed. I want to know something about a homicide. It's your beat"—the Vanderveer address was Kingsley Drive—"so you probably know something about it. One Jan Vanderveer."

"Oh, that," said Clock. "What's your interest?"

"He had an appointment with me this afternoon. I don't know what was on his mind—I'd only seen him once, years ago, made a will for him. When he didn't show, Jean called, and found the fuzz in possession."

"Oh," said Clock. "Well, I'm on it, yes—Petrovsky and I got

called right at the end of shift yesterday. The daughter came home
from work and found them—both Vanderveer and his wife dead. It
looks like a run-of-the-mill thing—and that's the hell of a comment
on modern city life, but there it is. There doesn't seem to have
been a break-in, but I suppose the old man could have opened the
door, and he or they just bulled their way in. Right now I'm bet-
ting it was juveniles, maybe a pair."

"Why?"

"There wasn't any ransacking of drawers and so on. The lab's
still poking around dusting for prints, something may show. Of
course the daughter was pretty shocked and shook up, but we
asked her to look around for anything missing and she didn't
come up with anything. My bet is that it was juveniles, maybe with
petty records or no records, and they panicked and ran when they
realized what they'd done. It has that kind of smell."

"How were they killed?"

"Banged around and beat up—we won't see autopsy reports for
a while, but that was obvious. And I don't suppose it would have
taken much, they were both elderly and frail. Kind of thing that
could happen without intention. The old woman was evidently
partly crippled, she used a walker. She'd been knocked away from
it against a wall. It looked as if he might have tried to put up a
fight. The poker out of the fireplace set was alongside him with
blood on it—maybe he grabbed it up and somebody got it away
from him, or when he tried to put up resistance they, whoever,
went for it as a weapon. There were things around could have
been hocked for a little loot—portable TV, typewriter, but none of
it was missing."

"Yes, I see," said Jesse. "And I suppose not a hope in hell of
any leads on it."

"All up in the air. That's a working-class neighborhood, not
many people at home during the day, and it was raining like hell
most of yesterday. We'll go through the motions, but it'll probably
end up in Pending."

"The hell of a thing all right," agreed Jesse. "But what I'm really calling about—I'll have to get in touch with this daughter. Immediate family. Find out about his bank, start the red tape. Do
you know if the daughter—"

"Well, she was all shook up, naturally," said Clock. "We got a

policewoman up, and she called some relative for her—a sister, I
think—and then a Mrs. Griffin showed up and took her off. I
meant to talk to her sometime today, but we had a gang rumble go
down at Hollywood High—just a second, I've got both addresses
in my notebook." There was a hiatus. "Lessee—the Griffin woman
lives in West Hollywood, Harratt Street. The sister's Marcia Coleman, it's an address in Claremont. Mrs. Charles Coleman."

"O.K., thanks. I think you're supposed to be coming to dinner
some night next week, if Fran feels up to it."

"I tell you, I don't like it at all, she's seven months along and
she shouldn't—" Jesse heard Fran in the background sounding annoyed; and then she came back on the line and said, "If you're
finished with Andrew I want to talk to Nell."

"All right." Jesse put the phone down and called Nell, who said
she'd take it on the kitchen extension.

While he waited for the girls to finish chatting, he slid farther
down in the desk chair and reflected, the hell of a thing indeed.
Inoffensive old people peacefully in their own home, set on suddenly by the violent ones. Killed for nothing and no reason—and
that could have been the juveniles, not yet quite hardened enough
to go on and rob when they saw they had done murder. A very
elderly couple indeed, they'd have been—Vanderveer had probably
been in his mid-seventies those years ago.

And the odds were, no leads on who had done it. And he
thought, Kingsley Drive—a very plebeian address. The chances
were the old man hadn't had much; it would be a piddling little estate to settle, just the red tape and paper work.

When the phone finally hummed blankly at him, he dialed the
number in West Hollywood, explained. The voice on the other
end was high and girlish. "Oh, what did you say your name— Are
you police, or— Oh, the *lawyer!* Oh, yes. Isn't it the most dreadful,
dreadful thing—I just couldn't believe it, but the awful things that
happen nowadays—when Marcia called, I just couldn't take it in—I
went *right down*—that police station on Fountain Avenue, you
know—of course it would take Marcia nearly two hours to drive
up—but she and Charles *came,* of course, but of course they took
Dulcie back with them—the house—the police were there, and Dulcie said there was blood—oh, it's just too dreadful— What? Oh,

I'm actually not a relative, just an old friend, my husband and Johnny Vanderveer were partners and of course—"

Jesse got away from her at last and called the Claremont number. Here he got a very different female, who sounded tired but crisply efficient. Mrs. Marcia Coleman. She also sounded surprised. "Oh, yes," she said. "You said Falkenstein? But I don't— how did you know? There isn't anything in the papers—" Jesse explained about the appointment, and she said, "Papa had an appointment—I don't understand. It's very odd you should call just now, you know, because it wasn't half an hour ago that Dulcie remembered Papa had made a will, but she couldn't remember your name."

"I'll want to see both of you, Mrs. Coleman, when it's convenient. We'll have to sort out the estate, start probate. There's no special hurry, I realize you're both upset— Do you know if your father kept a safe-deposit box?"

"Yes, probably. He must have, of course. He banked at Security-Pacific, I'm not sure which branch."

"I'll have to set up a date with the IRS, you see. I know this seems like an intrusion at such a time, but—"

"But," said Marcia Coleman dryly, "life goes on and the red tape has to get tied up. Yes. I understand that."

"Your sister would know definitely which bank?"

"Mr. Falkenstein," she said, "I'm not going to wake her up to ask her now. She's been through a very bad time for the last year or so, and she's exhausted—the shock of finding Mama and Papa murdered was just enough to put her right over the edge. I got my doctor to prescribe some sleeping capsules for her today, and she's knocked out. The police want to talk to her too, naturally, but it'll just have to wait. Maybe Monday we can come to your office."

He didn't know offhand what appointments he had on Monday; if there was a conflict one of the Gordons would have to sweet-talk another client. He agreed to a suggested two o'clock meeting, and she thanked him and rang off briskly.

When they came into his office at two o'clock on Monday afternoon, he thought at first glance that they were very unlike to be sisters; and then he realized that they were alike—it was the contrast of clothes and manner that differentiated them. Marcia Coleman looked to be in her mid-thirties, and was neatly and smartly dressed in a well-cut navy suit with an ivory tailored blouse. Her dark brown hair was smoothly, smartly cut, her makeup discreet; she was a good-looking woman, with regular features, intelligent blue eyes, a generous mouth. Her sister might be a few years older, and she had the same regular features, small straight nose, brown hair, and blue eyes; but she was plumper, and gracelessly dressed in a dowdy-looking beige knit dress, low-heeled oxfords, a too-large camel's-hair coat. She said correctly, "How do you do," in a dull voice, and obediently took the chair indicated. Marcia Coleman sat down beside her.

"We'd better get right to business," she told Jesse. "But I'm afraid neither of us can be much help to you. We don't know at all what Papa had, how much, or what it was—except for the houses he owned. But I expect you'll find accounts or something in the safe-deposit box."

"He kept an account book at home," said Dulcie. "I've seen it. I don't know where he kept it, though."

"His desk probably," said Marcia. And then, unexpectedly: "Oh, God, it's Mama—to think of that happening to her— And didn't we tell him! Didn't we try to tell him!" She drew a long breath. "Going on living in that neighborhood—but nobody could talk to Papa." She opened her bag, got out a cigarette, and lit it before he could reach for his lighter. "Oh, I suppose you think it sounds pretty cold and crude, Mr. Falkenstein, but Papa—he just wasn't a man anybody could be fond of, he didn't—"

"Except Uncle Howie," said Dulcie.

"Oh—" Marcia shrugged. "Yes, of course, but they'd known each other so long, they'd been young together."

Dulcie looked at her and a large tear slowly slid down one cheek; she got out a handkerchief and wiped it away. "Oh, Marcia, it's just—I can't stop thinking about it—how sort of pitiful it was. He aged five years when Uncle Howie died, and ever since then—you know how I've told you it's been, the last couple of months—he just hasn't been himself—Uncle Howie was really the only close friend he ever had—and how he kept saying, we'd be better out of it, your mother and I—and Mama—" She put the handkerchief to her mouth.

"Oh, God, I know," said Marcia.

Dulcie raised her eyes to Jesse's. "I don't know how many times Mama's said to me, I wish I could die and be at rest—but to have it happen—like that—"

"It's no good talking about it, Dulcie. It happened. And, my God, it's a terrible thing to say, Mr. Falkenstein—it's a terrible thing even to think—but at least it is a solution. We'd been feeling rather desperate—and after that awful row a week ago Saturday, the things Charles said to Papa—of course just the plain truth—I've had nightmares about it." She fumbled for another cigarette; she'd stabbed the first one out half-smoked; this time Jesse held his lighter for her.

"It wasn't anybody's fault," said Dulcie tiredly. "Just how Papa was."

"That sums it up neatly," said Marcia. "I suppose you think we're pretty—unfilial, if that's the word. That I am, anyway. But another month of it and Dulcie'd have been in the hospital with a nervous breakdown or whatever it's called now. What the situation was, Mr. Falkenstein—Papa must have been a very wealthy man. I don't mean a multimillionaire, but there must be quite a lot of money somewhere. He and Uncle Howie—Howard Griffin—had their own construction company for over thirty-five years, and they bought and sold land, apartment houses, I don't know what all—with the building boom after the Second World War they must have made a lot of money. But Papa never spent a dime more than he had to—he was always tightfisted and of course he just got worse as he got older." She gestured fiercely. "Uncle Howie used to—to kid him about it, but—men!—he never realized how it was for us, and anyway even he couldn't change Papa. He—Uncle Howie, I mean—that's how you can judge it, because they were equal partners until they dissolved the business about fifteen years ago, and retired. Uncle Howie and Aunt Flo had that beautiful house in West Hollywood, and good furniture, and nice cars, and they went out to theaters and—oh, Uncle Howie wasn't extravagant, but they always had nice things and—lived like civilized people. Anybody could tell there was money, big money even. And Papa must have had just as much, maybe more, because I've heard Uncle Howie say Papa was a smarter investor than he was—and what did we have?" She was wound up now, her tone bitter. "Nothing! Even when Dulcie and I were kids, Aunt Flo had a cleaning woman and her own car—and when I think how Mama had to slave—the fuss he made about buying a washing machine! And that house on Kingsley—my God, most of old central Hollywood running down for years, the crime rate up, but he wouldn't hear of moving. The house was good enough, taxes cheap compared to anywhere else, he had good locks, and what did it matter where you lived?

"You just summed it up, Dulcie—just how Papa was. But it was all his fault, obviously." Marcia drew strongly on her cigarette. "You see, Mr. Falkenstein, they weren't young when they were married—Mama and Papa. Papa'd been married and divorced before. He was forty, and Mama was only a year younger. Papa would have been eighty-two next month. And his parents were old country, and Papa was pretty old country too. Females just for waiting on men, and doing housework. My God, when I wanted to go to college—foolishness for a girl, he'd never gone to high school and he'd gotten on all right—I stood up to him, and when I got my first job I got out. And then when I worked to earn my own way at LACC, and met Charles who was a college *teacher,* you'd have thought I wanted to marry a queer or— But forget about me. It was Dulcie who came in for the brunt of it.

"Papa's arthritis was getting worse all the time—he could hardly get around some days, and he would go on trying to take the bus, too cheap to take a cab, he'd had a couple of bad falls lately. Lucky not to break a hip, I suppose. But Mama—she had her first stroke five years ago, and then another last year, and she had arthritis too, and when Papa found out Medicare wouldn't pay for the therapy, he said she didn't need it. They'd gotten her walking with the walker, but she couldn't do much. Dulcie had it all, you see? She works a regular job, and on top of that she had all the housework and cooking and taking care of Mama—I was no help at all, I'm an hour and a half away on the freeway, Charles is at Pomona College, and we've got four children, fourteen down to six—I've got to be at home. I couldn't help at all. And Mama needing more and more attention—and he couldn't see it—"

"It was just," said Dulcie, "that I had to be up with her so much at night. She couldn't help it. We got the bedside commode for at night, and the last six months I slept in her room, Papa moved into the den—she couldn't help getting me up three or four times a night, she didn't sleep very well."

"And try to talk to him!" said Marcia. "Oh, Dulcie could manage! She always had! They had the visiting nurse coming in—you know that county service—three times a week, to give Mama a bath and a hot lunch, do a little cleaning up—that helped. But it couldn't have gone on—Mama could manage to get to the bathroom, even make a cup of coffee, but she was getting worse, it was obvious that there'd come a time she'd be bedridden—it was just the week before last that that nurse, I forget her name—"

"Mrs. Gibson," said Dulcie. "It was just, you see, I didn't feel it was fair to Mr. Klein. I've worked for Mr. Klein for twenty years, since I was nearly nineteen, and he's been good to me. Sometimes I felt so queer, as if I wasn't all there, if I'd been up a lot with Mama, and I made mistakes in taking phone calls and writing orders—"

"This Mrs. Gibson," said Marcia, "called Dulcie and said we should realize that Mama would have to be in a convalescent home pretty soon, she'd be helpless and need attention around the clock—but Papa simply wouldn't listen. And what could we do? He said those places cost too damn much money and he wasn't going to pay for any such folderols. With Dulcie about to die of exhaustion—and I couldn't do a thing—and we know he had plenty of money to take care of her properly, what's money for except to keep you comfortable, buy necessities? But you just couldn't talk to Papa!"

"I see," said Jesse. "Frustrating."

"Oh, for the Lord's sake, water under the bridge," said Marcia, leaning back. "I'm sorry for the tirade. And it's a terrible way for it to end—but maybe you can see why I said it's a solution. Except for Mama—" She leaned forward to stub out her cigarette.

"I could have managed awhile longer," said Dulcie.

"My darling idiot, you were managing yourself to death. Look, Mr. Falkenstein. Neither of us knows much about what Papa had, or where it was, except that he owned two houses down there, one on Kingsley and one right behind his house, on Winona, and an apartment up on Fountain. He always went to collect those rents himself. The bank's the nearest Security-Pacific on Hollywood Boulevard." She stood up. "And you'll want to go through his desk, look at his account book. The police called this morning to say they were through at the house, and they sent back everything Papa'd had on him—when it happened. We can let you have his keys. You just go ahead and do whatever has to be done. I'm keeping Dulcie with me for a while, and you've got the address."

Jesse verified the safe-deposit box and duly contacted the local IRS office to set up a date for the official opening on the following Thursday afternoon. He had, by then, had a further annoying session with Lenhoff's attorney, and was about to leave the office for a quick lunch before foregathering with an IRS man at the bank when Jimmy put through a phone call.

"Oh, Jesse," said Clock. "I thought it'd be only neighborly to let you know that the D.A.'s office is probably going to charge one of your clients with homicide. At least I suppose you could call her a client."

"For God's sake," said Jesse. "Who the hell are you talking about?"

"Miss Dulcie Vanderveer," said Clock. He sounded irritated. "For once I seem to have been wrong. Some very funny evidence has turned up. I haven't had the definite word yet, but the assistant D.A. I talked it over with bought the case. It's offbeat, but—considering human nature—what you might call persuasive. If they bring the charge, it'll be Murder One, I think."

"My good God in heaven," said Jesse blankly. "What in God's name is the evidence?"

"I'll be happy to discuss it with you," said Clock. "Something very funny, Jesse."

CHAPTER 2

Jesse was still feeling somewhat stunned when he got to the bank; he'd hear what Clock had to say later. The IRS man was waiting for him, a fat middle-aged fellow by the name of Dobson. On Monday, Marcia Coleman had handed over the official little bag containing the effects from Vanderveer's body, including a ring of keys: a Yale house key and the long, narrow, warded key to a safe-deposit box marked 1370. On Monday, Jesse had duly verified the rental of safe-deposit box 1370 at this branch of the Security-Pacific bank and notified them of Vanderveer's death.

He fished the keys out of the little bag now, handed them over to Dobson. A blond woman led them into the vault incuriously.

It was everyday routine to the IRS man. The blonde used her key on the little door, he handed over the other, and she pulled out a good-sized steel box—one of the larger ones available. They took it into one of the cubicles and opened it.

"A very nice little pile," said Dobson five minutes later and opened a notebook and began to write busily, making a list.

Jesse regarded the loot in some fascination. It was a nice pile indeed. There was a fat sheaf of stock certificates, mostly preferred stock, and in respectacle blocks of a hundred, five hundred, a thousand shares—IBM, Sony, General Electric, Southern Pacific, New England Electric, Pacific Telephone, General Telephone, Texaco, Mobil Oil, Royal Dutch Airlines, Toyota— "Beautiful," said Dobson gratefully, making rapid notes.

There were deeds to four pieces of property, two houses on Kingsley Drive, one on Winona Avenue, one on Fountain Avenue. Which said that the property was free of mortgage, clear. There was a marriage certificate dated May of 1940, for Myra Ellis and Jan W. Vanderveer. And that was all; it seemed to be enough.

"I'll have to get current quotes on the stock," said Dobson, "but I'd estimate it as at least upwards of a million at current prices. All such very solid stuff, blue-chip, it'd have been paying very well."

"In spades," said Jesse. He shouldn't be feeling surprised about Vanderveer; that kind of careful, shrewd old fellow, the sort who did amass the money—and now and then got murdered for it. Dobson made copious notes, gave Jesse a copy of the list of contents, and an official release of the box to the estate. They proceeded upstairs to see the bank manager and request a look at Vanderveer's current account. The manager was a friendly-faced middle-aged man named Olderson, cooperative and amiable. This kind of thing was routine to him too: bank patrons died every day. He offered them cigarettes, then got on the phone to the chief teller.

Jesse reflected that at least he had put a clause in that will making Dulcie Vanderveer the residual legatee if the mother predeceased her— Dulcie. He conjured up the plump little figure with the oddly innocent eyes, feeling incredulous. But the most unexpected things did happen; and Clock knew all about the rules of evidence.

The chief teller was a sedate man of about fifty, rotund and bland and bald; his name was Parker. He acknowledged introductions with a nod and laid a manila folder on Olderson's desk.

"I hope this wasn't too much trouble," said Olderson pleasantly, meaninglessly.

Parker leaned on the desk and brought out a cigarette, eying Jesse and Dobson thoughtfully. "Oh, no, it's a very simple account. Always has been. Old Vanderveer's dead, is he?" He looked at the cigarette. "Natural causes, as they say?"

"As a matter of fact, no," said Jesse.

"Is that so? I'm not asking any questions," said Parker equably. "But—well, have a look at that latest statement, and I'll tell you something." It looked like a simple account indeed; there were just the latest posted figures here. Vanderveer had had only a checking account, and at the moment there was slightly under three thousand dollars in it. In the last month—they were coming up to the first of November—there had been just three checks written on it, in the sums of $67.10, $19.47, and $17.40.

"Yes?" said Jesse. "You've got something to tell us about the account?"

Parker blew out a thin stream of smoke. "I don't know if it means anything, but—well, I've been chief teller here for fourteen years. We've got a lot of customers, and the average account just gets posted and recorded automatically, nothing to notice, if you take me. But I could tell you something, not so much about the account, but the old man. Vanderveer used to deal in quite large sums of cash—you see, the girls would have to come to me for verification, pay out that much—or take in that much, come to that. I've known him to come in here and hand over ten, twenty, thirty thousand for a cashier's check."

"You don't say," said Dobson interestedly. Olderson sat up with a jerk.

"My God, man—did he ever offer any explanation, or—"

"Well, look," said Parker, "it was unusual, but what could I say to him? The first couple of times I said to him that walking around with that much cash wasn't very safe, and he snapped my head off—it was his own money and he'd handle it any way he damn well pleased." Parker shrugged. "It was his business—but naturally I wondered. He'd bring in dividend checks, other checks, and take cash—quite sizable amounts. Walk out of here with a couple of thousand on him in twenties. I just thought," said Parker cynically, "it could be he was one of those types—you read about one in the paper every so often—found dead of starvation or something, with a hundred grand in a suitcase in the closet."

"I will be goddamned," said Dobson avidly. Jesse surmised that Vanderveer's record with the IRS would be examined with a fine-tooth comb.

"You remember the last time anything like that happened?" he asked.

"Oh, I couldn't say exactly, it'll show in the accounts, but sometime back in the spring he bought a cashier's check for something like thirty grand, and paid for it in cash."

"My God," said Dobson, scribbling.

"Had he banked here long?" asked Jesse.

"Before my time," said Parker. "Probably. He had a big loan with us too, the records came through on his statement every month. I don't know anything about that."

Who did know was one of the officers in the loan department, Peter J. Metcalf. He was a spare elderly man with the banker's

proverbial gimlet eye, and at his word a pretty, dark secretary conjured up the records in short order.

The loan had been applied for and granted seven years back, and it amounted to just under a million dollars at the time. "Probably appreciated in value since," said Metcalf, "the property that is—in that location, Trousdale Estates." The property consisted of a twelve-unit apartment building in that very exclusive area, and Vanderveer had put down a tenth of the purchase price, getting the rest from the bank. The entire profit was applied to the loan monthly; the bank was handling it as a routine matter, billing for rents and paying the taxes, maintenance, and so on. "Of course it made a useful tax shelter," said Metcalf, eying the figures. "Interest and depreciation, et cetera. The principal wouldn't have been paid off for another twenty years, but meanwhile it was money in his pocket."

Dobson went off with a notebook full of figures. And Jesse should sometime see the officers of the trust department here, about that will; but until he knew exactly what was going to happen about that will, there wasn't much point.

It was four o'clock when he found a slot in a public lot up on Fountain and walked back to the new precinct station.

And his head was still full of figures—the monthly net take on that apartment house was fourteen thousand bucks; the house property in Hollywood would bring in a more modest return, he'd have to investigate that too, but together with those very solid dividends which would have been coming in from all that blue-chip preferred stock— A very cute old fellow, Jan Vanderveer, and Jesse could appreciate how Dulcie and Marcia had felt. Such a lot of nice money, and the old boy too tightfisted to hire a practical nurse or pay for his wife's care in a decent rest home. Well, they hadn't known how much he had, just that it was probably a tidy bundle; and so it was. That stock—Jesse didn't follow the market, and it had been up and down for the last year or so, but still—that kind of stock—

Where moth and rust doth corrupt, he thought, going in past the desk sergeant. Indeed, what was it but a medium of exchange? Hoarded for its own sake, it was meaningless, you could say; he thought of Marcia Coleman saying, what's money for?

What indeed, he thought ruefully. They had spent quite a lot of money, the money the old man had left, on Nell's house up on the hill; Jesse would rather have old Edgar back; but he knew how old Edgar would feel—money was to enjoy and use.

The big communal detective office at the rear of the precinct station, overlooking the parking lot, was starkly lighted with overhead fluorescent strip lighting. It was at the moment nearly empty; only Clock and Detective Petrovsky were there, heads together over a report.

"Well, I expected to see you sooner," said Clock.

Jesse pulled up a chair from a nearby desk and sat down. "I had an appointment with the Gestapo. But now suppose you give me chapter and verse on your funny story." He lit a cigarette and leaned back.

"It is a sort of queer one at that," said Petrovsky. His shortish rotund sandiness was in direct contrast to Clock, whose broad figure filled the desk chair. "But it hangs together, Mr. Falkenstein."

Clock passed a hand over his prognathous jaw and said, "You can say so." He looked annoyed. "Damnation, it looked like random violence—God knows we see enough of it—until a few funny things showed up. All right, you want to hear the evidence, it's easy to read. We talked to both the daughters at the time—Saturday, wasn't it, Pete?—not at length, but enough to get the picture. The unmarried one, Dulcie, was in a difficult spot, the mother to take care of, working a regular job, the old lady getting more helpless. That was just background, because of course at the time it looked like the possible juveniles, the random thing. But—"

"Yes," said Jesse, "and all the more frustrating because Vanderveer could have afforded the best hired help. He was loaded."

"Oh?" said Clock interestedly. "And everything left to the family?"

Jesse gave him a mirthless grin. "Depending on your evidence, I suppose the D.A.'ll be pleased to hear that most of it goes to Dulcie. And it won't impress you that I doubt very much if she knows it. What, for God's sake, have you turned up to tie her in?"

Clock said, "You don't say." He took up a large manila envelope centered on his desk and reached into it. "I've just got this packaged up to send to the D.A.'s office, don't suppose there's any harm in your seeing it. The first thing that showed—the lab men were still at the house poking around, you know what a hell of a time they take—was this." He handed it to Jesse. It was a small sheet of cheap stationery, with one typed line roughly in its center: *We are better out of it.* Jesse cocked his head at it. "The paper's from a box in Dulcie's room, and it was typed on her portable typewriter there. The note was under the grate in the fireplace. You know, that was a cold rainy day, and there'd been a fire lit there. It looks as if she thought it'd be burned, but it drifted under the grate and wasn't. But that's getting ahead of the evidence. When we got the autopsy reports, we did some rethinking. What it comes down to—usual bunch of six-syllable words—they'd both had an O.D. of the old lady's pain-killer prescription. It's some stuff called Ban Cap codeine capsules—the doctor prescribed it for her arthritis. The prescription had been renewed four days before the murder, so there was plenty available. Dulcie had gotten it refilled the previous Monday, at a pharmacy on Fountain. Both the old people had had a hot drink—eggnog for the old lady, cup of coffee for him—the glass and cup were still there, and used utensils in the kitchen, eggbeater, spoon, saucepan. The lab found traces of the stuff on everything. Both drinks had been laced with enough to kill. As a matter of fact that's what the old lady died of. Him, no. But you know, Jesse, we might have bought it, she might have gotten away with it. There was a little suggestion that the old man had thought of suicide. That pharmacist—sometimes Vanderveer got the prescription refilled, and the pharmacist said he'd heard him say people could live too long and they'd be better out of it at his age. This Griffin, Vanderveer's oldest friend, had just died in a convalescent home a couple of months ago, and apparently Vanderveer missed him, had been hit hard by that—he used to visit him every day. Of course it says nothing that Dulcie's prints were on the eggnog glass—she was doing the housework—but for what it's worth there they are, one good one, one not so good."

"Now really, Andrew—you're calling this evidence?"

"Just some. You see, we've got her placed there," said Clock. "She usually left home for work about eight-fifteen, got home a little after five-thirty. But that day she was seen to come home about ten-thirty in the morning. She works for a Bernard Klein, office down on North Spring, he's a salesman of some kind and it's a one-girl office. He's in and out, and he was going to be out most of that day, and she knew that. The other office people on that floor don't mingle—nobody would miss her. It was a dark rainy day, and a lot of people on that block on Kingsley would be at work—the Vanderveers didn't neighbor with anybody there, it isn't that kind of neighborhood. The chances were she wouldn't be noticed at all—but she was, just by a fluke. There's an apartment building next to the Vanderveer house, and this old fellow Richard Eberhart lives in the rear ground-floor unit on that side, his back door overlooks the Vanderveer drive. He says he saw her drive into the garage about ten-thirty that morning—swears he recognized her and her car."

"You can see how it was supposed to look," said Petrovsky. "She comes home with some excuse of Klein giving her the day off, and neither of the old folks pay any attention to what she's doing—she fixes the eggnog and coffee, slips in the overdose, and types out the suicide note. Intending to leave it propped up somewhere, and go back downtown, find the bodies when she comes home at the usual time. Only the old man must have realized what she was up to, maybe got a look at that note—and there was a struggle, and she snatched up the poker and hit him. The old lady"—Petrovsky sniffed thoughtfully—"from the photos we can deduce she was in the bedroom—where the eggnog glass was—maybe she heard the fight, was coming to see what was going on, and either fell from the walker and knocked herself out against the table or the girl knocked her down too. They both had O-type blood, which was on the poker. But she died of the O.D., anywhere between one and four. He died right then of a skull fracture. Call it eleven A.M."

"And," said Clock, "seeing the suicide setup was ruined, she threw the note in the fire and ran. Hoping, probably, that we'd put it down to the daylight burglar—but I'm inclined to think that by then she was pretty well unnerved, which would be understandable, or she'd have at least tried to fake a break-in. As it was, she just panicked."

"Now I will be damned," said Jesse. "It hangs together—but queer all the same, Andrew. No prints on the poker, I suppose."

"Not a hope."

"No, but that prim little soul—don't tell me, murderers don't conform to any type. And human nature, yes—what the sister said —maybe she wasn't altogether responsible. Tired out, going without sleep, not seeing any way out of the tangle—and resenting the old man's attitude, also understandable. Naturally. The girls both seemed fond of the mother, but not of him. With good reason. And—another thing she said—mother wishing she could die and be at rest— It could all have boiled up in her overnight, and she saw how it could be set up—not in her right mind, maybe. A psychiatrist might say—"

Clock laughed. "Is that the defense you'd put to a judge?"

"Not much criminal practice," said Jesse, brooding over his steepled hands. "I don't know if I'd take on the job of defending her, Andrew. But I can see that happening all right. A damnable thing. And what has she got to say about it? Have you questioned her since all this showed?"

"No," said Clock. "We just got the autopsy reports yesterday morning, and kicked it around with the lieutenant, and went out looking around Klein's office—"

"We heard Eberhart's story on Tuesday," said Petrovsky, "but it didn't seem important until we heard about the times of death. We'd been out asking any neighbors at home if they'd noticed anybody at the house that Thursday, naturally—drew a blank until we got to Eberhart."

"We'll be talking to her to get some answers," said Clock. "I'm bringing her in tomorrow morning. And you never know—she might come apart and admit it right off the bat. But I think the D.A.'s office has more or less decided to bring a charge. It might be Murder Two, of course."

Jesse drove home feeling sad and also uneasy. Thinking of those two women in his office last Monday—Dulcie's reactions just what anybody might expect, perfectly natural— But he didn't know the woman, after all; and most women were born natural actors. But she hadn't struck him as a very complicated woman— of course it hadn't been a very complicated crime. And it could be, as Clock said, that confronted with the evidence, she'd admit it readily. Didn't know what she was doing—or claiming a mercy killing. Human nature, he thought. And that shrewd single-minded old man, supremely unconscious of his narrow despotism, bringing it on himself—

He was late. Nell had just gotten the baby to bed; and it was cool enough for a fire in the living-room fireplace. They had a leisurely drink before dinner, and Athelstane leaned his bulk on Jesse's legs and had his ears fondled. "He was out there all afternoon again," said Nell amusedly. "I think he's fallen in love with that cat—it's too absurd." Jesse agreed absently, and she cocked her head at him. "You're worried about something, or just mulling over a case?"

"Just brooding on human nature." He told her about Vanderveer, and she was horrified.

"But what an awful thing, Jesse—the poor woman—"

"Yes, you can see how it could have happened, in a way. Without excusing her. And dammit, even if she's convicted on a lesser charge, second or third degree, nobody can profit by a crime—there may be some litigation over the old man's loot. Marcia Coleman would have to get that will set aside as the next blood relative. It's a hell of a thing all right."

He had two divorce hearings on Friday morning, but both were straightforward and brief; he was out of court by noon, and back at the office by one-thirty. Fifteen minutes after he came in, Jimmy put through a call, and it was Marcia Coleman. Her voice was frantic, with overtones of panic.

"—got to see you, I never in my life expected anything so wild as this—the police think *Dulcie* had something to do with it—stupid *cops*—but she ought to have a lawyer—and Charles says—I don't *believe* this, but—Charles said to—"

Jesse was just about to start drafting a new will for an old client, but he hadn't any appointments the rest of the day, and agreed to see them. They landed there hardly an hour later; whoever was driving must have broken some speed laws on the freeway.

Charles Coleman shook hands formally and said with a forced smile, "Shall we say a family crisis seemed to warrant canceling my afternoon classes." He was a tall fair man with a quiet voice, a quiet manner; his eyes were watchful.

"But it's just wild!" Marcia burst out. "I don't believe it—sending a police car, they kept her there all morning—those stupid cops —when she told me what they said, what they asked—"

"Marcia," said Coleman, and she subsided. "I must say we can't understand this at all, Mr. Falkenstein. This is supposed to be a competent police force, I shouldn't think they would act without evidence."

"No," said Jesse. He got them to sit down, offered cigarettes. He opened his mouth to tell them something about the evidence, but Dulcie, silent until then, forestalled him. She was looking more animated than he had seen her before, with color in her cheeks, and her voice was fuller and stronger.

"Mr. Falkenstein," she said, "I just want to say that they're wrong. I couldn't take it in at first, what they were talking about, why they were asking me all that—but when I realized what they were thinking, I was just so surprised. Not even frightened—just surprised. How could anyone think such a thing? That I could ever do a thing like that? I just don't understand it. But that big officer kept asking the same things over and over, and he kept saying, clear evidence—they asked all sorts of queer things, about my learning to type, and Mama's prescription—"

"Yes," said Jesse. He sat down in his desk chair. "You'd better hear about the evidence—I've talked with the sergeant." He told them about the autopsy reports, the fake suicide note, Eberhart. Against his expectations, it was Marcia who began to cry and protest incoherently. Coleman just looked wary and more watchful.

And Dulcie just sat and looked at him. She was dressed a little more smartly today, in a dark-blue dress. He hadn't noticed how square her little chin was, or the firmness of her rather wide mouth. And she said, cutting across his voice without apology, "But I didn't do that, Mr. Falkenstein. Believe me, I'd never, never have thought of doing such a thing. Do they think I'm insane, even to think about such a thing?"

Jesse said equably, softly, "That could be a line of defense, Miss Vanderveer."

She thrust her chin at him. "For heaven's sake," she said, "I'd been awfully tired, never enough sleep, but I knew what I was doing all the while! I'm not so crazy or plain wicked as ever to have thought of that. I don't know anything about that note, but I certainly didn't come back home that morning, and I don't know anything about what happened." Her voice was strong and sure and oddly calm.

"What about Eberhart's story, Miss Vanderveer?"

"They kept on and on about that, they told me I'd been seen coming back—they didn't tell me who'd said so, and I'm afraid I was just confused at first, all the questions about different things—those two officers, the big man with the big jaw and the other one, they kept asking the same questions and after a while I began to see what they were thinking, and I was just so surprised. But when they kept saying that, that I'd been seen coming back that morning, all of a sudden I remembered—a couple of days before that, it was Tuesday, I'd forgotten my keys to the office and had to come back. I got all the way downtown, I'd changed handbags the night before, and I had to go back for them. Mr. Klein wasn't coming in that morning, but he'd remember because I mentioned it to him later on. But it wouldn't have been as late as ten-thirty, it'd have been more like nine-thirty when I got back home. I thought maybe whoever it was who said he'd seen me had just confused the days. That could be, couldn't it?"

"Oh," said Jesse. "Did you tell the sergeant about that?"

"I most certainly did, as soon as I remembered it myself," she said sturdily.

"What car do you drive?"

"It's a two-door Ford, tan, it's ten years old." She was sounding indignant now.

"But they can't really think—just this rigmarole—I can't believe anything like this could happen—" Marcia was in a panic.

"It isn't any use to cry about it, Marcia," said Dulcie a little impatiently. Whether fear or righteous anger had animated her, today she was the stronger of the two. And she sounded as if she were telling the flat truth. He wondered how Clock felt about Dulcie now, after hearing her answers. "Mr. Falkenstein," she said, and she flushed deeper and leaned forward. "I don't suppose it's any good my saying it, because anybody can say anything. Papa wasn't at all religious, but Mama'd been brought up in the Presbyterian Church, and she sent us to Sunday school. I haven't been to church in ages, well, I haven't had time—but I'm a Christian. I believe in the Commandments—about doing no murder, and honoring your father and mother. I just couldn't have done—what they seem to think."

Jesse was interested in this woman now; the colorless personality had burgeoned into something more forceful. With animation in her expression, the resemblance between the sisters was more strongly marked. And he thought, indeed, she might always have been the stronger of the two, the one who had for those long years withstood the monotonous daily grind, staying home with the old people. The warm sincerity in her tone was unmistakable.

He said slowly, "Well, this may put a little different complexion on it, you coming up with an explanation of that witness—a possible explanation."

"But all the rest of it," said Coleman. "The autopsy results— that's very odd indeed, isn't it? It makes it look—" He stopped, and Jesse finished the thought for himself: like an inside job. Yes.

"But what can we *do?*" burst out Marcia. "They can't possibly—"

"We wait and see what happens," said Jesse. "All we can do at the moment."

Clock and Fran came to dinner that night. In spite of bulging considerably in the middle, Fran looked her usual pert dark gamine self, and said it hadn't been so bad this morning. Over dinner, with Athelstane scrounging for tidbits, the talk was general; but when Nell and Fran retired to the kitchen, and later upstairs to look at the new bedroom drapes, Jesse asked Clock how he was feeling about Dulcie now.

"I heard about the keys this afternoon."

"Oh, yes," said Clock. He massaged his Neanderthal jaw. "Well, I sent another report to the D.A.'s office. It's something on the other side of the ledger, Jesse, but not all that much. I saw Klein this afternoon, and he said he remembered her mentioning it. Yes, she sounds quite honest and straightforward, but you can't get away from the evidence, you know. The note, the overdose. Who else knew those capsules were there? They weren't social people, seldom had anyone come to the house. Who else knew the old man's phrase, better out of it? Who else could have arranged the overdose so quiet and easy? And we can't shake Eberhart's story. He's absolutely certain of the day, and he's got good reason

—it was his late wife's birthday, he wanted to go and put flowers on her grave, and he kept looking out to see if the rain was letting up. He's sure of the time because he always has a second cup of coffee about ten-thirty, and he was in the kitchen getting it."

Jesse said ruminatively, "There's some evidence that Vanderveer's mind could have been running on suicide, Andrew. One thing that occurs to me—what that visiting nurse said. There was a family row about it, I'd like to hear more about that—they were trying to get across the truth about his wife's condition, persuade him to put her in a rest home. He just wouldn't listen, Marcia said, but he must have taken some of it in. It could have been working away in him, and he decided they'd be better out of it indeed. He could have arranged the overdose just as easily."

Clock made a derisive sound. "Oh, now, Jesse. Coincidences happen but that'd be one hell of a long one. And the same day, nearly the same hour, he inadvertently lets in a violent burglar who bangs them both over the head and then runs off without ransacking the place? And another thing, that note—I talked to Questioned Documents again yesterday, and they say it was typed by a professional. Even touch and no errors. Vanderveer had probably never used a typewriter in his life, but it's how Dulcie earns her living."

"And that, of course, is another thing," said Jesse, but his voice was dissatisfied. "They knew he must have a good bit tucked away, if not how much, and that when he shuffled off they'd get it. But at that, could they be sure? He was a secretive old gent, and funnily enough, I don't think the money had much to do with it. And you'd better hear about that." He told Clock what they'd come across at the bank, and Clock whistled respectfully.

"That would be a dandy extra motive."

"By the way, did somebody say he kept chains on the doors? How did she say she expected to get in that night? She couldn't—no, I'm not thinking straight, of course."

"She told us," said Clock, "that he knew what time she generally got home and unhooked the chain for her—there was a TV program he liked to watch at five-thirty. So she didn't think a thing about it, walked in as usual. Well, of course she couldn't very well hook the chain after herself when she went out after killing him. That's all perfectly natural."

"But—well, of course, yes. But that girl—I really don't think she did it, Andrew."

"For God's sake," said Clock. "You've let the baby face and innocent look convince you?"

"I think she convinced me this afternoon," said Jesse.

"Just tell me who else could have done it, then."

"Yes, that's the difficulty." And about then Fran and Nell came back, and Nell began telling Clock about Athelstane's love affair, and the conversation became general again.

It had drizzled for an hour or two on Friday afternoon, but Saturday was clear and cold; they were in for an early winter. Jesse drove down into Hollywood and started hunting the address on Kingsley. When he found it, he pulled into the empty drive of the Vanderveer house and contemplated the house, the block.

A good many years ago, this part of central Hollywood had been a generally good middle-class area; never anything fancy, but safe and respectable. But it was an old area, and there were houses and apartments scattered around these sixty square blocks that would date fifty and sixty years back. After the war, this whole area had started running down, and the character of the population had changed. Ten years ago most of the residential blocks off the main drags here had been shabby, slatternly, sinking toward something not quite a slum. Where once most of the single houses had been lived in by owners, by then a majority of residents were tenants. Then a change had come, with developers tearing down the oldest places to put up garden apartments, smartening up a block here and there, so that now many streets like Kingsley were a combination of old and new.

This block on Kingsley was one of those. Jan Vanderveer's house must be one of the oldest on the street, a little frame California bungalow with a wide front porch, a narrow drive made of twin strips of cement with grass between, an old single garage with old-fashioned double doors. It could have stood a coat of paint; its once white walls were faded to a grayish tone. It probably dated from the twenties.

On the right of it as Jesse faced it was another single house only slightly newer; it was a cracker box of a pseudo-Spanish stucco, with no front porch at all. To the left of the Vanderveer house was a garishly modern small apartment building, its stucco painted bright yellow with brown trim. It was built in two wings running front to back, with a walk and strips of lawn down the middle, and a driveway adjoining this one. Jesse measured it mentally and decided that each wing might contain eight apartments, four up and four down.

He fished in his briefcase again for the little bag Marcia Coleman had handed him: effects taken from the body, handed back by the police. Now, reaching in for the keys, he dumped out what else was there. There wasn't, he discovered, very much. An old man at home on a rainy day wouldn't have had much in his pockets. An ancient dime-store address book; he'd look that over later. Thirty-seven cents in change. A dirty handkerchief. A ball-point pen.

He thought about that safe-deposit box, looking at those things. *—brought nothing into this world, and it is certain we can carry nothing out,* he thought sadly. He had a brief memory of the gaunt old man in his office that day, suspicious, grudging, prejudiced.

There had been a police seal on the front door. And he thought, the crime rate up, leaving a house empty is inviting the burglar: not that he supposed there was anything of much value here that either Dulcie or Marcia would miss.

There hadn't yet been a burglary, and it was a dingy tired house full of dingy gimcrack things. The narrow combination living-dining room ran straight across the front, with a hall going off the living-room end, which gave onto two bedrooms with a bathroom between. The kitchen, large and square, adjoined the dining area, with a service porch and a back door on the driveway. All the furniture was cheap and old. Sometime after the house had been built, a third bedroom had been added at the rear; the floor level was uneven where a door led straight from the end of the hall into a box of a room about twelve feet square. That was Dulcie's room: there was a narrow wardrobe, a single bed, a thin rug, white organdy curtains at the one window looking out on a bare backyard with a long-unpainted picket fence around it. There was a portable typewriter on a tiny metal table opposite the bed, a narrow mirror over a dressing table. The typewriter was an old Smith-Corona.

The middle bedroom had been turned into a den. There was an

ancient scarred rolltop desk, a studio couch, a vinyl-upholstered
recliner with some stuffing coming out, and one metal file cabinet.
Here, and in the front bedroom and long front room, the carpeting
was wall-to-wall, much worn, a faded beige.

In the front room he looked at the marks left by murderer and
detectives, and read the simple story. The fireplace was at one end
of the living-room area, on the side wall: a conventional red-brick
fireplace with a painted mantel. Under the front window was a
couch, and at the other side of the fireplace a fat square chair and
ottoman faced a portable TV on a metal stand in the corner.
There was a rough chalk outline of a body between those two, and
rusty marks on the carpet: where the old man had died. Just down
from the door to the hall, the cumbersome metal walker lay on
one side, and there was another chalk outline: the woman had
fallen, or been struck down, close to the old-fashioned round oak
table, and there were more old bloodstains.

He wandered back down the hall, remembering that Dulcie had
said she'd been sleeping in her mother's room; in the front bedroom was a pair of twin beds, in one corner the ugly necessary
bedside commode, a metal affair with its plastic bucket concealed
by a plastic lid.

The odd thing was, of course, while this house, or anything in
it, was worth very little, the land it was sitting on in central Hollywood might add a respectable sum to the estate.

—*or anything in it.* The chief reason he was here, of course, was
what that chief teller had said. From what they knew of Vanderveer, he'd have been exactly the type to keep the wads of cash at
home; indeed, with that modest checking account, what had be-
come of all those nice dividends?

He started looking in the old man's den, the obvious place. He
looked behind the three pictures, tore the paper backing off. He
went through the desk quickly, not stopping to examine anything
in detail, and came on this and that: a box of current-year bank
statements, a large account book. The drawers were sparsely filled.
He found a steel cash box in a bottom drawer with sixty dollars in
cash in it. The pigeonholes were stuffed with meaningless odds
and ends: paper clips, old pens, rubber bands. When he had been
through the drawers he took them out one by one and looked at

their undersides: a favorite place to tape valuables. There was nothing.

The file cabinet was no more productive: there were a few long-out-of-date construction contracts, statements and receipts from seven different local brokerage houses, the most recent dated last spring. Nichols-Neuman, Meyer and Salmon, Rettig and Rettig—all respectable well-known houses. He took down the addresses. The statements, dating back a good many years, listed sales and purchases of stock very different from that solid blue-chip stuff in the safe-deposit box now. He abstracted the whole wad to go over at his leisure.

He looked into the narrow built-in wardrobe. It held a collection of shabby old clothes, slacks, jackets, sweaters, shirts; the narrow shelf was stacked with old cardboard boxes, which were neatly packed with old copies of *The Wall Street Journal*—the bottom box went back to 1942.

"And didn't Solomon have the word for it," said Jesse to himself. *"Riches profit not in the day of wrath."*

He turned the file cabinet upside down, and found nothing. He removed a collection of old shoes and stacked clothes from the wardrobe floor and looked for evidence of a trapdoor or concealed recess: nothing.

It was very unlikely that Vanderveer would have hidden anything where the women might have come across it, but just in case, Jesse investigated the tiny coat closet beside the front door and discovered several boxes of Christmas ornaments, a collection of umbrellas, and a silver-headed cane. He looked behind all the pictures through the rest of the house and went through the old woman's room methodically, but it was going through the motions. If Vanderveer had had a hidey-hole for the wads of cash, it would have been in his own domain.

Frustrated, he stood on the front porch and ruminated. To hell with the chief teller: that was just imagination. Whatever else you could say about him, Vanderveer had been an eminently shrewd man; he had made his money work for him, and been smart and lucky in investments. Was it so likely he'd be so foolish to keep the hoard at home? So he'd liked to deal in cash, he was an old-fashioned, cautious fellow. What it came down to, had he had another safe-deposit box? Somewhere? Or—another thought—had all that dealing-in-cash, with the anonymous cashier's checks, been something to do with a tax dodge? He could imagine what Vanderveer had thought of the Gestapo.

And he thought, *Where moth and rust do not corrupt—* It had turned a good deal colder and he hadn't worn a coat; he shivered suddenly.

About one o'clock Nell went out to the garage to empty wastebaskets, and was surprised to find it so cold. "Climate's changing," she said to Athelstane, who had accompanied her.

The chain-link fence ran beside the garage, with a tall growth of shrubbery against it, and when Athelstane uttered a pleased whuffle and started over there, she looked after him.

The Siamese cat was huddled under the thick shrubbery there, barely visible, motionless. This time she could see that it was a dark seal point. But Siamese were generally pampered by owners; on a day like this it ought to be inside, she thought. She said coaxingly, "Pussin—come, pussin—" Nell was fond of cats and had never had one since long before her father died.

The cat fled away, long and low, and disappeared behind the shrubbery. Athelstane uttered a minor whuffle.

CHAPTER 3

When Jesse turned down the walk leading between the wings of the apartment house next to the Vanderveer house, he was reflecting: a working-class neighborhood, but it was Saturday. He could see a row of garages at the rear of the property. On the front step of the first apartment to the right in from the street, a rather blowsy-looking woman with dyed red hair was taking mail out of one of the two boxes between the doors.

On the forlorn chance that Clock had missed her, Jesse stopped to ask questions.

"You another cop? I already told the other one, I wouldn't have noticed nothing that day, I was at work. I wouldn't have noticed nothing at that house anyway, living upstairs like I do. But a murder right next door—it's scary these days, killers and robbers all over. What? Oh, the people live downstairs here, I told the other cop that too, they wouldn't have noticed nothing—the Lutzes —they've gone off on a trip somewhere, I think they left that day or the day before, I don't remember."

Jesse went on down to the rear units, and found the name slot in the ground-floor front door. R. J. Eberhart. The chief reason he wanted to see Eberhart was to gauge what sort of witness he might sometime be facing in court.

Eberhart looked at his card and invited him in, listened to his questions. "About that business next door," he said. "Siddown. That's short answered, sir. Sure I'm sure. What I saw and when." Eberhart was a peppery, perky little man around seventy, with once fiery red hair turning gray; he had a pugnacious bulldog face, shrewd little blue eyes, a quick sharp voice, and he was obviously in possession of all his faculties. "Look here," he said to Jesse, "I don't know those people—don't know anybody along here—I got my own friends and family. I only moved over here from south

Pasadena when my wife died five years back, so as to be closer to my daughter, she and her family live up on Outpost Drive. But you can't help noticing people, just casual. Roundabout five-thirty or a bit later, I'll usually be in the kitchen fixing something to eat, and the window and back door give on the driveway and the driveway of the house next door. I didn't even know the people's name, see, but three-four times a week I'd see that young woman drive in. About that time. So when I saw her drive in that morning I recognized her. Naturally."

"And you're absolutely sure of the day and the time?" asked Jesse.

Eberhart said exasperatedly, "How many times do I have to say it? Look, son, I may be seventy-one come January, but I've still got all my buttons and my eyes are as good as they ever were. I only retired a couple of years ago—worked for Kellogg Plumbing and Heating in Atwater for nearly forty years, and you can ask Jack Kellogg, Jr., if I showed any signs of senility."

"Nobody's suggested it," said Jesse.

"It's nothing to do with me," said Eberhart, "one way or the other. But I know what I saw, and when. Didn't take but casual note of it at the time, but I noticed it. The young woman next door driving in there. Drove right into the garage. It was around ten-thirty that morning."

"And you're positive which morning."

"Certainly I'm positive. It was Alice's birthday, October twentieth. She died five years ago, she's buried out at Rose Hills, and I never missed taking flowers to the grave, her birthday and Christmas and Memorial Day. But it was raining cats and dogs that day, I was hoping it'd let up. Kept looking out to see. It never did, and I finally went out anyway."

"And you're sure of the time," said Jesse.

"Well, I am." Eberhart looked at him belligerently. "Like I told the cops, I always have another cup of coffee along middle of the morning. I was in the kitchen fixing it, only reason I saw her drive in. Ten feet off across the apartment drive. That old tan Ford. She drove right into the garage."

"Mind if I take a look at your kitchen?"

"Help yourself."

The little apartment was neat and clean, the kitchen spotless and uncluttered. The window over the sink was a generous size, with a clear view past the driveway on this side to the Vanderveer drive and part of the Vanderveer garage.

"Do they think she did it?" asked Eberhart at his elbow. "The daughter? Did the murder?" He sounded avid. "Will I have to go in court?"

Jesse looked at him thoughtfully. He wore an eager expression. "I couldn't tell you, Mr. Eberhart. Possibly."

"Oh. Well, all I could do is tell the plain truth," said Eberhart. "What I saw. What I'm sure of."

And Jesse was thinking about witnesses. Good, bad, and indifferent. Eberhart was one kind: dogmatic, stubborn, arrogantly sure of himself. Sometimes judges and juries were wary of that kind, and sometimes they were quite right to be. Of the man convinced he couldn't make a mistake.

He stopped at a coffee shop on Sunset for a sandwich, and went to take a look at the other places Vanderveer had owned. Owned outright, and always collected the rents himself. One of them, a block down on Kingsley, was nearly a twin of the Vanderveer house, but its front lawn was greener and neater and there were rose trees lining the front walk. The other house fronted on Winona Avenue and was back to back with the Vanderveer house. It was an ugly square stucco house with a neglected front yard.

The apartment house on Fountain was one of the newer garden apartments, square and modern and brightly painted. There were sixteen units on two floors, and considering rents now, and that he'd owned it clear, it would be paying a very respectable profit. But none of these tenants would have known Vanderveer personally; they wouldn't have seen him in a month. Yes, and those rents would be due on Monday, and somebody would have to attend to that. A nuisance; have one of the girls type notices to leave in mailboxes, send checks to his office.

He drove on up Fountain until he spotted a public phone and called the Claremont number.

It was a pleasant wide street, Redwood Drive, in a neatly manicured residential area, and the house was a rambling ranch type on a wide lot, with a stretch of lawn and flower beds in front. Dulcie Vanderveer opened the door to him. "Is there anything—different?" she asked anxiously. "When you called I hoped maybe—"

"Just a few questions," said Jesse. Her face fell a little but she welcomed him in, to a comfortable homey living room furnished in early American. "Marcia had to take Jay to hockey practice, and Charles is out working in the yard— Sit down. What do you want to ask?"

"The day you forgot your keys," said Jesse. "When you got home, did you drive into the garage? And if so, why?"

She thought. "Yes, I did. Of course I was going right out again, but if you remember, it was raining. At least it was then—it hadn't been predicted, it started when I was driving downtown, and I didn't have an umbrella in the car. So I drove into the garage because it's closer to the back door. I had an awful time making Papa hear me, to come and unhook the chain and let me in."

"He always kept the door chains up?"

"Yes. Except when he knew I'd be coming home, at the usual time."

"Would you have any idea," asked Jesse, "whether he was in the habit of keeping much cash in the house? And where?"

"Well, I don't know," she said doubtfully. "Some, yes. Just for expenses. He gave me thirty-five dollars every Saturday to go marketing with—"

"For God's sake!" said Jesse. "A week's marketing?" He thought about the bills Nell reported, and she wasn't an extravagant shopper. Inflation—

Dulcie laughed a little bitterly. "Papa was supposed to be smart about money. Investing it, maybe. But I don't suppose he'd been in a grocery store for years. It wasn't any use trying to tell him. I used to put some of my money with it, to get enough—and little treats Mama liked, like fresh strawberries and Roquefort dressing. But about the money—I think he kept some in the den. If there wasn't enough in his wallet when I was ready to go to market, he'd go in there and get some. I don't know where he kept it, his desk probably. He never told us—Mama and me—anything about his money, he thought women were all fools, you know, about that kind of thing." Her little smile was mirthless. "He used to pay the newsboy in cash, before he stopped taking the paper—it got too expensive, he said. He used to subscribe to *The Wall Street Journal*. He stopped that too when the subscription rate went up—he used to go to the library and read it there." Suddenly Dulcie let out a huge sigh. "You're all thinking he was an ogre," she said unexpectedly. "He wasn't really, Mr. Falkenstein."

"Well—"

"No, really." She looked down at her clasped ringless hands. "He was lonely, you know—especially after Uncle Howie died, really his only close friend. We always called them aunt and uncle, but we really never saw much of them, even when we were children—Aunt Flo is pretty social, bridge and things, she hadn't the same interests as Mama, and of course Mama didn't drive. But you mustn't think he was a—a tyrant, Mr. Falkenstein. It was just the last few years—since he'd retired from business, he hadn't much to interest him, you see. Marcia's right, he wasn't always so bad—I can remember, when we were growing up, he was more cheerful, he'd make little jokes, even bring home little presents sometimes. He never liked to go out places, movies or restaurants, but Mama and Marcia and I did sometimes—he'd fuss about the money but we did. And after I was driving, that was after Marcia left home, Mama and I used to go out shopping and to movies, while she was still getting around all right. But the last couple of years, he was lonely," said Dulcie sadly, "and he hated getting old. He was so cross-grained he'd snap at you if you looked at him—but he wasn't always like that. Fighting with everybody."

"Had he had any—er—fights with people recently? There was something about a row in the family, when the nurse—"

"Oh, that," said Dulcie. "That! He didn't want to believe it, you see, that Mama was getting so much worse, so he wouldn't let himself listen. I hardly know Mrs. Gibson, she's the visiting nurse who'd been coming most of the time—sometimes they change around, you don't always get the same one, but it was her mostly. She came Mondays, Wednesdays, and Fridays to give Mama a bath and so on, and Mama said she was nice—and when she talked to me on the phone she sounded, well, efficient. I should have had better sense, but I talked to Marcia and we thought if we all went at him—you know. Of course he just shouted us all down. He didn't want to listen. And he was furious because Charles was there—"

"Why?" asked Jesse.

"Oh, he always hated Charles. You see, Mr. Falkenstein, he always blamed Mama for not having a boy—he didn't think much of girls—but at the same time, we sort of belonged to him and he'd, well, always have found some reason for—for hating anybody who tried to take us away. He wasn't really—prejudiced or—" She blinked. "He sort of despised what he called fancy education, he said Charles was a prissy old maid. And the children—you'd think he'd have been glad to have two grandsons, but it didn't work out that way. It was sort of impossible. Whenever Marcia brought the children, Mama loved to have them, but he'd be forever saying they weren't being raised right, indulged too much, given a lot of fancy ideas—it just made trouble, and Marcia just gave up. She'd come to see Mama when she could, and we talked on the phone—"

"I see," said Jesse. All that was expected.

"You can't help the way you're made," she said. "He never had much education, he started out as a carpenter. And after he retired from the business he didn't have anything to keep him interested. You asked about anybody he'd argued with lately. He'd had trouble with some of the tenants in the apartment house on Fountain—they were always late with the rent, and he told them to get out, and they left the place in a mess. He was trying to get damages from them—the place needed a lot of repairs, the stove and dishwasher. And about a month ago he had a terrible fight with somebody who came to the house, I don't know who it was. Mama told me about it. She'd been taking her nap when she heard the doorbell, and Papa let somebody in, and then there was a lot of yelling and shouting—but it took her a while to get herself up and into the walker, and she said when she got out to the living room Papa was just banging the door and yelling something like, 'Don't you ever dare try that again, goddamn liar'—and he just told her it was some drunk—but why would he have let him in? And he was mad at one of the other tenants, I don't know who that was either. It was just after the other thing. I answered the door, it was in the evening, and it was a young man, very polite, he had a little accent, I think he was Mexican. He just said he was one of Papa's tenants. I'd been busy getting Mama to bed, so I don't know what it was all about, but after he left I could see Papa was just furious about something. And then," said Dulcie resignedly, "he had a fight with the gardener because he was raising his price. It infuriated him that he couldn't cut the lawn anymore, had to hire it done, and the same man took care of the apartment house, the lawn and bushes there. He's a Mexican fellow, sort of excitable, and I thought they were going to kill each other. Oh, it all sounds so silly. But the least little thing would upset him, lately. I know he stayed out all day that next day, and he forgot all about that TV program he always watched."

"Did he watch TV much?" Jesse was still thinking about the money.

"Oh, not much. There isn't much worth watching anymore, and I never had time. There were a few things Mama liked. But he had three or four programs he usually looked at—not anything Mama and I liked, they were, well, what I'd call a little risqué, if you know what I mean."

Jesse felt vague surprise. "Did he go out very much? Do you know where?"

"Not as much as he used to, it was getting hard for him to get on and off the bus, and cabs are so expensive. He'd go to the bank for the housekeeping money, I suppose, and he went to the library, the one up on Santa Monica—and of course he went to the rest home a lot. Where Uncle Howie was. He had diabetes, you see, and they finally had to amputate his leg and it never healed properly—Aunt Flo couldn't take care of him at home and he had to go there, he was there nearly two years. Papa used to spend a lot of time there—he'd get me to take him on weekends, and the rest of the time took the bus. He was still going there sometimes, he'd gotten friendly with a couple of other old men who live there and went to see them even after Uncle Howie died. You know, it's sort of frightening, Mr. Falkenstein," said Dulcie soberly. "How people get when they get old. Changing, and at the same time more—more like themselves. And sometimes—like Uncle Howie— That was pathetic, it really was, Marcia and I both said. It was at the funeral, I took Papa of course, and Marcia came—sort of a mark of respect—and after it was all over, Papa said to Aunt Flo, I'm glad Howie's gone, the last while he wasn't the Howie we

knew, just a childish old man, he's better out of it. Mr. Falkenstein."

"Yes?"

"That—that queer note. I've been thinking— Do you think Papa
could have done that himself? Planned to take Mama with him—
like that—and then something went wrong, or—?"

"Well, it is a thought," said Jesse noncommittally.

"I've wondered." And then she looked up, turning her head.
"There's Marcia back." Automatically following her gaze, he saw
a middle-aged tan Chevy parked in the drive, and Marcia Coleman and a teen-aged boy getting out of it.

He spent Saturday evening poring over Vanderveer's account
book, a big stiff-covered ledger. It was evidently the latest one in
use; it had been started on January first four years ago, and was
about half used.

The old man had hardly been a trained bookkeeper, but he was
painstaking and methodical, and had his own method of record
keeping. Everything was scrupulously entered, from utility bills,
grocery bills, medical fees to the occasional large purchase or sale
of stock. Income, outgo—once Jesse figured out the system it was
easy to follow; but mathematics had never been his strongest
point, and he sat scribbling figures, hunched over his desk, mutter-
ing as he tried to add and subtract.

He went back over the year before this, and this year, and
wished he had a calculator. The wastepaper basket accumulated
discarded sheets as he multiplied and added, made mistakes and
did sums over.

When Nell looked in and said, "Are you coming to bed? It's
nearly midnight," he muttered at her, "Presently." He sat back
and looked at several pages of figures rather incredulously.

The real property, modest though it looked, had been bringing
in a very healthy income. Both the little houses rented for three
hundred and fifty a month. There were sixteen units in the apartment building, the singles renting at two-fifty, the doubles at three-
fifty. Of course the taxes and maintenance took a bite out of that,
but it had still been a nice income. And the dividends from the
blue-chip stock had added a pile to that. The gross income would
have put him way up there in a high tax bracket, but of course

there were convenient write-offs in real estate—Jesse remembered that there had been some 1040 and 540 forms, copies of tax returns, in that file cabinet, he'd have to take a look at those—and that heavy loan at the bank, a sizable write-off there, would have lowered Uncle Sam's take.

He gave it up half an hour later. It was a job for a CPA. But as far as he could figure it, if the amounts were true ones, there was anywhere between fifty and a hundred thousand dollars unaccounted for. Twenty-eight hundred in his checking account. Sixty dollars in a cash box at home. And where the hell was the rest of it? Where the hell?

If he knew IRS men, Dobson had been ferreting out Vanderveer's back records. See if he had come up with any attempted evasion to suggest where Vanderveer might have channeled the money. Turn the whole mess over to a CPA, and see what the trained mind made of it.

He opened his briefcase to put the big ledger into it, and as he did so encountered the little bag that had held the effects from the body. He hadn't looked at that address book, and took a minute to glance at it now.

It was very old and worn, and had been a cheap one to start with. Riffling through it, he realized just how obsolete it was; it must date from the years before Vanderveer's retirement, for it was largely filled with the names of realty companies, building-supply firms, and the like; there were very few personal names. But here and there through the little book he came on cryptic notations. They didn't seem to mean anything.

The first was on the first page, printed minutely at the very top. A Archer 1459. The next under B—BC Brown 730. The next under C—C Canning 1240. He studied them, frowning; they said nothing to him.

He found himself yawning, and put out the desk light and started up to bed.

On Sunday morning he went back to the house on Kingsley to pick up those tax records, and being in the vicinity wondered if he could track down the young man with the accent who had annoyed Vanderveer: what had that been about? The tenant of the house on Kingsley was listed in the ledger as Roberto Renaldo; the tenant of the place on Winona was R. Perez.

He got no answer at the first place; the doorbell chimed emptily. He drove up a block to the ugly little house on Winona.

The woman who opened the door was in the forties by her face, a once-pretty rather vapid little face, but she had kept a good figure. She had golden blond hair. She was chewing gum, and wore a fluffy pink housecoat. "Oh," she said to Jesse's self-introduction. "It's about that? Yeah, I heard about the old man getting killed. Who owns this place now, do you know? The rent's due tomorrow. And I'll bet the old bastard asked for it, too, whoever did it. I'll bet he left a bundle of money. He'd raised the rent on me twice the first year I was here, and it's tough to find anything much cheaper now—and I got two kids to raise and that no-good Mex husband of mine ran out on me four years back."

Jesse regarded her with interest. "Why should you say he asked for it?"

She pressed her lips together and then said drearily, "Oh, I don't suppose it matters now, only I still wouldn't like Bill to know about it. That dirty old bastard—that Vanderveer—just a nasty old man like they say. He hadn't ever done that before, but along last April or May, when he came to get the rent he said it was going up again, and I said I couldn't pay any more, and he laughed sort of funny and he started pawing at me—said if I was nice to him he'd be nice to me and not raise the rent. Dirty old bastard—what I had to put up with—every time he came since, pawing and slobbering over me, and I had to stand it. He couldn't do much more, he was about a hundred, but he sure had the urge. And all the time, I was scared to death Bill'd find out—my boy—he's got a temper on him, he'd have knocked the old bastard into the middle o' next week, and he could do it too, he's over six feet now already. When I heard that old bastard was dead, I just said thank God. Do they know who killed him yet?"

Astonished, he stared at her. And then he remembered the dirty TV shows. There hadn't been a hint at this facet of Vanderveer's character; had the old man started to go senile? Just along that line? Or just a little queer? And if in one way, maybe in another.

He handed her a card and explained that she could pay the rent to his office until the estate was settled. He wondered about Bill.

He got back in the car and started for the apartment on Fountain, and halfway there he suddenly slid the car in to the curb and switched off the engine. He asked himself what the hell he was doing. He wasn't a private eye. And it didn't matter a damn who Vanderveer had had arguments with, how many people had had some reason to hate him or to want to be rid of him—the same difficulty was still there: the difficulty of setting up that inside job. That very funny inside job. Of having the knowledge to do it. Conceivably, Vanderveer would have admitted the gardener, one of the tenants, almost anybody he knew even slightly who claimed legitimate business—even the meter reader, whoever—and how wild could you get? But, obligingly fetching the eggnog, the coffee, prying into the medicine cabinet—

Woolgathering, he thought disgustedly. And he wasn't a detective. He sat up to start the car, and idly noticed that he was parked across from a little cluster of shops, one of the neighborhood blocks of small independent places that might eke out a modest living from local residents. There was a pharmacy on the corner, a cleaner's, a variety store, a beauty salon. The door of the pharmacy was open, and it struck him suddenly that this would be the pharmacy where that codeine prescription had been on file. Clock would have heard about dosages from the coroner's office, but Jesse felt he could bear to know more about that, and also whether that last refill had been at a usual time.

He walked across to the pharmacy and went in. It was an old building, high-ceilinged and dim, and very untidy, with counters piled all down the center. He didn't locate the pharmacist until he had penetrated to the very rear of the store and came on him behind the prescription counter, a thin bald man in a dirty white smock.

"I'd like to ask you a few questions about that prescription of Mrs. Vanderveer's—" He reached for a card. "I expect the police asked you about it last week."

"That's right." The man looked nervous; he clutched the card without looking at it. He was about fifty; he had pale china-blue eyes behind metal-framed glasses. "It was all in order, the doctor's office said it could be refilled whenever she needed it. I told the police before—"

"How often was it refilled as a rule?"

"Oh, it varied. There were a hundred capsules to a bottle. The dosage is no more than two every four hours. She'd usually use up a bottle every couple of weeks, around there."

"And when had it been refilled the last time? I mean, before Miss Vanderveer got it refilled a week ago last Monday?"

"I had to look it up for the other officer—it was about two weeks before. The old—old gentleman called the order in that day, said his daughter would pick it up on her way home from work."

"Oh, said Jesse. "By the way, I'm not police—I'm the lawyer. What are you nervous about?"

The man stepped back a pace and said angrily, "I'm not nervous—but that's a dirty trick to pretend to be a cop, mister. You might have come right out and said what you were after. All I can say is, you can't get blood out of a stone, like I told the old man— I'm sorry, I'm an honest man and I like to pay my debts, but the way business has been—I said I'd pay him something as soon as I could—"

"You owed him money," said Jesse softly.

"As if you didn't know." The pharmacist was sullen.

"As a matter of fact, I haven't come across any record of it yet," said Jesse.

"Oh, sweet Christ—and I have to open my big mouth—"

"Of course I haven't been through everything."

"He took an IOU," said the pharmacist. "He offered it. He was in here, an old customer, I was just telling him about it—that fire inspection, how I had to have the whole building rewired. I own this block of stores, and they all had to be done, or we'd lose our business licenses. It was going to cost over five thousand and I didn't have it. He offered. Said he'd give me half percent less interest than the bank. That was way last year, I was supposed to pay so much a month, and he was here on the dot to get it too. But the last six months business has fallen way off, I just couldn't squeeze it out, and he'd been nasty about it."

"Well, well," said Jesse. "That's interesting, Mr.—"

"Schultz."

"Mr. Schultz. It'll be a while before the estate's settled, we can sort it out. Nobody's going to harass you about it." But he thought, back in the car, such a canny old man. Such a secretive old man. And just getting more so as he got older. And still busily raking in the money wherever and however he could. That IOU had to be somewhere. That rolltop desk—there could be a secret drawer somewhere? Damn the old man. And that funny business with the Perez woman—that really rocked him. Nobody had suggested that sort of thing about Vanderveer up to now.

Suddenly he remembered that Vanderveer had made that appointment with him, wondered about it again—and then at least one thing fell into place with a little click. Those tenants at the apartment who had been kicked out. Vanderveer had wanted damages out of them and had probably decided on legal action.

But he was wondering now just how many people there were around who, hearing that the old man was dead, had said a fervent thank God.

He had to be in court on Monday, on that other damage suit, but the bench was either bored or lazy and dismissed the court at four o'clock. With any luck it would go to the jury tomorrow. On his way back to the office, Jesse stopped at the CPA offices on the second floor and talked to a young fellow named Thurlow. He handed over the ledger, the bank statements for this year and last, the copies of the tax returns. Vanderveer had figured his own taxes, and to give him credit had had everything filed quite neatly by year. He explained what he was after.

"I'm no good at figures, and besides I'm busy. You've got all the handy calculators. By all I come up with, this old boy was living on a pittance and raking it in with both fists, and what the hell he's done with it is a mystery. I've got to settle his estate, and I'd like to know exactly what there is to settle."

"Don't worry," said Thurlow with a grin, "Uncle Sam's Gestapo will locate it for you, Mr. Falkenstein. I'll see what it looks like."

Reminded of that, when he got to the office he called Dobson, who said they'd been back through Vanderveer's account with them and he seemed to have an absolutely clean record. "Never delinquent a day, never been audited, never any suspicion of any fiddling. But considering that bank account, and a few other things—"

"Yes, I know," said Jesse. "Where is it, and how much? Well, it's more my worry than yours."

"You can say that six times," said Dobson. "I suppose it's occurred to you what sort of inheritance tax will be slapped on all that gold-plated stock, and the heirs with just that checking account to pay it."

"The thought had entered my mind," said Jesse irritably.

Jean had left a memo on his desk. Lenhoff's attorney had called and wanted to set up a meeting on Wednesday. "Damned shyster," muttered Jesse, but he supposed he'd better see him. At least Rose Lenhoff was out of town somewhere. And ten to one, if that judge decided to quit early tomorrow, the damned court case would drag over into Wednesday and he'd have to postpone the meeting.

It was one of the days when he wished he'd gone in for anything but law.

He got home just after six; but of course they'd gone off daylight saving time last Saturday night and it was pitch dark. Up here at this end of the canyon the street was unlighted; the first thing he'd insisted on was a couple of good bright lights at the gate, at the front door. He could see the lights at the gate as soon as he swung onto Paradise Lane, shining out a welcome; and as he turned into the drive the twin floodlights on the garage glared at him. The gate was open: Athelstane was in. As he slid down the drive, something small and light-colored fled across his path and he slammed on the brakes.

Nell was just setting the table in the dining room. "Athelstane's friend was out in the front yard," said Jesse, bending to kiss her.

She looked concerned. "At this hour? Cats ought to be in by dark, and a Siamese—"

Athelstane came bounding up with Davy hanging onto his collar. "Daddy! Fee kittens!"

"My God, how long does this phase last? All right, all right, we'll read about the three kittens just once, and then it's bedtime." And as he swung the sturdy little figure up in his arms, he thought of crabbed, suspicious, despotic old Vanderveer, who had exchanged all his chances of love and respect for the bundle of money.

"I'll be in to bed him down in ten minutes," Nell called after them.

* * *

When the phone rang at nine-forty he was getting on with the job of cataloguing all his records and knocked over a stack of Bach fugues getting to the desk. "Oh, Jesse," said Clock. He sounded very tired. "This is the first chance I've had to call you, sorry, but we've got two men off sick and we're all doing overtime." A sharp yip in the background cut across his voice, which suddenly turned fatuous. "That's my sweet girl, you just wait a minute and I'll get out your brush—"

"Just wait," said Jesse, "until your offspring arrives, and that hairy floor mop will get her comeuppance. And you won't be sounding so doting. Get a little education."

"What are you talking about?"

"Fee kittens," said Jesse darkly. "Do you want anything?"

"Just to break the news. The D.A.'s office is going for a charge of second degree. The warrant's applied for and will probably be waiting in the morning. We'll go out to arrest her as soon as it comes through."

"I was afraid of that."

"You still think she didn't do it."

"I can't know for a hundred percent sure. I just feel it's—out of character."

"You don't deal with crime by using intuition," said Clock. "It's out of my hands now. Red tape set in motion."

"Yes. Well, thanks for letting me know. And dammit, I've got to be in court— Look, Andrew, will you just tell her I'll get there as soon as possible?"

"Will do."

The case went to the jury at eleven o'clock, but what with the nice free lunch at an uptown restaurant, they didn't bring in a verdict until nearly three o'clock.

He got down to the Sybil Brand Institute, the women's jail, at three forty-five, and a few minutes later a wardress brought her in to him in one of the visitors' rooms, a bare little cubicle with a square table and two straight chairs. She looked quite calm, but the square little jaw was in evidence.

"That sergeant said you'd get here as soon as you could. Isn't that the queerest thing, him being your brother-in-law. I thought— you know—I thought if it ever happened—I'd be frightened, being arrested I mean, but I wasn't. It just all seems so awfully silly. That anyone could think I committed murder. Mama and Papa. Mr. Falkenstein, what happens how?"

"You'll be brought up for arraignment," he told her. "Probably the day after tomorrow. Later on you'll be indicted. You do know that there's no bail granted in homicide cases, you'll have to stay here."

She nodded. "The sergeant told me. It's all right—just like a little room, and very clean. But—do you think"—she leaned forward, her hands tightly clasped—"Mr. Falkenstein, all I can do is say it again—I didn't do it."

"If you plead guilty," said Jesse deliberately, "it'd just be a hearing before a judge, and the sentence very probably something like three to five years. You know all the evidence seems to be against you."

"I couldn't do that," said Dulcie. "Are you advising me to do that? As a lawyer? You don't believe me?"

"Against all common sense, I guess I do," said Jesse slowly. "Look. Can you tell me who would have known your parents' routine, have been admitted to the house—would have been able to arrange—what was done?"

She said helplessly, "But there's nobody—I mean, nobody who'd have done that! The family—Aunt Flo—Marcia, Charles— There weren't many visitors the last few years. Some of Mama's friends had died, and the ones left didn't come to see her often, they're all too old and don't get around much. Mrs. Fellowes went back East to live with her daughter—Mary Bright's in a rest home —and after Alice Hope moved to Long Beach, Mama used to write her letters, until her hands got so crippled— Oh, there might be a lot of people who knew things about us, but nobody we knew, you see. We didn't know any of the neighbors—most of them out all day, and not old neighbors."

"What do you mean, lots of people knew about you?"

"Oh, you see, Mama was just starved for talk," said Dulcie. "She hadn't anybody to talk to all day, she'd never been one for reading—I could sit and read all day, only I never had time—and if anybody came to the door when Papa was out, she'd talk to them as long as they'd stay. If I know Mama, tell them what time we had dinner and anything came into her head! She was so pleased when the Avon lady came, but she hadn't been back in a while, because Mama never could buy anything."

"Something else," said Jesse. "You knew your father had money somewhere, but you don't think he kept a lot of cash in the house—just what he gave you for shopping and so on—"

"Well, I don't know, but there wasn't a safe in the house like the one Uncle Howie had at home. Papa was smart about money, and he knew about the crime rate. I don't think he would have kept a lot around." She was silent, looking down at her hands, and then she said, "I know how it looks, Mr. Falkenstein. As if nobody else could have done it—that queer note—and no door broken in or anything. But I didn't, I don't know anything about it."

"All right," said Jesse. "Now I'd like you to go over that day in your mind, and think about this. Could there be anybody who might be able to testify that you were in your office downtown, say, between ten and noon?"

"I've already thought about that," said Dulcie. "The office door was closed, naturally, and Mr. Klein didn't come in that day until about two o'clock. I always took my lunch, there's no place right around there to get a sandwich, and we've got a little refrigerator and a coffee maker off the front office. But that day— I went down to the ladies' room about, maybe, a little after ten-thirty, and there was another woman there, just washing her hands before she left. I don't know if she'd remember it. I'm pretty sure she works in the tax office at the end of the hall—a blond girl about twenty-five, she's thin and always wears a lot of jangly bracelets—I don't know her, but of course everybody in the building would run into each other occasionally, see each other in the halls and so on—and maybe she'd remember. Of course I'm alone in the office a lot, Mr. Klein out seeing customers—"

"What's the business?" asked Jesse to keep her talking.

She brightened a little. "Oh, it's a very interesting business, Mr. Falkenstein. He's a wholesaler for fabrics, we deal with all the big department stores, furniture stores, upholsterers, dress factories, places like that. Most of the textile mills are in the South, you know, and Mr. Klein's the middleman supplier. I've gotten to know a lot about fabrics since I've worked for him—and he's always been so nice to me, he's a nice man."

"Well." Jesse stood up. "I can't tell you not to worry, Miss

Vanderveer. The court calendar's always full, I don't know when the trial might come up."

"It's funny," said Dulcie, "but I'm not worrying. Maybe I'm just being naïve to say I know I'm not guilty so it'll all come out all right. It was Marcia who went to pieces when they came with that warrant. And I'll be all right here, I've got my own things, clothes and like that. When I called Mr. Klein—after it happened —and told him, he was kind and said to take a couple of weeks off. And Marcia packed some clothes for me to take while I stayed with her, and they let me pack a bag this morning." Suddenly she yawned widely, and said, "Oh, excuse me. It's awful—I don't think I've caught up on my sleep yet. All I seemed to do at Marcia's was sleep, and right now that nice clean bed is all I can think of. I must be a funny client, Mr. Falkenstein. But I'm not worried."

CHAPTER 4

"What the hell are you giving me?" asked Bernard Klein incredulously. "Dulcie arrested? For homicide? That's ridiculous. This I've got to hear about."

Jesse had found him hunched over a typewriter in this rather cramped two-room office in an old building on North Spring Street at ten o'clock on Wednesday morning. Klein was a middle-sized stocky man about fifty, with thinning dark hair, a big crooked nose, a prominent gold tooth, an incipient paunch, and cynical dark eyes. His herringbone suit wasn't off the rack, but he was the kind of man whose tie went crooked ten minutes after he put it on. "What the hell?" he said blankly.

Jesse rather liked the look of him: a plain man, a man without any subterfuges. He sat back, lit a cigarette, and told him all about it. Klein listened, and commented with one succinct four-letter word.

"Dulcie!" he said. "Dulcie'd never in God's world have done that. 'S ridiculous."

"Well, she says she didn't."

Klein swiveled around in his desk chair and lit a cigarette with an angry snap of a disposable lighter. "My God," he said, "do I know my Dulcie! Better than her own family, I swear-- God knows she spent more time here than at home! She's a good girl, Falkenstein, a nice girl. With me nearly twenty years, God, how the time goes—a green young girl when she came to me, but she caught on fast, she's a smart girl. Hell, I'm out calling on customers, showing samples, most of the time—I just need a girl here to answer the phone, take orders, do a few letters. I cover the whole damn county, all over, I'll be in maybe a couple of hours a day and that's all. But twenty years—you're telling me the law thinks Dulcie did a murder?" He used the succinct word again.

"There's evidence," said Jesse.

"You can shove the evidence," said Klein. He looked at his cigarette. "She never said very much about her home life—but sometime last year, around there, I figured she wasn't having it so easy, she'd mentioned about her mother's having another stroke and having to use a walker, and getting worse. And the last couple of months she'd been looking like hell, all tired out. I told her to take a couple of weeks off if she wanted, but she wouldn't. Said she'd had the usual two weeks in May, she'd be all right." Klein stabbed out his cigarette and got up to stand at the window, looking at the view over the city, gray and bleak and cold-looking.

"It hadn't been easy for her, certainly," said Jesse.

"That's a rough one, what you say about the way things were— that old bastard of a father." Klein laughed sharply. "My God, we're supposed to be the misers and skinflints, hah, but at that, there are a couple of things Mosaic law has to say about it—"

"He who maketh haste to be rich shall not be innocent," said Jesse sleepily.

Klein laughed again, sharp and high. "I don't remember that one. Talk about biting off your nose to spite your face— What the hell did he think he was piling it up for? That's damn foolishness. All very well to stack it up, take care of it, but when it comes to going without necessities just to sit and gloat over the damn bank balance—" He turned to face Jesse. "I'm sorry for that girl. A good girl, Falkenstein. I always have been sorry for her. When I thought about it. Come to think, she never had much. Stayed at home, looked after the old folk, looked after my office. You could say sort of thankless jobs."

"She never said much to you about her home, you said."

Klein shook his head. "Not a complainer, our Dulcie. Always bright and cheerful. A good girl. God, I can't take this in. But an old bastard like that—all the work, her mother— But I'll never believe she could do a thing like that. No way. It's a funny word to use, maybe, but she's a gentle girl, Dulcie. A nice girl. She wouldn't be capable of a thing like that."

"Rather what I thought. Don't know her as well as you do, of course."

"Like I say, maybe better than anybody else," said Klein. He turned abruptly and sat down at the desk again, lit another cigarette. His dark eyes were sad. "Nice to think there was some rhyme or reason to things. People getting what they deserve, good or bad, eventually. God. A thing like this—I'd felt so damned sorry for her, you know, when Dan Wolfe showed up so unexpected—I thought she was going to pass out when he walked in, I happened to be dictating a letter to her—but Dulcie's a pretty game girl, she pulled herself together and put up a good show. I'd always thought there was something there, on her part anyway, and the way she looked, after all those years, I guess there was, in spades. I thought at the time—"

"Who's Wolfe?" asked Jesse.

Klein was staring out the window again. "Oh, he used to work for Wechler Brothers, down the hall, they're candy and novelty brokers. God, how time gets away, that's twelve or fourteen years back. He and Dulcie had dated some, back then. God, how old would Dulcie be now?—getting on to forty, I guess, it doesn't seem possible. She wasn't ever a spectacular beauty, you know, but— pretty. Nice skin and hair and eyes. Pretty in a quiet sort of way. A quiet girl. I know at the time I was kind of surprised at a young fellow like that having the sense to appreciate her."

"Oh," said Jesse. "Serious on his part?"

Klein met his eyes. "Well, I kind of had the feeling it was. Nothing definite said, but she— Well, I had an idea it was serious. Then all of a sudden it was kaput. Wolfe went into business for himself about that time, wasn't around anymore, and Dulcie never mentioned his name again, never said anything. Not a girl to talk about her troubles. I hadn't laid eyes on Wolfe since, but he turned up one day last month, seems he had some business with somebody down this way and dropped in to see his old boss—he came in here to see me and Dulcie."

"I see," said Jesse thoughtfully.

"About this trial," said Klein abruptly. "I don't suppose she can lay her hands on that money. Now or ever. It's a goddamned shame. And you don't work for love. Just take it that I'll guarantee your fee, Falkenstein. Nobody gets rich at the rag trade, any part of it, what this business amounts to—but Dulcie's a good girl, I'd like to see her through this. Do you think you can get her off?"

"I've got no idea," said Jesse. "There'll be enough money—however things turn out—but thanks for the offer. Any idea where I'd find Dan Wolfe?"

Klein looked curious. "Sure. He's in candy, novelties, souvenirs —he'll be in the phone book. Can she have visitors?"

"Anytime."

"I'll go and see her. She's a nice girl, Dulcie."

Down at the end of the hall from Klein's office was a door with a frosted glass top which bore the legend C. P. BAKER TAX ACCOUNTANT. On his way down the hall Jesse had noticed the door with the LADIES sign on it, sandwiched between Mason's Moving Service and W. F. Gunn Insurance.

Past the frosted door was a front office with a counter halfway across, two females, a row of file cabinets, and two desks with typewriters. Beyond an open door at the rear was a glimpse of a larger office where a broad-shouldered dark man in shirt sleeves was bent over a desk.

One of the females was plump and dark, the other thin and blond; the blonde was wearing a purple sheath and an armful of charm bracelets.

"Yes, sir? Mr. Baker's busy right now, but if you'd like to make an appointment—"

"Think it's you I want to talk to." He gave her a card. "I'm looking for a possible witness, Miss—?"

"Mrs.—Mrs. Linda Orley. What's it about? You're a lawyer?"

He told her what it was about. "It was October twentieth. A Thursday. If the date doesn't mean anything, the day it rained so hard for the second time. It would have been between ten-thirty and eleven, when you were in the ladies' room down the hall. There was another woman who came in just as you were leaving."

Her gaze was blank. "Heavens, I wouldn't remember."

"The woman who works for Mr. Klein in one-ten. A woman about thirty-eight, short, plump, brown hair. Miss Vanderveer."

"Oh, I know her. I never heard her name before. But goodness, I just couldn't say—I don't remember. Any of the girls working on this floor, we'd run into each other occasionally in the ladies' room, but it isn't a thing you remember particularly. If you know what I mean. I just couldn't say—yes, I'd seen her there sometimes, but I couldn't swear to the day or the time, anything like

that. If it came to going into court or anything." She looked
vaguely alarmed. "One day's like another in this place. I just
couldn't say."

Jesse hadn't really expected anything else; but it was frustrating.
He thanked her and started back for the elevator. And it wasn't at
all relevant—or was it?—but he found himself curious about Dan
Wolfe. Anything about Dulcie Vanderveer interested him at the
moment.

He was in the book, at an address on Olympic Boulevard. It
was an old office building, middling rents, nothing fancy; Wolfe
was on the top floor. The hall door led into a tiny front office
where a freckle-faced red-headed girl asked his business briskly.
"Mr. Wolfe? If he's in, like to see him."

"Well, I'll see, he's on the phone." She went into the inner
office. In a minute a man appeared in that doorway.

"What can I do for you?"

Jesse handed him a card. "Few minutes of your time."

"Well, all right." He led Jesse into a small square untidy office
with a littered desk, a couple of straight chairs. "Am I getting
sued, or have I inherited a bundle?"

"Neither. You remember Dulcie Vanderveer?"

Wolfe's half smile vanished. "Well, sure. What about her?"

Jesse told him economically, and Wolfe said, "Oh, my God. My
God, what a—what a hell of a thing. I'm damned sorry to hear
about it. Damned sorry." He looked as if he meant it.

And Jesse looked at him with interest. Wolfe would be about
Dulcie's age, a year or two older. Twelve, fourteen years ago he'd
have been a very handsome young fellow; he was still handsome
in maturity: a tall, dark, well-built man with sharply chiseled features, thick eyebrows, a head of gleaming black hair, a firm well-
cut mouth. He looked back at Jesse blankly and said, "The hell of
a thing. I hadn't seen her for over thirteen years—just happened to
be near my old office one day last month, and dropped in. She
hadn't changed much—I was a little surprised—but what—"

"What's it got to do with you? Nothing at all. And you'll think
I've got a damned nerve to ask you," said Jesse. "But back there
quite a while ago, you'd dated her a little. Klein thought it might
be serious. Was it?"

Wolfe got out a cigarette and tapped it slowly against the desk top before lighting it. "I don't know why the hell I should tell you anything about that."

"Neither do I. Just take it, it wouldn't go any farther."

"What the hell?" said Wolfe. "It's ancient history, it doesn't matter now. Dulcie was a nice girl. Not the prettiest girl around, but that isn't everything, and when you got to know her— You could say I was halfway serious about her. I thought she liked me pretty well. She'd never had any boy friends, she was a shy sort of little thing. We had maybe half a dozen dates, and I was thinking —well, put it that I was getting serious about her. Then—well, she'd always asked me to pick her up at the office, and then she finally told me that her father didn't like her to date, he was old-fashioned, but we'd have to meet sometime, and she asked me— that next date—to come to her house. I did. It was a place in Hollywood—old house in the middle of town. That old bastard," said Wolfe. "How the hell do people get that way? She introduced me, and right away he started in yelling—I thought he was going to jump me—he wasn't having his daughter going with any dirty Jew, and all the rest of it. You can fill in the blanks for yourself." He shrugged.

"Oh, yes," said Jesse. And he remembered how she had said, anyone who wanted to take us away—and, he wasn't really prejudiced. The excuse. Even the useless daughters had belonged to him, part of his possessions.

"Well, for God's sake," said Wolfe. "Even if I'd been all the way serious, there's no profit in that sort of thing, is there?—hardly the basis for a settled marriage." He laughed shortly. "I was planning to start my own business about then, I don't think I stayed with Wechler more than a month after that. I didn't see Dulcie again. Hadn't seen her since, until that time last month. End of story."

"Short and sweet." Jesse looked at his own cigarette. "Are you married, Mr. Wolfe?"

"Yes, Ruth and I got married the year after that, we've got three kids now."

"Well, sorry to have raised a ghost," said Jesse, getting up. "It was just a loose end."

"I'm very sorry to hear about this," said Wolfe formally. "I don't suppose there's anything I can do, but—"

No, there wasn't, thought Jesse in the elevator. That surprise visit to the old office probably a pure impulse. And maybe he'd showed some proud pictures of the three kids. He thought of Dulcie saying so steadily, I don't know anything about it— A last straw? The only man who'd ever acted serious about her, that could be inferred, and a handsome man, a virile man. She could have been deeply in love with him. And the irascible, reasonlessly jealous old man driving him away. The long dull years going by. And lately, coming home day by dreary day to the increasingly helpless old woman, the fierce despotic old man—

That chance meeting with Dan Wolfe last month just could have waked some slumbering passions.

He had believed her. He'd like to go on believing her. But he hoped the D.A.'s office would never hear about Dan Wolfe.

Lenhoff's attorney came into the office at three o'clock and to Jesse's surprise brought a counteroffer which nearly matched the settlement Rose Lenhoff was asking. It was probably the best deal they could get, and Jesse accepted it provisionally. He told the other man he'd contact her and let him know. But it appeared that Mrs. Lenhoff was still out of town, and the daughter who answered the phone when Jean called couldn't say when she'd be home.

Jesse felt annoyed with the wayward clients.

And it was out of his way, but he left the office early and drove into West Hollywood to see Florence Griffin. He had nearly forgotten her; he had discounted her as irrelevant to the case. But Dulcie had reminded him that she was indeed one of the relatively few people who would have been admitted to the house without question—an old friend—would have been given the freedom of the house. But what possible motive could she have had?

It was a block of older homes, in a quietly elegant neighborhood of manicured lawns and solid wealth. The house was French Colonial, on a wide lot; he contrasted it with the mean little bungalow on Kingsley.

She answered the door promptly; he remembered the high girlish voice on the telephone that night. She was a small, neat woman with fluffy silver-gray hair, a peaches-and-cream complexion, and she greeted him warmly. Not ever an intellectual woman in any sense of the word, he judged her, but she had a warmth of personality, she was friendly—and a talker. "Of course Marcia called, I just couldn't believe it, there must be some mistake—as if Dulcie would do a thing like that! I don't know what the police are thinking of—but"—she regarded him with her head on one side —"you look like a very good lawyer, Mr. Falkenstein, you can show them how wrong they are. Do come in and sit down and tell me how I can help you."

"Well—" He wasn't sure what he wanted to ask her. "When was the last time you saw any of the Vanderveers?"

"At the funeral," she said promptly. "Howie's funeral. It was really awful of me that I didn't go to see Myra oftener, but time goes by—Johnny came to the funeral, of course, with Dulcie and Marcia, and they said if I felt up to it Myra'd like to see me, so I went over there for an hour or so afterward. Of course I'd seen Johnny nearly every day at the rest home. Howie liked Johnny to come—of course they'd known each other so long, and been part-ners in business. Frankly, I always detested the man—it's funny, I suppose men see something in other men that makes them friends, but they weren't at all alike—oh, Howie was ambitious too and liked money well enough, but at least we enjoyed it—not being ex-travagant, I don't mean, but just living nicely and being comfort-able, and trips and theaters and things like that. Oh, I was sorry then—that day—that I hadn't gone to see Myra oftener, I was sorry for her, you know. What with Howie so bad, I hadn't realized— But Myra and I never had much in common, she was so much older. And Dulcie looked just terrible. It was killing her—taking care of them. I hadn't seen Dulcie in ages—but she just looked exhausted." She accepted a cigarette with a little nod.

"What did—" But she had flown on.

"When the children were small they were told to call us uncle and aunt, but we never actually saw much of them socially—Myra and Johnny I mean— He wasn't so bad back then, more talkative, if he always was an old grouch—but then he had the business to give him an interest in life, men need that the way women need bridge and shopping, it's funny. I wasn't surprised when Aline left him, his first wife—you knew he was married before—"

"I didn't realize you'd known her."

"Oh, yes. Let's see, Howie and I were married in 1935—we

wanted a family, of course, but I guess it just wasn't meant to be. He and Johnny were both working for Keene Construction then, and lucky to have jobs at all, but things were awfully slow—the Depression was still on, you know. It was a couple of years later that Howie's father died and left him a little money, and Johnny had some savings, and they decided to start their own company. Johnny and Aline had gotten married the year before we did, and she was a lot younger than Johnny—he was five years older than Howie, you see—she was about my age, and I was twenty-one. She left him about six months after Howie and I were married, and as I say I wasn't surprised—all his penny-pinching and ordering her around. I said money was tight—the Depression—but you could still have fun and enjoy yourself—movies twenty-five cents and there was always the beach—but Johnny always grudged every penny. And then there was his chasing around—"

"Oh, did he?" asked Jesse.

"Well, I couldn't prove it but I know in my bones he did. Men are funny," she said ruminatively. "Whenever I mentioned it to Howie, he just laughed. Now, Howie'd never have played around on the side, he wasn't that kind of man, but I guess a man can overlook that sort of thing in another man—it was like Johnny telling the dirty jokes, but not in front of women unless it was by accident, and Howie'd never repeat them to me. But Johnny had an eye for the girls—only I don't suppose he did *much* about it because it'd cost him money. And he only married Myra to have a cook and housekeeper. She was nearly his age, he was forty then, she'd never been married, worked in an office somewhere. I always thought she was so grateful to be able to call herself Mrs., she just put up with him, but maybe I misjudged her. I don't know how she did put up with him. She was a good mother to the girls, I will say, but he never let her forget she ought to have had a son."

Jesse remembered that that was nearly the first thing Vanderveer had said to him.

"Poor Myra—I ought to have gone to see her oftener, but it was all pretty depressing, you know—that horrible little house, and the walker, and Johnny grumbling around like a bear. It was the girls I felt sorriest for—I always thought Myra could have stood up for them better. Of course Marcia was the rebellious one—she stood up for herself. When she wanted to go to college Johnny had a fit, what good would college do a girl, he never finished high school and he made out all right, and Marcia just got herself a job and moved out, started to go to LACC part time, and of course that's where she met her husband. It was poor Dulcie got the short end of the stick, ending up taking care of them both, but then she's the kind— Well, Howie always used to say, there are two kinds of bravery, you know. There's the kind that makes you rescue somebody from a fire, or stop a dog fight, and then there's the kind that makes you able just to stand things, however bad it is, just grit your teeth and bear it. "

"That's perfectly true," said Jesse.

"But when I saw Dulcie that day—as bad as I was feeling about Howie—I could just have cried for her. She looked awful. It was killing her, all that work and no rest. And of course Johnny would never even notice it." She put out her cigarette and looked at him seriously. "You've just got to make everybody see that Dulcie would never have done such a thing—*killing* them. It's just impossible. But"—and suddenly her light voice sounded almost fierce— "I'll say one thing, Mr. Falkenstein. If I thought Dulcie had done it, I'd say Johnny Vanderveer just brought it on himself."

The arraignment was set for ten o'clock on Thursday morning; there wasn't any need for him to be there, but he showed up to give Dulcie a little moral support.

And he intended sometime today to talk to some of those stockbrokers; but he'd just gotten back to the office when Jimmy came in and said the Colemans were here.

"Oh, Lord," said Jesse. "All right."

They came in and sat down, looking very grave and miserable; but Marcia was in control of herself, her voice was steady. Coleman was looking very worried. "Mr. Falkenstein," she said, "we thought we'd better come and talk to you. About money. Dulcie's got some savings, but we haven't got much at all—the children, and it's expensive to live now, and—"

"Oh." Jesse was surprised. "I wouldn't worry about it, Mrs. Coleman. It'll all be all right."

"All right!" said Coleman roughly. "You'll want some sort of retainer to defend her—I know these things don't come cheap. I'm not sure how much I might manage, but—"

"But there's money available, or will be. You knew that your father had a bundle," Jesse said to Marcia.

"I know we always suspected it. But what he did with it, how he left it—"

Jesse said, "My God, that's my fault—I should have known, of course it wouldn't have crossed his mind to tell anybody. I should have told you about the will."

"Dulcie remembered a will. His making one. But—with all this going on—I'd forgotten about it. Is there a lot of money?"

"Quite a bundle. But it'll be tied up." He told them about the will, and Marcia shut her eyes and leaned back in her chair.

"Oh, isn't that typical. Just exactly what he would do. Stupid woman with not enough sense to handle money, appoint a bunch of men to do it for her. And he always resented my getting out from under his thumb, of course." Coleman was looking very relieved. "Why will it be tied up?"

"Well, you see, legally nobody can profit directly from a crime. If your sister is convicted, that will can't be proved. It'd be a little legal mess, I'm afraid. The estate was left in trust, so the trustees at the bank would have some say—but it might take a while to straighten it out."

"What would have to be done?" asked Coleman interestedly.

"Mrs. Coleman would have to petition the court to set the will aside and award the estate to her as the next blood relative. I think it'd go through without much trouble, but it'd take time. Maybe a lot of time—the law's like the mills of the gods, doesn't get things done overnight."

"That's if—if Dulcie's found guilty. What happens if she isn't?"

"Why, then the will goes into probate and she gets it all. Except for your hundred bucks. But that's another tie-up, you see, because as matters stand I can't put it into probate. We'll have to wait until we know the outcome of the trial."

"I see," said Coleman.

"Either way we'll get the money, you mean," said Marcia. "Both of us. Because I know how Dulcie'll feel. If she got it all she'd share with me. If I get it all, I can give her half, can't I?"

"If you want it that way."

"But you might have to wait quite a while before you get paid for your services," said Coleman.

"Don't fuss about that. I can stand it. Lawyers get used to that sort of thing."

"Mr. Falkenstein," said Marcia in a small tight voice, "what—what do you think is going to happen?"

He didn't pretend to misunderstand her. "I think we've all got to realize," he said gently, "that the chances aren't very good for your sister to be found innocent. It may seem to you that it's rather vague evidence against her, and mostly what's called circumstantial evidence. But what a lot of people don't realize is that circumstantial evidence is perfectly valid. In this case—well, you can see it for yourselves, it isn't so much a question of her possible guilt as the near impossibility of anybody else having done it. Maybe that's oversimplifying, but you see what I mean."

They looked at each other in wretched silence. "What kind of sentence would she get?" asked Coleman.

"Well, it's second degree. It's barely possible that a judge might hand her a ten to twenty, but I'd be more inclined to expect something like five to ten, and that would mean she'd probably get parole in about two years."

"Two *years*," said Marcia, and gave a little dry sob.

"Better than the other," said Coleman shortly. "When do you think the trial might come up?"

Jesse shrugged. "The calendars are always full. A couple of months—it could be longer."

"Oh, my God," he said.

"There was a story in the *Times*," she said. "Not much, and on a back page— But there are the children, you can't lie to them, and Jay and Ann are old enough to be sensible, but—"

"Excuse me," said Jesse, "for prying, Mrs. Coleman. Just an academic question. Your sister doesn't seem to have any close friends. Any friends period. I mean, rallying around as it were. I realize she'd been living a restricted life lately, but surely—"

"Oh, for heaven's sake," said Marcia. "Excuse *me* to say that's just like a man. Of course she had friends—at school, and later on. Good friends. If not a squad of them— Dulcie's not the kind to have a lot of friends. But all the other girls went on to get married, some of them pretty young, and they started their own families, and married women have different interests, different concerns, and not much time for gadding around. For a while there'd have been the phone calls, the occasional get-together—and then when Dulcie had to be home most of the time she wasn't working, they just—dropped away. I know exactly how it would happen. First it'd be, I haven't seen Dulcie in ages, I really must call her, and later on it'd be, I wonder what ever happened to Dulcie, and then they'd stop thinking about her."

"Yes, I suppose so."

"It's just, I feel so d-damned guilty," she said suddenly. "I could have helped more than I did—gone to spell her once a week or something—"

"Now, Marcia," said Coleman.

"I could have. And now this—I don't know how she can be so—so calm about it. When I saw her yesterday—that enormous jail, and guards—"

Coleman got up. "We'd better not take up any more of your time, sir," he said heavily.

Before he could get away, Thurlow called him from the CPA office downstairs. "Say, I've been over all these figures, and very interesting they are. I wish the old boy was alive to tell me how he lived so cheap. But what I come up with, adding up his gross income and subtracting expenses, property taxes, and income taxes, he should have come out on the right side of the ledger—I'm talking about this year—by eighty-nine thousand, six hundred and seventy bucks and ninety-two cents."

"For the Lord's sweet sake," said Jesse.

"Did I understand you to say you don't know where he was putting it? It's just gone?"

"That's about the size of it. Oh, there's a lot of stock, and real estate, but this'll be the net income derived from that, and it doesn't seem to be anywhere visible. My God. As much as that?"

"Last year it added up to more—the market's been down. Let's see, it came to a hundred and five thousand, seven hundred something. Net."

"Thank you so much," said Jesse. "Send me your bill, and all those figures."

"Oh, I won't forget."

He got down to Meyer and Salmon, one of the oldest and most conservative brokerages in town, at one-thirty. It was housed on the ground floor of a newly refaced office building on Spring Street, and it was a large busy place with a lot of smartly groomed secretaries and young executive types. After talking to several of those, he was finally introduced to a Wallace Halliday, who took him into a private cubbyhole in a row of those at the rear of the office. Halliday was in his forties, with a cheerful round face and bland dark eyes. He was the broker here Vanderveer had dealt with.

"Oh, yes, I remember the old boy, Mr. Falkenstein. He'd been dealing with the firm since before my time—Brett was handling his account, and when he retired and I took on some of his clients, Vanderveer didn't think much of me at first." He laughed. "What do you want to know? You said you're settling his estate?"

"That's right. There's a lot that isn't very clear, evidently records missing. When was the last time he did any buying or selling?"

"Oh, a good five years ago," said Halliday. "He never did much speculating, chopping and changing around—we didn't see him all that often. Sometimes he'd hang onto something just awhile and then sell, usually did himself some good too, but mostly he just bought the stuff to sock away and sit on—the blue-chip stuff. He never asked me for advice, he knew just what he wanted to do. I remember the first thing he bought through me was a block of Pacific Telephone, and he never let go of it."

"How did he handle the transactions?" asked Jesse. "Personal checks or what?"

"Well, when I first had his account it was checks—that was about fifteen years ago. He was still in business then, and able to drive. He'd drop in here once in a while, talk over the market, tell me what was on his mind—sell this, buy into that—and if there was anything due, he'd hand over a personal check. Later on, I suppose when he was older and not feeling so spry, he'd do business by phone. I'd get him a current quote if he wanted to buy anything, and he'd mail me a cashier's check. Or if he was selling, we'd mail him ours. But he hadn't done any business with us in a good five years. I could check, but I think it was along in the spring of 1976, might have been 1977. I was thinking of that, oddly enough, just the other day," said Halliday thoughtfully. "He wanted to sell a block of G.M. common, and I told him he was crazy. Let me look it up." Halliday rummaged in the bottom drawer of the tall file cabinet behind his desk. "Inactive accounts— never know when they'll come to life—R, S, T, U, here we are—" He straightened with a manila folder in one hand and sat down again. "Yep." He riffled through statements and found what he wanted. "G.M. common, like money in the bank, I said he was nuts. He knew me then, and he just laughed. He said, wait and see. He just had a hunch that pretty soon the American manufacturers were going to find themselves in trouble, it was time to get out. And wasn't he right indeed, if it took a while. He was a smart old boy, Vanderveer. But he was pretty old then, he'd been retired for some time, and he couldn't drive anymore. He hadn't been doing much dealing for a few years before that—" Halliday had been leafing through the statements and now clicked his tongue again rapidly. "Oh-oh, there was that—I'd forgotten that. Yep. 1965. He sold off a great big parcel of stuff, different bundles of stock—some good stuff too—and took it all in one big check. He said he was buying an apartment building with it, paying it off clear. It came to a hundred and seventy-seven thousand, six hundred odd. I said he was crazy then too, and he laughed and said, a good rule always was to diversify your holdings, and real estate was always the first thing to go in a depression and the first thing to come back."

And that would be the apartment on Fountain, Jesse surmised. At today's inflated prices, it might change hands for nearly double that. He said, "He'd dealt with other brokerage firms. Rettig and Rettig, Neuman—"

Halliday's eyebrows shot up. "He had?" He sounded incredulous. After a moment he laughed. "That's damned funny. Damned funny. As a rule, an investor picks one broker and stays with him —unless, of course, he's the kind of investor who takes the broker's advice and it turns out to be not so hot. There's no difference in commissions, what's the point of going to two or three?"

"Could you suggest any reason he shopped around?"

Halliday passed a hand over his round well-shaven face. "Old Vanderveer," he said thoughtfully. "He was a queer old codger all right. He had some funny ideas. About women, for instance. Old-fashioned. Now you take my wife, she's got quite a nose for the market—a smart girl. But that old boy—I'd lay a bet he was pretty secretive about his private business. You know? He was what they call a self-made man—liked to boast about it—told me how he'd started working at fourteen, got to be a master cabinetmaker and went on to start his own business—construction. It just could be that he didn't want any one broker knowing all about what he held, all his assets. All I can think of." Halliday grinned. "Uncle Sam would know, of course, but that he couldn't avoid. Like not putting all his eggs in one basket."

"Um," said Jesse. "Do you think he was an honest man, Mr. Halliday?"

Halliday looked serious, and massaged his round cheek again. "Now that's not a thing always easy to guess about another man. But I'd say he'd have been honest to the letter of the law. He might cut corners a little—always a way to beat the devil round a gate—but it'd all be perfectly legal. On the other hand—well, he was mighty fond of money, that old boy."

"Yes," said Jesse. "Well, thanks very much for nothing."

"All the same, you have to admire a fellow like that. Pulled himself up from nothing and died worth a small fortune."

"The hand of the diligent maketh rich," said Jesse, "so Solomon says. Thanks very much." He got up.

He stood in the entry beyond the elegant smoked-glass front door with the gold lettering and reflected dismally that he'd have to see every one of these brokers personally. He hadn't looked at those statements in Vanderveer's file cabinet. Vanderveer hadn't had any dealings with this house in over five years, but he could have had with others; and if he had been starting to go a little senile, he could have destroyed statements; it wouldn't say anything if the statements in his files weren't recent.

That IOU of Schultz's was somewhere. That secretive, sly old man—not putting all his eggs in one basket—

No, of course he'd have to report everything all honest to Uncle. Uncle had so many snoopers now—the automatic reports of all bank dealings sent to Uncle, any other deals—all the duplicate paper work— He couldn't have gotten away with keeping other bank accounts. Even bank accounts in different names, because he'd need different addresses for the statements—and come to think of it, different Social Security numbers. Social Security numbers didn't appear on bankbooks, weren't recorded by the bank, but all bank reports and tax returns, ending up in Uncle's hands, got tied to Social Security numbers, and when there wasn't one on file for the fictitious name, no tax returns, Uncle would investigate. The mills of the gods— Vanderveer couldn't have hidden away any of his take that way. And that, he'd know.

And what Halliday had said—the letter of the law. And maybe not, too.

The phrase ran teasingly across his mind again, not putting all his eggs in one basket. Jesse swore, fumbling for his car keys as he started for the parking lot. Vanderveer always close-mouthed, a loner, and secretive—but— As he came up to the car he amended that in his mind. Vanderveer had discussed his affairs with Halliday, probably to a much greater extent with his former partner and close friend Howard Griffin, very possibly with other men, while he was still active in business. It was women he thought were stupid about money—he hadn't wanted the foolish women to know anything about his cache of cash in the house, what business deals he was into, how much he had— And something else. Liked to boast a little, said Halliday. Lonely, said Dulcie. Yes, he'd been in the habit of a busy active life, mostly among other men, and when he retired he hadn't had much to do with himself. Reading *The Wall Street Journal* at the library— And Dulcie had also said, Uncle Howie at that rest home for two years, and Papa friendly with a couple of other old men there.

It was a thought. And it was five minutes past three, and he had an appointment with a new client at four.

On Thursday afternoon Nell started out to the market about three, with Davy strapped into the seat beside her. When she went past the nearest house, a quarter mile down the hill, there was a woman bending over a flower bed near the street, pulling weeds. Impulsively Nell braked and got out.

The woman stood up and Nell introduced herself. "We just moved in last month, and we do like it up here so much—it's so quiet, isn't it? You really feel as if you're away from the city." The woman was about forty, thin and angular, with a narrow jaw and a thin-lipped mouth.

"Oh. You're the people bought Miss Spicer's house. I'm Mrs.

Tidwell. We didn't know her at all, she was a sort of peculiar woman, an artist, you know."

"Yes, I know." The realtor had told them that: Miss Bertha Spicer had been a well-known illustrator of children's books. "What I stopped to ask you—"

"Artists are always peculiar," said Mrs. Tidwell.

"Well, what I wanted to ask you, do you have a Siamese cat? Because—"

"Heavens above, no," said Mrs. Tidwell. "I can't abide cats and neither can Martin. Nasty sly dirty things. Have you seen it up there? I don't know where it belongs—it's come into our backyard hunting birds, I'm always chasing it off, I called the pound once but they said I'd have to get it in a box before they'd send a truck, and of course you can't lay a hand on it—not that I'd want to—cats always carry germs."

Getting back into the car, Nell reflected that at least Mrs. Tidwell didn't live nearer and wasn't inclined to be neighborly. She stopped at the only other house at the bottom of the street, but there was nobody home.

CHAPTER 5

On Friday morning a new client had a damage suit in mind; it would be a rather complicated business, and Jesse took a couple of pages of notes in his finicky copperplate. The client left a little before eleven, and Jesse swiveled around in his desk chair and stared unseeingly out the window, wondering what he was going to say to a judge and jury about the deaths of the Vanderveers.

Call Klein as a character witness. Such a nice reliable girl, she'd never do such a thing. Very useful. And there was Eberhart—Eberhart the dogmatic, couldn't have made a mistake, know what I saw. Oh, yes? Jesse sighed to himself.

There was Dan Wolfe. Could have been the unwitting spark that triggered her—Dulcie, meekly looking after the old people, efficient at her job, all those dull years, reminded of what she had missed.

Eberhart could easily have confused the days. Tuesday when she forgot her keys, Thursday when the Vanderveers had died. But he didn't have any idea what story he might spin to a judge and jury.

Just before he went out to lunch, Rose Lenhoff called. "I know you've been trying to reach me, Mr. Falkenstein—I'm sorry, I've been in San Diego, my sister had an emergency operation—but thank God she's going to be all right, everything's fine. I just got back." He told her about the offered settlement, and she was pleased. He explained that they would have to get legal evaluations of all Lenhoff's property—he was into land development, had holdings all over—and after that it might be a while before they got a court date.

"I think what we're looking at here is sometime in early February. I know it's already taken some time—"

"So long as it's settled," she said. "I'm very grateful, Mr. Falkenstein. You'll be in touch then."

He started out for lunch, and as he came into the front office Jean was saying, "Well, I wish he had a twin brother to date me, it was just your luck I backed out of Gina's party and you got to meet him first—"

Jesse regarded the Gordons suspiciously. "Neither of you thinking of leaving me for the rich husband?"

They laughed at him. "Not yet," said Jimmy. "They don't grow on every tree, Mr. Falkenstein."

After lunch he went to see another stockbroker. Rettig and Rettig was another respectable conservative brokerage, not as venerable as the other one, or as large. It was out on the Sunset Strip, in a newish high-rise office building.

He got passed around a little, but ended up with Mr. Anthony Rinaldi, who belied his melodious name by being square and phlegmatic and businesslike, with a New York accent. "Oh, yes, I remember Mr. Vanderveer," he said. "I handled his account, but it didn't amount to much—he bought and sold stock infrequently. What exactly did you want to know?"

"When was the last time he did any business with you?"

"Oh, it's been some time ago. Five or six years at least." Rinaldi brought out a thin cigar and squinted at it before lighting it. "Oh, yes, I remember him. He dealt with us for ten or twelve years, just now and then as I said. A very decided character." Rinaldi looked thoughtfully at the cigar. "The last time I saw him —your asking about him just reminded me—well, I wonder if he was right."

"About what?"

"To the best of my recollection it was early in 1977. He came in and wanted to sell a block of some preferred stock, I forget what it was, and I tried to persuade him into buying some South African gold stock. A very sound investment and paying quite well, but he just laughed at me and said I'd lose my shirt, go in for that." Rinaldi looked a little disturbed. "Five years ago, but the headlines yesterday— Vanderveer said that was the next Communist goal, reason for all the trouble there, and anybody fool enough to invest money there could kiss it good-bye."

"Oh," said Jesse. "And doesn't it look as if he was right. He hadn't done any business with you since then? Well, thanks so much."

When he left there he was thinking again about that convalescent home and Howard Griffin. Had anybody mentioned which one it was? He stopped at a public phone and called Mrs. Griffin to ask; but nobody answered the phone. He called Marcia Coleman and she couldn't remember, had only been there twice. He finally had to chase all the way down to the jail—they wouldn't summon a prisoner to the phone on the mere claim that it was her lawyer—and Dulcie told him that it was the Golden West Convalescent Home on Vermont.

It wasn't very far out on Vermont. There were a couple of big hospitals in that area, a Kaiser hospital, the Hollywood Presbyterian Medical Center, and there were several convalescent homes not far away; this was one of them. It occupied nearly half a block, a tan stucco building with a red tile roof, and had its own small parking lot.

Beyond plain double doors he found himself in a little lobby with a counter built halfway across at the back, vinyl-covered banquettes, a couple of low tables spread with magazines. There was a vacant-eyed old lady strapped into a wheelchair sitting on one side of the lobby, and a stout young woman with sandy hair behind the counter.

She listened with perfunctory interest and said, "Well, most of the old people are always pleased to have visitors, whatever kind. I'd better let you talk to Mrs. Seager." She led him out of the lobby into a wide hallway.

As such places went, this one seemed to be a nice enough place. It all looked very clean and bright and tidy. As he followed her along the hall, he had glimpses into rooms with open doors, small rooms with two single beds each, but airy and neat. They passed a cross hall, and down there to the right was a double exit door propped open, beyond it a neat quadrangle of lawn and trees and brick walks. Not inviting today, with an overcast gray sky and a chill wind moving the trees, but in nice weather it would be a pleasant place for the patients here.

Patients. Euphemisms, he thought. The majority of people here, as in most of these places, were the old people—senile, or just physically incapable, or without responsible family, for whatever reason sitting here waiting for death.

Up the hallway another cross hall cut through; they passed a uniformed nurse's aide pushing a wheelchair with an old man in it. There was an L-shaped counter, a desk with a telephone, and a couple of uniformed nurses.

"I don't want to disrupt any routine," said Jesse meekly.

Mrs. Seager regarded him benignly. "Don't worry about that." She was a rather tall thin woman in her forties, with a plain no-nonsense face, defiantly gold-tinted blond hair, an inquisitive long nose; she looked very efficient. He noticed her severe little cap, the gold badge on her uniform, remembering that these places had to have a fully trained RN for every so many rooms or patients. "Of course I remember Mr. Griffin very well," she told him. "And his friend—I'd forgotten the name until you said it—Mr. Vanderveer. He used to come nearly every day while Mr. Griffin was here. We were sorry to lose Mr. Griffin, such a nice old man, and he always tried to keep cheerful in spite of all the pain he had."

"I understand Mr. Vanderveer had gotten friendly with some of the other patients here. I'd like to talk to any of those."

"Oh?" she said a little blankly. "Well, of course the ambulatory patients sit in the TV room a good deal, and on his good days Mr. Griffin would be there—I know he was friendly with a few of the other men, I suppose he could have introduced the other old gentleman. I wouldn't know about that, it's the aides and LVN's who have the most to do with the patients, you see. But you can ask, of course—it's just down this hall." She slipped off her high stool and led him down the cross hall. "We call it the TV room, but actually it's more than that—we have card tables set up and various amusements for the ones still able to function. There are a couple of church groups who are very faithful about coming in, and we have a director of hobbies who supervises little arts and crafts projects and games, to give them some interest in life. That's very important, of course." They passed a wheelchair with an ancient wrinkled man sagging to one side, mumbling to himself, and came into a very large room, vaguely like a hotel lobby. It was at least forty feet long, and well furnished, if not expensively, with couches, chairs, low tables. There was a color TV in one corner, and an old lady in a wheelchair was hunched in front of it watching a soap

opera; the sound was turned low. There were a couple of old ladies in wheelchairs talking animatedly to three women sitting on a
couch. At the opposite end of the room four men were sitting together, two in wheelchairs, one flanked by a couple of heavy
canes.

"Oh, there's Mr. Ott," said Mrs. Seager cheerfully. "He and
Mr. Griffin were great friends." She led Jesse up there and introduced them, and went away with the air of washing her hands of
him.

Ott was the man with the canes. He had once been a big man,
but he had shrunk with age; he had bright little blue eyes and his
mind seemed to be working all right. "Oh, sure," he said at once
to Jesse's question, "Griffin and I were good pals, had a lot in
common, I was in construction too if not one of the bosses. He
was a nice fellow—shame he had to have so much trouble with
that leg of his. His wife's a nice woman, came to see him every
day. It makes a difference when you have people coming, my
daughter and son come as often as they can, a'course I lost my
wife last year. Sure I know Vanderveer, Griffin's old partner, he
was here most days and he's come back a few times since Griffin
died, that was the end of July." He introduced Jesse to the others:
Fischback, a big fat man in a wheelchair, Perloff, a smaller man in
the other wheelchair, a Mr. Nettleton. "He's not incarcerated
here, just our visiting preacher." Nettleton was a middle-aged man
with a thin face and fine gray eyes with a twinkle in them.

They had all known Vanderveer. They were surprised but not
shocked to hear he was dead. "Of course he was older than
Griffin," said Ott. Jesse didn't elaborate on the death and nobody
asked questions. "Do I remember what he used to talk about?"
Ott repeated doubtfully. "Well, Griffin and Vanderveer talked
about old times mostly, guess that's what old people usually do
talk about, isn't it? Jobs they'd done when they had their own
business, deals they'd made—they'd both done pretty well, I gathered—"

Fischback said somberly, "And families and wives and good
times when we were all young. Like that."

"Why do you ask?" asked Perloff curiously. Jesse explained:
settling the estate, and some records not clear. "I just wondered if

he ever mentioned much about what he owned, how much he had and what it was in—anything like that."

"Oh," said Ott. "Well, I dunno. I know Griffin told me that Vanderveer had parlayed his take into quite a pile, investing in the stock market—me, I was never smart enough to fool with that even if I'd had the money. Griffin said Vanderveer used to give him lots of tips, he'd made quite a bit too. Now I do recall that Vanderveer said he owned real estate too, I think he had quite a bit tied up in that."

"I guess he was pretty damn smart about making money," said Fischback gloomily. "The way he talked. And what Griffin used to say."

"He thought we're heading for a big economic crash," said Ott. "Something real bad. He said he figured there'd be bank failures and a lot of businesses going down the drain. Oh, I don't know if it'd mean anything to you, but he said once that he used to keep a big savings account at the bank, but when the government was going to slap the withholding tax on savings, and seeing you get such piddling little interest, he closed it out."

"Yeah, I remember him saying that," agreed Fischback. "Must be nice to have money, all I can say. That much money." He sounded envious and angry. "He said that—about another depression, and the banks—he said anybody had very much was a damn fool to leave it all in one bank. Something about diversifying, he said. My God, I got little enough in one bank account—"

"My God!" said Jesse. "Oh, yes, I see. That's enlightening."

"He was a queer mixture—an interesting man, Vanderveer," said Perloff. "He was actually quite proud of the fact that he'd had very little formal education—oh, excuse me, I'm a retired schoolteacher, you see, I taught math at Marshall Junior High for nearly forty years. But he had a very quick mind, it was rather remarkable at his age. I always did say, if one has to end up incapacitated, I'd rather have it physical than mental," and he looked ruefully at the blanket across his legs. "I'm very thankful my mind's as good as it ever was. Do you know, I taught him to play chess—Mr. Nettleton very kindly comes in to give me a game when he has time—and Vanderveer took to it right away, even beat me a few times. But I don't think he'd have talked about his private affairs to us, except in general terms. He probably did with

Griffin. The days when Griffin wasn't so well they'd be in his room, not out here."

"Griffin had old Ortiz in with him mostly, didn't he?" said Ott. "Well, he died before Griffin did, so that's no good. He didn't speak very good English anyway. It was that temporary patient was in with Griffin just before he died—Dickey, that was the name, Adam Dickey. Had his knee crushed in an auto accident, he was here a couple of months having therapy. I remember they moved him the night Griffin died—I never saw that Mrs. Seager ruffled before, but she was then—I guess Griffin started to pass away before they rightly expected it, and they don't like a patient in the same room—" Ott sighed sharply. "Not a thing anybody likes to think about, but we all come to it. I guess we're not much help to you, sir."

"Well, have to keep poking around," said Jesse. "I just wish he had thought some about dying, and realized somebody'd have to do the tidying up."

"Left things in a mess, did he?" asked Fischback. "Must be a nuisance for the family."

"Yes. *We brought nothing into this world and it is certain we can carry nothing out*—isn't it the truth—"

Nettleton coughed and said, "Excuse me, but I have always thought that that line is much misinterpreted, Mr. Falkenstein. That's not strictly true at all. We bring a good deal into this world with us—what brain we have, our physical bodies to use at useful work and play and procreation, what talents we may have, what characters we develop. And we take a good deal with us when we leave, too—all that's eternally important to us, the good or evil we've done, the love we've given, kindnesses done, the whole results of how we've employed our characters, our lives, what we've given our children of moral training, the responsibilities we've borne. The least important thing about any person is what material possessions he may control while he's here—that is so ephemeral. The most important is what we take with us when we leave."

"And that's true too," said Jesse soberly. *"His own iniquities shall take the wicked himself, and he shall be holden with the cords of his sins."*

Nettleton beamed at him gently. *"The Wisdom of the Torah.* Oh, yes, indeed that is true."

That damned wily old sinner, playing both ends against the middle, thought Jesse as he drove home. Not dreaming up any tax dodges at all: just hedging his bets. Expecting some banks to fold, maybe the big ones shored up later, just protecting his assets—scattering money around in different banks, and my God, there were ten thousand in the greater L.A. area—what a hell of a job—but there must be some way to narrow down the hunt. And where were the bankbooks, the bank statements? It wasn't likely he'd have used banks out in the valley, or down at the beach, probably nearer home—

Oh, yes? Those accounts would be inactive, he wouldn't have had occasion to visit the banks—he could have done the whole thing by mail. Yes, and according to that woman at the apartment the other day, the mail was delivered about eleven o'clock, and Vanderveer would have been the one to take it in; and the chances were that on Saturdays, even if Dulcie was home and not at the market, he'd get it then too. What the hell had he done with the statements?

Trying to second-guess the old fox, Jesse felt halfway certain that he'd had a hidey-hole of some kind at home—and more than sixty bucks in it. Emergency provisions, for when the banks shut up. The stray thought slid across his mind—that visiting nurse, he forgot her name, Gibson—how long would she be there when she came? The old man used to her coming and going in the house, and he didn't pay much attention to women anyway—except, Jesse amended, in one way, and he marveled again at what the Perez woman had said. Would the nurse possibly have noticed anything? By God, he'd go over that house inch by inch, in case there was a hidey-hole of some kind. He couldn't get at the banks until Monday anyway.

The gate was open. He drove through, got out and closed it, drove into the garage and went in the back door. Nell was taking something out of the oven. He said to her, "You've got duplicate keys to the office, and access to the safe-deposit box and checking account. You know where my will is, and where to find the combination to the office safe. You do know which insurance company we're with, don't you?—well, it's in my address book at the office. I can't think of anything else—oh, don't forget we're both members of the Neptune Society—cheap disposal, cremation, and ashes scattered at sea. Very hygienic."

Nell stared at him. "You've suddenly found out you've got an incurable disease?"

"I feel fine," said Jesse crossly. "But I tell you, these damned secretive people can leave utter chaos behind, without intending to. What a mess. Come and sit down and hold my hand and I'll tell you about it."

"You sound as if you need a drink," said Nell sensibly. "For once the offspring's peacefully playing in his room. He can have another half hour before bed."

He felt a little better for the drink and dinner. It was getting on for eight o'clock when he called Clock and brought him up to date.

"Tomorrow's your day off, and you're the expert on where people hide things, after covering all the burglaries. You can come and help me hunt."

Clock swore. "It's not a police case any longer, it's all your own baby."

"Listen," said Jesse, "I keep reminding you, I've got a lot of money, maybe to leave some to a niece or nephew. You'd better keep on good terms."

"Oh, hell," said Clock and laughed. "O.K., I'll meet you there at nine o'clock. And Fran's feeling a lot better, she hasn't been sick in a couple of days."

"Good. I'll see you in the morning."

"I'll tell you one thing," said Clock on the front porch of the house on Kingsley on Saturday morning. "If there's anything here worth anything, you'd better locate it and take it away. An empty house in central Hollywood is a standing invitation to the burglars."

"The thought had crossed my mind. None of the furniture would be any loss, but I'd better ask the Colemans to pack up all Dulcie's things. Now look, Andrew. I think the chances are that if he had a little hidey-hole here, it'd be in the den. Under his own eye. I think we start there."

They went down to the little room and Clock surveyed it dubiously. "I'm not all that much of an expert. The carpet's fastened down, that's no good." They took everything out of the wardrobe, tapped the floor and walls. They emptied the file cabinet—Jesse wanted all the contents anyway—and looked at the undersides of its drawers. They took the studio couch apart to look under the mattress. They turned the old-fashioned desk chair over.

Clock stood in the middle of the room eying the rolltop desk. "My grandfather had one something like this, and it had a secret drawer in it. I remember him showing me the trick. Let's see. It was at the back of one of the pigeonholes, a place you pushed—" He fumbled around in the pigeonholes, one after the other, without result, finally found an old steel letter opener and prodded with that.

Suddenly part of the ornamental carving below the pigeonholes shot out with a little click, revealing a small drawer about an inch deep and four inches long.

"Not very secret or very big," said Jesse.

"Don't be so ungrateful."

The drawer held just two pieces of paper. One proved to be Schultz's IOU on an ordinary piece of bond typing paper. The other one was another piece of Dulcie's stationery with one line printed on it in a crabbed hand. *G. W. 411-0219.*

"Now what the hell?" said Jesse.

"He couldn't stash away much cash in there," said Clock. He was looking around the room. "Now I do wonder—places this old don't usually have too many electric outlets." There was an overhead light with a switch by the door; an outlet behind the desk; and one across the room under the window, with nothing plugged into it. "Well, let's have a look." Clock kneeled down in front of it. "There's this new gadget out—of course it's not very big either, handy place to hide jewelry, little items like— Ah. There you are." The electric outlet wasn't an outlet at all, but a little box built into the baseboard; it tilted out under Clock's questing finger. The inside was about three inches deep and a couple of inches wide.

Crammed into it, tightly folded, were ten hundred-dollar bills.

"Well, very pretty," said Jesse. "The man was a carpenter, he could have installed that quietly while his wife was taking an afternoon nap. But my God, nobody knowing." He tucked the money away.

"Could be little caches like that all over the house for all we know," said Clock. Fired with the hunt, they carried it to the rest of the house. But all the other electrical outlets were just ordinary outlets. They took everything out of the front closet and sounded the floor, walls, and Clock got a splinter in his thumb off the shelf. They rummaged through the Christmas ornaments. They looked under the cabinet beneath the sink in the kitchen—"A good place to put a trapdoor," said Clock; but there wasn't any loose board.

"My God," said Jesse suddenly, "those boxes of *Wall Street Journals*—there could be bills tucked between every page—"

Clock emerged from crawling under the sink and stood up, brushing at himself. "At least we can look at those sitting down. I've had a rough week, and I'm beat. How you get into these things, Jesse—"

They dumped all the old *Journals* out of those boxes and went through them thoroughly page by page, but didn't find any more money hidden there. It took a while.

They gave up at two o'clock and went out for a belated lunch.

Jesse had called that Visiting Nurse service and gotten the name and address of the woman who had gone to the Vanderveers'. She was Mrs. Amelia Gibson and she lived on Courtney Avenue. Clock had gone home after lunch, claiming that he was entitled to half a day's rest. Jesse found a public phone outside the restaurant and tried her phone number. She was in. No, she wouldn't mind talking to him.

It was an old apartment building on an old street on the border of West Hollywood; probably these places were larger and more comfortable than a lot of the jerry-built new ones. She lived on the second floor, and when he'd pushed the bell the door opened on a chain, and she took his card through the crack before asking him in, unhooking the chain.

"Sorry, but you can't be too careful these days, the things that go on." Amelia Gibson was a plain woman in her fifties, with a sallow horseface and short gray hair. The living room was neat, plainly furnished, with no frills, utilitarian. She offered him a chair, sat down in another, and rather to his surprise accepted a cigarette.

"I don't know how I can help you," she told him. "I never knew the daughter at all."

"I know that. You'd been going to Mrs. Vanderveer how long, Mrs. Gibson?"

She thought. "About a year. I went Mondays, Wednesdays, and Fridays for a couple of hours. I think before that she had Miss O'Hagan. And sometimes the schedule gets changed, with temporary patients turning up, there were a few times I was sent to somebody else and another nurse substituted. The permanent patients usually get the same nurse, of course. Poor woman, she was getting more helpless all the time. It was a terrible thing her getting killed like that, I could hardly believe it when Mrs. Borchard told me, that's our supervisor—so much violence these days, but her own daughter—"

"Do you remember," asked Jesse, "any time you were there, Mr. Vanderveer having any visitors? Or maybe you happened to overhear something he was saying on the phone—not to suggest that you'd eavesdrop deliberately, but maybe you couldn't help hearing—"

She didn't acknowledge the invitation to gossip. "He was a crusty old man, not very sympathetic to his wife." She glanced at Jesse, and away, hesitated, and went on, "They couldn't have gone on like that much longer, she would have been bedridden before long, and needed a lot more care. I'd told him that, or tried to tell him, that they should make other arrangements. Put her in a rest home, or have more practical nurses in. I couldn't make him understand it, he just said his daughter would manage, she always had. I talked it over with Mrs. Borchard, and she said I ought to talk to the daughter. I never saw her, you see, because she was working all day. So I called her on a Saturday, and talked to her about it. I must say," said Mrs. Gibson uneasily, "she sounded quite sensible. She said she knew her mother was getting worse, but it was going to be difficult to make her father see it, that she'd try. Well, it was the family's business after all, nothing to do with me. Of course I was annoyed"—she drew down the corners of her mouth—"but that wasn't her fault—"

"About what?" asked Jesse.

"What? Oh, she happened to mention that my supervisor had called to ask if I was satisfactory and coming when I was supposed to—really I was very put out at Mrs. Borchard, of course she checks up on new nurses who haven't worked for the county before, but after all I've been with the service for nearly ten years, she knows I'm quite reliable. I didn't say anything about it, of course, but I was annoyed. But you were asking about any visitors or— He was really a most unpleasant old man. I remember once, quite some time ago, there was a young man came to pay his rent, Mr. Vanderveer owned rental property, you know, and he was quite ugly to him, Mr. Vanderveer I mean, shouting and threatening him because it was overdue."

"Mmh," said Jesse. "Remember anything else?"

"Well, yes," she said. "It was your mentioning phone calls that reminded me, and at first I wasn't going to say anything, but maybe I'd better. I did hear something once, something that really did disgust me." Her mouth drew tight. "You're quite right, Mr. Falkenstein, I wasn't trying to hear, but I'd be going back and forth from the kitchen to the bedroom and bathroom, you know, and of course it's not a large house. And the phone was on his desk in the den. This was just a couple of months ago, by the way. He was talking on the phone, and I couldn't help hearing what he was saying as I came past—and he was talking to a woman named Gloria, sounding like an old lecher—he was actually making a date with her, of all things, saying about the usual place on Saturday afternoon."

"Well, well," said Jesse. So Flo Griffin had been quite right.

"And him eighty if he was a day!" She sniffed. "They do say, no fool like an old fool."

That was all she could tell him, and it was interesting, but hardly helpful on any of his problems. He sat behind the wheel of the Mercedes and got out that little old address book—there hadn't been any general address book at the house—and hunted through it again. He realized again just how obsolete it was, most of the ink faded; all the old building-supply houses, names of realty companies—he recognized the name of one well-known developer whose obituary had been in the *Times* a couple of years ago. There were few personal names and no women's names at all. He puzzled briefly again over those cryptic little notations; no rhyme or reason to that.

And then suddenly he thought about that other paper in the little secret door of the desk. G.W.—G. for Gloria?

*   *   *

"You know, Jesse," said Nell, ladling out lima beans and passing the dish to him, "that cat. I don't think it has a home—I think it's lost, or abandoned. I asked the other people down the hill today, and they don't know anything about it either. Where it belongs. And we're so far from any other house—I suppose it would be attracted up here by all the underbrush, mice and things on wild land. That Mrs. Tidwell is a horror. I got another look at it this morning, it was sitting by the side fence, and it looks awfully thin. Siamese are usually pampered pets, but something could have happened, someone died or— And people do just abandon cats, the kind of horrible people who think cats can fend for themselves."

"It's a five-hundred-dollar fine in this state to abandon an animal," said Jesse. "You'd better start feeding it, then. Can't have Athelstane's friend going hungry."

"Oh, I will. I always liked Siamese, and if it ever had a good home it might make friends with people again."

Ensconced in the study after dinner, Jesse looked at that slip of paper curiously. G.W. Well, you never knew where something might show up.

He dialed the number, and after three rings a voice answered: a pleasant woman's voice, sounding educated and mature. "Is Gloria there?" asked Jesse.

"Who is this?"

"I just want to talk to Gloria, set up a date."

"I think you must have the wrong number," she said remotely. "This is the Worth residence."

"Sorry," mumbled Jesse, and hung up. Worth. G.W. He picked up the phone book. He had all six of the books covering Los Angeles County, but he was pretty sure that that prefix was local and tried the west central book first. And there it was as big as life. Robert Worth, an address on Glentower Terrace, and the same phone number. That would be up in the Hollywood hills, up near Griffith Park. Quite a classy address. What was this? He sat back and wondered.

But like Mr. Kipling's Elephant's Child, he was always curious, and whether this was relevant to anything or not, he'd like to know what the hell it was all about.

Early on Sunday afternoon he looked up the address in the *County Guide* and drove up there. It was one of the short streets curving off Beachwood Drive, and when he found the house, it was a handsome old Spanish place with a smooth lawn and rose beds in front, and past the end of the drive a hint of a pool behind. It said money, it said class, and just what its connection had been with Vanderveer he couldn't imagine. Well, you didn't get answers if you didn't ask questions. He parked in front, went up to the door, and pushed the bell.

The woman who opened the door might be in her late forties, not looking it. She was an attractive dark-haired woman with a fine fair complexion, a professional coiffure, smartly dressed in a navy sheath and tasteful costume jewelry. She had a very nice figure.

"Mrs. Gloria Worth?"

She looked at him in small surprise. "Why, yes."

"I think," said Jesse gently, "that you were acquainted with Mr. Jan Vanderveer."

Terror filled her eyes, stark and sudden. "No. I'm afraid I don't know anybody by that name."

"He had your phone number in a rather special place," said Jesse, watching her.

"What do you want?" she demanded sharply. "I don't know you—either."

"No, but I'm perfectly respectable, Mrs. Worth." He handed her a card; she didn't look at it. "Did you know he's dead? I'm the lawyer settling his estate, I'm just clearing up loose ends, that's all."

She said dully, after a long moment, "It was you—on the phone last night. So it starts up—all over again. You'd better come in. Thank God, Robert's out, he and the children went riding."

It was an elegantly furnished living room, expensive furniture, everything in excellent taste. She didn't ask him to sit down. She faced him coldly, and asked, "How much do you want?" And her voice was sharp and contemptuous.

Jesse said, "My God. He was blackmailing you? That old bastard— Look, Mrs. Worth, it's all right. I'm just tying up loose ends, as I told you."

She stared at him for a full minute, as if she were trying to see into his soul. "Oh, my God," she said in a strained voice, "I saw in the paper that he'd been killed, and I was never so thankful for anything in my life. Please, please—I have a husband and family, it would kill Robert to find out—Johnny didn't tell you, leave anything written down, did he? Oh, my God, haven't I paid enough in —in being so ashamed, for something twenty-eight years in the past?" That was passionate. "I've got a good decent husband, a son and daughter—I couldn't stand it if they knew—please, please don't—"

"Now calm down," said Jesse. "Take it easy." She was shaking all over; he took her by the shoulders and walked her over to a chair, made her sit down. He sat down on the couch opposite. "It doesn't matter what he had on you, there's no record. I don't know anything about it and if I did I wouldn't put an ad in the *Times* about it, or write your husband an anonymous letter. Everything's all right now, Mrs. Worth."

She stared at him again, and this time he saw her beginning to believe him.

"Oh, my God," she said, and drew a long unsteady breath. "I nearly died when I saw him—I hadn't seen him in twenty-six years— And of course it had to be that day my car was in the garage, and I had to keep a dental appointment—I had to be on the same bus. And he had to see me, and recognize me. I was—on my way home—and he followed me. Saw which house. I nearly died when I saw him on the porch—like an old dried-up mummy, he was old when I knew him—back all that time ago—standing there grinning at me like a fox, saying, you've got a nice house, Gloria, maybe a husband with money, a nice family—you think your husband 'd like to meet one of your old cust—" Her hand went to her mouth and her eyes were terrified again.

"Oh, I see," said Jesse. "Don't look so scared—I'm safe. That old bastard. Do you mean to say he—well, what did he want?"

"Money," she said bitterly. "Oh"—and she gave a hard laugh— "he'd be past wanting—anything else, wouldn't he? I've been paying him fifty dollars a week out of the housekeeping money, I couldn't manage any more, Robert's easygoing but he'd wonder if I asked—" Her voice had gone dull again. "Just a silly stupid kid, I'd gotten into drugs in high school, pot was just starting to be the 'in' thing then—and one thing led to another—it was only a couple

of years, I straightened up and pulled myself together—but it
would kill Robert—"

"Well, by God," said Jesse, "I wish the old bastard was alive to
get his teeth kicked in. That's the damndest— Whoever did kill
him deserves a medal, all I can say."

She managed a bitter laugh. "Amen to that."

"Look, don't worry. This won't go any further, I'll forget all
about it. Sorry to upset you all over again."

And she was glad to see him go, if she did believe him. But as
she shut the front door on him her eyes were still anxious.

He got into the car consumed with seething contempt for his
late client. You'd think the man would have been more concerned
with his immortal soul, as close to death as he was at eighty-one,
instead of still fanatically concentrating on raking in the pennies
and dimes wherever, however he could. The old bastard.

He sat at his desk on Monday morning and thought, how the
hell to track down those probable bank accounts? Banks didn't
give out information about their customers for the asking. Clock
could do it, but Clock was a busy cop—the police weren't concerned in the case any longer.

I'm a fool, he thought. The statements. It was just past the first
of the month, and the statements ought to be coming in—what the
hell had the old man been doing with them? Such a convoluted
mind—and Jesse could swear that they had searched that house
thoroughly, there wasn't another hidey-hole, but—they hadn't
looked in the garage, dammit. Never mind, the old man had had
somewhere to keep the statements—if he'd kept them at all. Very
likely the inactive accounts, though if he destroyed the statements
you'd think he'd have kept a record of the amounts somewhere.
Conceivably, of course, he could have had another safe-deposit
box at another bank, but if so where the hell was the key?

He called Marcia Coleman and asked about the mail. "Well, I
thought of it, of course," she told him. "I told the post office to
put a hold on it. Stop delivery. They wouldn't have gotten much
mail, mostly ads—a couple of Mama's old friends wrote to her occasionally. Why do you want to know?"

"I've just discovered he probably had some other bank accounts. The monthly statements ought to be drifting in, and it's the only way we're going to find out where and what."

"Do you want me to come and pick up what's there? Right now?"

"It's a long drive," said Jesse. "I apologize, but you couldn't authorize me to do it over the phone. Uncle's so persnickety about custody of the mails."

"I'll come up right away and bring it to your office," she said at once. "I can authorize you to get it from now on while I'm there, can't I?"

She must have gotten right on the ball; she came into the office at eleven o'clock and handed over a little package of mail. "I've got to get back—pick up Bobby at nursery school, and Marion's got a music lesson. But you can get the mail from now on."

Jesse was grateful and told her so. And when he went through the pile—catalogs, ads, no personal letters at all—there were two bank statements. One on the account they knew about, at Security-Pacific. And a statement from a Bank of America on Western Avenue. He ripped that open and looked at it and said, "Well, there we are. Good God. A mind like a corkscrew." The statement showed a checking account in the amount of twenty thousand even. No checks written on it in the last month—or probably ever.

Jesse lit a cigarette and thought about it. Why a checking account? In a savings account, he'd be earning the little interest at least—yes, but the withholding tax automatically abstracted to offset that—and the other way, the money immediately available.

He called Dobson and told him about it. "Probably some more will show up. I'll let you know."

"What a character," said Dobson. "Just keep me informed."

Jesse was just starting out for lunch when William DeWitt came in without being announced, as a privileged person, and said, "I forgot all about our ledger, Jesse. Miss Duffy just ordered some new letterhead stationery, and you know how fussy she is about keeping records. She reminded me to pick it up." He sat down in one of the clients' chairs, briefcase on his knee for once. "I've got a rather interesting transcript with me, a session with Wanda and a new sitter last night—some rather evidential material. I'll take you out to lunch and you can look it over."

"Fair enough," said Jesse. "And what's the latest on your ambiguous seeker after truth?" DeWitt looked blank. "The lady who thinks the medium's reading her mind."

"Oh, the Finch woman," said DeWitt. "My God, it makes you wonder about people, Jesse. If she's open-minded enough to go to a psychic, she ought to be willing to accept what she gets and evaluate it logically, good, bad, or indifferent. But that damn fool of a woman—worse than the other damn fools who are ready to swallow anything and everything a psychic says as gospel truth—she wants to believe it, but there's a lifetime of agnosticism, no conviction of survival, and when she comes out of the emotional jag she's got to hunt for the rational explanation. Telepathy!" said DeWitt, as if it were a four-letter word.

"Oh, yes," said Jesse. "Survival. It'll be interesting to find out what happens next, William. To what we take with us when we leave. I do just wonder what's happening to a late client of mine. Don't think anything very pleasant, William. Trust not, anyway. Where are we going for lunch?"

CHAPTER 6

Athelstane's friend or not, Nell knew that dog, and if he found anything edible around he wasn't going to leave it for anyone else. She spotted the cat about the middle of the afternoon, coming out from under the trees at the back of the yard and sliding under the shrubbery by the fence. She wondered, hunting for mice, gophers? She called Athelstane in and, as she had done yesterday, took out a paper plate heaped with fresh hamburger. She was careful not to go too near to where she'd seen the cat vanish, but she talked to the cat coaxingly, put the plate down on the edge of the lawn, and came back to watch at the kitchen window.

After about five minutes, the cat cautiously came out onto the lawn; it had waited longer yesterday. It approached the plate warily, and took its time about sniffing carefully at the contents. But then it hastily bolted down the hamburger, not in the normal leisurely way of a cat confident of routine meals, but seizing a windfall before it should vanish. The cat was certainly very thin, and its fur rough-looking, but now Nell had a good look, it was a once-handsome seal point Siamese.

"I wonder," she said aloud to Athelstane, "where on earth you came from and what happened to you."

Jesse descended on the precinct station in midafternoon and interrupted Clock typing a report on a burglary. Clock was the sole occupant of the detective office, and he told Jesse he was busy. "I need somebody to talk at," said Jesse, dragging up Petrovsky's desk chair and sitting down across from Clock's desk. "Discuss what's showed up. I think you were all a little hasty about sending the reports down to the D.A.'s office on this one, Andrew."

"Oh, hell," said Clock, "I guess I'm due for a coffee break."

They brought paper cups of coffee and napkins from the machine down the hall. "What's on your mind now?"

"Dammit," said Jesse, "I suppose we'll uncover all the loot eventually. It's more important to me right now to think about this trial. How the hell to handle it. There are other possibilities here than the single-minded theory you relayed to the D.A. And especially, when I got to thinking about it, this Worth female." He told Clock about that: Clock was safe, and wouldn't pass it on; at the moment there was nothing to warrant any more police work on the case. "Think about it. She had, God knows, a motive. Vanderveer was in the phone book, she'd know where to find him. She could have done a little rudimentary snooping around, found out that Dulcie was out all day, even when that visiting nurse was there. Dammit, I wouldn't like to throw her to the wolves, but— And Vanderveer would have let her in."

"And just how could she have managed to set up that funny situation?" asked Clock.

"Well, I can think of ways," said Jesse uneasily. "She could have pretended to come to ask him, oh, to take one big lump sum once and for all and leave her alone. Maybe she brought a gun along intending to shoot him, for all we know. He was in the habit of ordering his wife around, he could have told her to stay in the bedroom while he and Gloria talked."

"And before she got around to shooting him, she asked to use the bathroom and just by chance opened the medicine cabinet and happened to notice the codeine capsules," said Clock. "So she offered to make him a cup of coffee in his own kitchen. And why kill the old lady too?"

"Well, if she'd seen her— And dammit all to hell, Andrew, there's an even likelier possibility. As I said before, the coincidences do happen—not everything in life is reasonable. The old fellow was getting shakier, feeling his age, missing his lifelong pal, and realizing whether he admitted it or not that his wife was getting worse. I don't think he cared much about her, but at the least she was going to start costing him a lot more money. It is just possible that he's the one arranged the overdose that morning—thinking they'd both be better out of it—and Gloria Worth walked in on him just afterward. She may not have planned to kill him—just plead with him—and there was an argument, and she lost her wits and grabbed up the poker when he got abusive. The autopsy report said it was just as likely that Myra Vanderveer fell out of her walker—hurrying to see what the noise was all about—and knocked herself out."

Clock sat back and scratched his big jaw. "Well, it's a little forced, but you've got an imagination."

"The back door," said Jesse. "Somebody went out that door after the old man was incapable of rehooking the chain." He was silent, and then he said, "Hell and damnation, I wish I had some vague idea of how to handle the case in court. What with Eberhart— Eberhart so sure and certain of his story—" And then he stood up and said loudly, "But, *Eberhart!*" He dropped his cup on Clock's desk. "Eberhart! Eberhart—suppose—"

Clock leaped up and snatched papers off the desk, began to mop up spilled coffee with a paper napkin. "For God's sake, what bit you? Look at this mess—"

"But suppose—" said Jesse. He sat down again. "I've been taking it for granted that Eberhart remembered seeing Dulcie come home for her keys on Tuesday morning, two days before—but suppose he was absolutely right and it was Thursday? My God, Andrew, don't you see it? It just suddenly struck me—it could have been the other one he saw—they're alike—and Marcia drives a tan two-door Chevy."

"For the love of Christ," said Clock, and stared at him. He dropped the sopping napkin into the wastepaper basket and lowered himself into the chair. "From out in left field. But—"

"And now I see it, it makes a hell of a lot more sense," Jesse said.

"Why?" asked Clock.

"Let me go on thinking, get it straight in my mind." Jesse stared into space for three minutes and then uttered a deep sigh, sat up, and lit a cigarette. "And it fits like a glove. I like it—it makes sense. What did everybody say? Marcia was the rebellious one, who got away, out from under his thumb. She has her own life, busy wife and mother, fond husband. But she's fond of her sister too, and feels guilty she couldn't help her more, as the situation got worse— Yes, and she wouldn't have gotten up to Hollywood often—once a month, less than that?—talked on the phone with Dulcie, that's all. But Griffin died at the end of July, and when she saw Dulcie at the funeral she realized just how exhausted she was, almost at the end of her rope. And she felt guiltier. Didn't know what to do about it, went on worrying about it. And then we get that family row after the visiting nurse talked to Dulcie, when they tried to persuade the old man to put his wife in a rest home and he refused to listen—that must have brought matters to a head. The girls were both fond of their mother, but Marcia had nothing but dislike for the old man—and Dulcie would have told her how Mama kept saying she just wanted to die and be at rest. And the more she thought about it, the more she saw it as a solution. She'd escaped, but Dulcie had sacrificed her life to the old people, and the mother's life was only a misery to her, the pain and helplessness. It would be a kindness to put her at rest, same as we have the decency to do for an animal we're fond of who's suffering. And how easy it all falls into place from there, Andrew."

"I see it," said Clock slowly. "It's possible."

"Yes, the busy wife and mother, children at school—even Bobby at nursery school—and Charles at his English classes at the college. She'd always have errands to do, out every day in her own car. Ask where she was? At the market—busy supermart where nobody'd remember if she was there or not. And the times fit so nicely too—she'd have gotten up to Hollywood about eleven, surprise visit to Mama and Papa. And of course she had the freedom of the house. She knew all about the codeine capsules. And they were both used to being waited on, the old man because that's what women were for, the old woman because she couldn't do much for herself. And another thing you said, that other story sounds forced—yes, the reason I don't halfway like it. Because Vanderveer wasn't at all the kind to think of suicide. He was too passionately interested in the affairs of this world, in the material possessions."

"Yes," said Clock. "But when it went wrong—how did it, do you think?"

"The same way you said it went wrong for Dulcie. She thought the old man was already unconscious, brought out the suicide note too soon—and he realized what she was up to and lashed out at her. He was old and shaky, but he'd been a powerful man in his prime—if he had the poker—and she grabbed it and got in a lucky hit. The old lady, coming to investigate, fell out of the walker."

"What I was going to say," said Clock, "when she saw the fake suicide wasn't going to stand up, why didn't she fake a break-in? It'd have been easy enough, make it look as if some casual thief had pried open the kitchen door. Wouldn't she have realized that Dulcie might be blamed?"

"I don't think," said Jesse, "that she would have been thinking very clearly right then. She'd had to nerve herself up to do the thing at all—the physical struggle would have finished her for any straight thinking. She just ran." He got up and stood looking out the window, to the parking lot below. "It wasn't until later she realized what the police thought. What she'd inadvertently let Dulcie in for. And she'd be feeling a hell of a lot guiltier now. I think if I tackled her on the stand she'd come right apart and admit it. Think even if I tackled her right now—or if you did—she'd admit it." After a silence, he added, "And I can imagine how Dulcie would feel about that."

"Oh, so can I," said Clock heavily.

Jesse got back to the office at four o'clock. There was paper work to do. The girls were turning down appointments for this week and next; he had to have time to think about all this.

Ten minutes after Jesse came in, Jimmy announced that Mr. Renaldo wanted to see him. A Roberto Renaldo. Jesse put down his pen.

He was a handsome young fellow in his early twenties, dark and romantic-looking like the hero in a young-adult novel. He was tall, and he had brooding dark eyes, arched thick brows, a mobile mouth. He was neatly dressed in casual sports clothes. He greeted Jesse with formal courtesy.

"There is a notice in the mail, that this is where the rent is to be paid? You are a lawyer who processes the will of the old man, his property?— Ah, I thought this when I see the door outside, attorney at law. I have come to give you notice that we leave the house."

"Oh," said Jesse.

"The atmosphere of the house, it disturbs my wife, Lucia. Since the old man is murdered. He was a very wicked old man, and since he first upset Lucia we have thought of moving anyway. Now he is murdered she is more upset, naturally, to think of a murderer about, and so we will move. It is expensive and a great trouble, but there is no choice."

Jesse asked, "How did Vanderveer upset your wife?"

Remembered fury came into the dark eyes. "Ah, it was an outrage! Imagine, this ancient, this old *padre caballo lascivo,* he has made the dirty advances when he came to collect the rent—imagine, a man as old as that, it was an outrage! He thought because we have not much money, we are not born Americans, he can take the liberty with a respectable girl! Lucia is upset and frightened—perhaps he has another key to the house, she says—I went to see this creature, and I am calm, I do not shout or swear at him, I merely tell him if he comes again to do this I will have the police arrest him, and if they will not I will kill him myself with a knife."

"Fine," said Jesse. "Did you scare him?"

"Oh, he sneers and swears, but I do not think he will come again, and he did not," said Renaldo. "And I put the chain on the door to calm Lucia. But the atmosphere—like all women she is a little superstitious, and says the spirit of a man murdered will still be about. Myself, I do not believe this. But we will move." He fixed Jesse with a royally fierce stare. "We will not always be poor, you understand. Now I drive a taxi, but I study the accounting in night school and someday will have my own business."

"Well, good luck to it," said Jesse.

Renaldo gave him a correct little nod. "I thank you, sir." He added casually as he went to the door, "It is devoutly to be hoped that the old man has now found his home with the devil, as no doubt he has." He marched out stiffly.

And Jesse thought, dammit, he wasn't a real estate agent. Another empty house. Better turn it over to an agent and let somebody else worry about it.

On Tuesday morning he faced Dulcie in one of the bare little rooms at the women's jail. "I just think we'd better lay a few things on the line, Miss Vanderveer. I don't want to sound pessimistic, but facts are facts and as your lawyer it's my job to tell you the truth."

"I should hope so," she said. She looked plain and washed out in the ugly tan uniform dress, without much makeup, her brown hair flat and uncurled.

"You'd better realize," he said expressionlessly, "the cumulative effect of all the evidence. First of all, of Eberhart's evidence. He's so very positive that he saw you drive in that morning, and he apparently has good reason for being positive."

"He's wrong, that's all."

"Well, he says he has a plausible reason for being sure. But beyond that, there's the entire background—the family situation. Your parents had very few close friends, very few visitors. There weren't many people who would have had the automatic freedom of that house, to locate those codeine capsules, to arrange that fake suicide setup so easily—to prepare the eggnog, the coffee, type that note, and so on. It would, as anyone can see, have been very easy for you. You didn't know any of the neighbors, or they you—most people on that block are out at work all day. The chances were good that nobody would notice you coming home that morning. You knew that Klein would be out, wouldn't miss you at the office. You see how it builds up—to anyone who doesn't know you."

"Yes," she said. "Do you think I haven't thought all that out for myself?"

"Let's just think," said Jesse, "who else might have been able to do it. Who would be automatically admitted, could wander around the house without causing any surprise. Now there's Mrs. Griffin. She's known you all your life, and she felt sorry for you just lately. She always disliked your father, felt sorry for your mother. She might, let's say, have decided to do a good deed and rescue you from a difficult situation. But it seems a pretty big responsibility for her to have taken—a double murder—and as you told me, you'd never really been close with the Griffins, though you called them aunt and uncle."

"No, that's ridiculous," said Dulcie with a faint smile. "She'd never have thought of such a thing, of course."

"Well, now, who else is there? There was a woman who had a great fear and hatred of your father—I needn't go into details—and he'd have let her into the house. But she wouldn't have known about the codeine capsules, and if she'd gone prying around he'd have objected, been suspicious, wouldn't he?"

"I don't want to know anything about her, Mr. Falkenstein. Yes, of course he would have been."

"The same thing holds true for a few other people—people he'd had arguments with lately. But there's a much better possibility we can think about. There's a fellow owed him some money, and he's a much better bet—he's the pharmacist where you got your mother's prescription."

She looked astonished. "Mr. Schultz?"

"That's right. Now, he could have come right in, and said there'd been some mistake in filling that last prescription, so he could get hold of the capsules. It's possible, say, that your father had already fixed the eggnog and coffee, and Schultz managed to slip the capsules into both. But it's a little hard to see how. It wouldn't be just one or two, but quite a lot. It wouldn't be easy to do, without being observed. Of course, he'd probably heard your father use that phrase—better out of it—he'd know enough to prepare that note."

"Oh, I don't think it could have happened like that," said Dulcie. She was looking at him calmly. "Papa often warmed up a cup of coffee for himself, I left a pot on the stove after breakfast. But he never bothered to get anything for Mama. On her good days she could get out to the kitchen, warm up coffee, or make a cup of tea. I left her a sandwich for her lunch. But that day she wasn't feeling well at all, I'd been worried about her all day. I don't think she'd have been able to fix herself that eggnog."

"Well, you can see how all this is going to sound in court," said Jesse briskly.

"You mean you think I'll be convicted?" She considered. "I've been thinking, Mr. Falkenstein, and I wonder if it was all just a terrible coincidence. Papa was always saying that, better out of it, if we never thought he meant anything by it. But he might have. He might have noticed Mama was so much worse, even if he wouldn't admit it, and decided to do that. Take her with him. And just afterward, some one of those people he'd had fights with came, and—there was another fight."

"Oh, yes, I thought of that too."

She said seriously, "But there's a good reason that that might

have happened. When the doctor prescribed those capsules for
Mama I wanted to know all about them, and I looked it up at the
library in the P.D.R—the *Physician's Desk Reference*—where all
prescriptive medicine is described. And one thing it said is that an
overdose causes excitability at first."

"Oh, really," said Jesse, taken off base.

She nodded. "If somebody Papa'd had trouble with came in just
after he'd taken that overdose, Papa might have been mad enough
and excited—by the overdose—to grab up the poker and attack
them. Him. It sort of makes sense, don't you think?"

Jesse said quietly, "Now, you might just have handed me the
line to follow in court, Miss Vanderveer. But there's another possibility, you know. We said Eberhart confused the days. Suppose
he didn't?"

There was a long silence. Faintly through the closed window
they could hear the hum of traffic outside. Dulcie turned a little
paler, but met his eyes, and the small square jaw looked squarer.
"You mean Marcia," she said quietly. "I was hoping you wouldn't
think of that, Mr. Falkenstein."

"So you thought it out too."

"Oh, yes. Our cars look alike, don't they? And we're generally
alike in size and coloring. And she'd been calling me oftener, she
said it wasn't until she saw me at Uncle Howie's funeral that she
realized how run-down I was, and she was feeling guilty at not
being able to help me more. Oh, of course I thought of it."

"And when it all went wrong and this happened, she'd be feeling guiltier, wouldn't she? She'd probably admit to the truth, if I
taxed her with it now. Or got her on the witness stand and brow-
beat her a little."

"No!" said Dulcie sharply. "No, Mr. Falkenstein, you mustn't
do that. I'm not going to say—if I think—she did it or not. But
there's Charles, and the children. It doesn't matter so much about
me. You said it would probably be two or three years—well, that's
not so long really. It doesn't bear thinking about, what it would do
to the family—if she was in jail instead. Please promise me—you
won't even ask her—please, Mr. Falkenstein! You can try—the
other story—at the trial, can't you? About the excitability—
because it's quite true—and it would have been somebody just
defending themselves, really. If they believe you, all right—and if

they don't believe you, that's all right too—because it doesn't matter much about me."

Jesse said gently, "Don't you think you've sacrificed enough of your life, Miss Vanderveer?"

She gave him that faint ghost of a smile. "It's been this much, this long—what's a little longer?"

And he had unexpectedly gotten a very cogent lead from those old fellows at the rest home, and another stray idea had occurred to him. Vanderveer had gone to the public library—to read *The Wall Street Journal,* she had said. Jesse wondered if he'd got talking to other men there, if it was worth asking about. The old man hadn't been much of a reader—there wasn't a book in that house except in Dulcie's room where a little shelf held a modest stack of light romances and some modern poetry. It was doubtful if he'd had a library card, or really had spent much time there. But Jesse drove out to that branch on Santa Monica Boulevard just on the chance.

The woman at the desk didn't recognize the name, and Jesse gave her a description—a tall thin old man with a prominent nose, in shabby clothes—he probably sat in the periodical section. Her expression lightened doubtfully.

"Oh, if that's the one you mean, yes, I think I remember him. He came in nearly every Saturday to read the newspapers, but he never checked out any books."

"Ever notice him talking to anyone here? Another regular patron?"

She shook her head. "I couldn't say. But I remember he asked to see the head librarian once. Only he just said, the boss here."

"Oh, really," said Jesse. "And where would I find her?"

"It's Mr. Underhill," she said disapprovingly. "His office is through that door, next to the children's section."

Underhill looked more like a pro football player than a librarian. He was a youngish sandy fellow, with an amiable expression. He listened to Jesse's description, grinned, and said, "That one. People do constantly surprise you, what they get up to. Yes, I remember that old chap all right—it was about six months ago. He came in here to ask me about dirty books."

Momentarily confused, Jesse repeated, "Dirty books?"

"The porn," said Underhill. "You know. He asked if we didn't have some stuff like that under the counter. An old fellow that age! I just laughed at him. I told him all the blue stuff was on locked shelves at the main branch, available to serious research students on request, and he just gave me a disappointed look and shuffled out."

"That damned old goat!" said Jesse. "All right, as long as I'm here, I'd better take a look at something called the P.D.R."

"Sure. The girl out front will find it for you."

It was an unwieldy tome, but once he got onto the system it was easy to find what he was looking for, and he scanned the description swiftly. Good material for the trial. *Ban Cap Codeine Capsules*—and a technical list of contents—*Warning May Be Habit Forming . . . provide effective analgesia in a wide variety of conditions. . . .* And on down through a long paragraph, until he finally came to *Dosage in excess of two Ban Cap codeine capsules may cause excitability.*

And dammit, no, Vanderveer hardly the suicidal type, but was there one? And it made a story—it was just possible he had decided to take the quick way out. And take her with him. Missing Griffin, and all that had happened to him lately, little things, but it was often little things that triggered suicide. The typing—what were six words?—with a little care he could have produced that note.

And that damned house—holding any more secrets?

On the way, he stopped at the local post office and collected the recent mail. There was another bank statement, from a United California Bank on Western, showing a checking account with a balance of ten thousand dollars, no checks drawn on it. Catalogs and ads, no personal letters, and then something different. An ordinary plain postcard, with its printed stamp, a Los Angeles postmark, and the address hastily scrawled on the front. On the back was another scrawl. *Couldn't reach on phone, thought as price down you might be interested in another deal. Won't last!* It was signed *K.A.* Jesse regarded this anonymous message with some exasperation, and proceeded on to Kingsley Drive.

They hadn't looked at the garage. Dammit, he and Clock had covered this place—there wasn't anywhere else to look. He looked at it now, but not long: it was just an old single-car garage, with

Dulcie's old tan Ford sitting in it. There was a workbench built across the back, and everything was very neat, out in plain sight. A metal box full of different bits for an electric drill. The drill itself in a box. Boxes of nails, a few tools hung tidily on the wall, a ladder against one wall. There were open rafters, but nothing on them. Both electrical outlets were genuine.

Jesse went on into the house for no good reason. Dammit, they had looked everywhere there was to look. And eventually the different bank accounts would be turned up via the statements. He wondered academically whether anybody would have found out about those accounts if he hadn't talked to the old fellows at the rest home; Marcia might have thrown the whole lot of mail straight out, knowing there was seldom anything personal, and would it have occurred to him to ask about it? Probably not. But— but— There wasn't anything else to look for here, was there?

But he still had the uneasy little conviction that somewhere here there could still be a secret hidey-hole, larger than the little ones they had found, large enough to hold a real wad of cash. . . . What indeed did get into the ones like Vanderveer? Flo Griffin was quite right; men of completely different temperaments could be good friends; but Griffin by all accounts had been a civilized human being, while Vanderveer— Well, they had probably split the profits down the middle: but look at their lives. Both of them shrewd investors, building up the capital. But while the Griffins had enjoyed it—the nice house, the cars, trips, theaters, clothes—as it came in, Vanderveer had squatted in this sad little house like an old toad, avidly putting the profits back to work, squirreling them away in sterile banks, living on the mean edge of nothing. . . . Dulcie, adding part of her salary to buy the little treats Mama liked. . . .

He wandered down to that cramped squalid den and looked at the stuffing coming out of the old chair. And what for? What did it all come to? *For unto a malicious soul wisdom will not enter . . . and in the death of a man there is no remedy.* "Ephemeral" was the word. A flash—eighty-one years; and what had he taken with him when he left? What of any value in the eternal importances? And he had been calling Vanderveer an old bastard, but just now, looking into the room where the old man had spent so many hours, he saw him as not so much evil as merely stunted. Perhaps evil was never the mighty wrathful force it pretended to be, but a whining, deformed, ignorant child without understanding of itself or anything else.

Getting philosophical in his old age, he thought. He didn't know what the hell he was doing here.

He reached into his jacket pocket for his keys, and suddenly said, "Oh, for God's sake! For *God's*— how stupid can two grown men be?" Tapping the walls and closet shelves, my God, and it had never occurred to either of them— He went across to the wardrobe and started to examine all those clothes, feeling in all the pockets. The simple, elementary thing, simply not occurring to them before.

The old man had run true to character about his clothes, of course. These had all been worn threadbare, and none of them had been expensive to start with. Most of the suits were styles years out of date, with shiny patches and missing buttons. There was only one fairly new one, a navy wool; he wondered if Vanderveer had worn that to Griffin's funeral. And there weren't many clothes—he had moved in here when Dulcie had to be up so much with her mother—his shirts, socks, ties, underwear would be in drawers in the front bedroom.

For the moment Jesse wasn't interested in those. He went through every pocket, even felt in the turn-ups of trousers; and he was rewarded with exactly one find.

It was crumpled into the side pocket of an old herringbone suit jacket, and it was a sales slip. At the top was a logo produced by a rubber stamp: The Red Knight, an address on Santa Monica Boulevard. Below was scrawled in ballpoint pen, *Rcvd. 2.10.*

The Red Knight. It sounded like a restaurant or a nightclub, but the amount didn't match that.

It was rather far out on Santa Monica Boulevard, on his left as he passed it, and a glance showed a rather tattered red and white awning bearing the name, fancy scarlet letters above on the face of the building. He found a public lot and walked back. As he walked, he realized that these blocks up here were rapidly running to seed, sidewalks cracked, buildings in need of paint, stores empty. When he came to The Red Knight, it was sandwiched between a defunct cleaner's and a dark old independent drugstore.

There were scarlet curtains across the store window. He opened the door and went in.

Immediately beyond the door was a table littered with books; it was a bookstore. He took one look and said, "Oh, my God," disgustedly. More waste of time.

"Just take your time, look around, buddy," said a friendly voice. "We gotta lot of interesting stuff here, cater to all tastes like they say."

There was a partition halfway up the length of the store; over to the left was a table with a cash box on it, and a hairy young fellow was sitting behind it.

"Why," asked Jesse, "The Red Knight? For a porno bookstore?"

"Hah? Oh, see, the name was on it. A restaurant or something folded. And I started with hardly any bread, see, I figured just leave it. Could I help you find something?"

"No, thanks," said Jesse. "Do you remember an old man coming in here—tall, thin, with a hooked sort of nose, shabby clothes? A fellow about eighty years old—"

"What the hell you got to do with him?" asked the hairy one.

"Do you remember him? He did come in here?"

"You're not a cop—I can smell fuzz. I don't know what you want that one for, but you can stop lookin' for him here. Do I remember him? I should live so long to forget him! In the first place, it's not natural, a guy that old, one foot in the grave, interested in what I got here—it sort of turned my stomach, if you understand me. I didn't like to see him come in. Well, it was about a year back, just after I opened the place. And he never spent much, just a little bit now and then. Did a lot of looking, and I make no bread on that. Well, we show movies in the back room on Saturday afternoon, and he showed up for that a couple of times. Just once he took me, see—the movie, it's no big deal, five bucks per, but five is five. He showed up one day with the rest of the crowd, I'm taking the money at the door, he says he'll pay in a minute, wants to use the john—it's just back of the partition—and like a damn fool I let him in. I forgot about it till after the show, but when he comes out I say, hey, you owe me five, and he says he forgot his wallet, he'll pay me next time he's in. If there is one thing I hate it's a cheapskate welsher. What could I do at the time, but next time he comes in I remind him, he makes with the excuses and I say that's all, buddy, you get out and don't come back. I never saw the creep again and I don't want to. An old guy about ninety—turned my stomach."

Dobson called on Wednesday morning. "I tried to reach you yesterday but you were out. I just thought I'd check with that Bank of America, and Vanderveer has a safe-deposit box there."

"The hell you say," said Jesse.

"That's right. One of their medium-sized boxes, sixteen dollars a year. Number five-thirty-nine."

"But where the hell is his key? That damned old lunatic, it could be hidden anywhere and it wouldn't take up much space—"

"Have you been all through the house?"

"Have I been all through the *house?*" said Jesse. "I'm beginning to feel like a burglar. I seem to have spent most of my time lately going through that old devil's house. But anything as small as a key, for God's sake— Would you like to help look?"

"We're not paid to do jobs like that."

"Just," said Jesse bitterly, "to abstract their own money from the citizens and call it a service. For *God's* sake—"

He sat thinking, which wasn't productive of anything; finally, grumbling to himself, he went out to the car and drove down to Kingsley Drive. He'd be having nightmares about this house before he was much older. He didn't know where else he could look, dammit. It was bad enough hunting the possible hidey-holes big enough to hold a wad of cash, but a damned key—the long narrow steel key, with its number stamped on it—of a bank vault's safe-deposit box—

Hopelessly, he started the hunt all over again. The den: they had really exhausted the den, he and Clock. They had even moved the studio couch. This again was a case where the old man wouldn't have put it where the women might come across it. He went into the living room and looked around. The TV, he thought. Dulcie and her mother didn't watch it much, but he did. Jesse looked it over, lifted it from the metal stand with a little effort; there was nothing underneath. He put it on the floor and turned the stand upside down. Nothing. His gaze wandered around the room and lit on the mantel. There was a brass match box hanging on one side of it; he picked the matches out and felt in the bottom. Nothing. He felt along the underside of the mantel without result. But a *key*—you could fasten it with tape almost anywhere— Suddenly inspired, he began feeling the undersides of windowsills. He went through the entire house on that inspiration, and came up empty.

He sat down in the living room to rest and have a cigarette, fetching a saucer from the kitchen to use as an ashtray—of course Vanderveer had never used tobacco or liquor, they cost too much —and suddenly noticed that the old-fashioned breakfront in the dining end of the room had an ornamental ledge running around its middle. He leaped up to feel under that. Nothing.

When he had finished the cigarette, he stared into space for three minutes, and a hazy recollection came to him of a detective novel he'd once read where a key was hidden in a jar of cold cream. The bathroom—

It was typical of its period, a square room with linoleum on the floor, painted walls; tub on one side, commode behind it; a built-in washstand with a medicine cabinet above the bowl, two drawers and a cupboard below. He looked into the medicine cabinet. Three glass shelves: aspirin, antacid, half-used tube of toothpaste, a patent cream to hold false teeth, one lone toothbrush on a metal rack inside the door. Dulcie's. Both the old people had false teeth, he deduced.

The left-hand drawer held a package of razor blades, Band-Aids, a styptic pencil; the old man's things. He yanked it right out and emptied it: old razor blades, tubes of shaving cream, more Band-Aids, a dime-store comb, a cheap and probably useless gadget supposed to sharpen old blades. He took the old newspaper out of the bottom and discovered another rusty blade and a dead silverfish. Dulcie would be mortified; she hadn't had time for thorough cleaning lately.

The other drawer would be hers, but he went through it to be thorough. Cosmetics, comb, brush, a packet of Kleenex, hairpins, a hand mirror with a magnifying second side.

He felt under the overhanging edge of the counter. He took the top of the toilet tank off and peered inside.

Frustrated, he went back to the den, making a detour to pick up his ashtray on the way, and sat down to rest again.

He was about ninety percent convinced now that Marcia had done that murder. He thought Dulcie was a hundred percent convinced. He felt abstractly very sorry for both of them. He could see exactly how the whole sorry thing had happened—human nature— Well, that was something both lawyers and cops saw a lot of. If it weren't for the husband and family, Marcia would probably have confessed as soon as Dulcie was arrested. And it was a question— She was a nervous, emotional, at the moment highly tense woman; would she on impulse, during the trial, break down and shout, I did it so let her go? Don't even ask her, said Dulcie. He wouldn't need to call her as a witness, but the other side would: and under the urbane handling of one of those slick assistant D.A.s—Mrs. Coleman, you were aware that your sister had been under a good deal of physical and emotional strain lately, were you not?—

He sighed and put out his cigarette. The trial was some way ahead. He was supposed to be thinking about something else right now. Pull yourself together, boy, he thought, and use some common sense on it. This safe-deposit key. Well, depending on what you kept in a safe-deposit box, it wasn't a thing you visited every day, every week, even every month; but if you went to it fairly often you'd want the key handy. Ordinary people without corkscrew minds kept keys on key rings, but if you didn't you'd want it somewhere fairly accessible.

The idiot boy and the lost horse, he thought. If you were a horse— If you were a queer secretive old man with a yen to hide things, where would you hide a key? He looked around vaguely.

At least the weather had cleared up. The sun had come out today, and it was slightly warmer. There was more rain predicted for the weekend.

He looked over the contents of the room again. Furniture: all examined. Carpet nailed down. Wardrobe examined. One window, nothing taped to underside of sill; heavy brown drapes at window, an old-fashioned double-hung window with a wooden box valance hiding the curtain rod—that was a thought— He went over and examined the hems of the drapes. They were intact, and he could feel nothing sewn into them.

"Hell!" he said. He straightened and collided with the straight chair beside the studio couch; it fell on its side and he picked it up. It was a humble old pine chair with a dark finish, and as he sat it upright the light from the window fell full on it and he noticed how scarred the unpadded seat was, with raw wood showing. An old chair, but it couldn't have had much use in here, the old man sitting in the desk chair—

He looked from the chair to the window. "By God!" he said. He set the chair under the window and tried the left side first, standing on the chair and feeling along the valance top. Nothing. He moved the chair to the right side and his groping fingers encountered what he was hunting—the loose key resting on top of the valance.

It was the right key: the long slender key of a safe-deposit box, and it was stamped 539.

He met Dobson after lunch at that Bank of America and got the IRS authorization to open the box. The short fat woman who presided over the vault said of course she had known Mr. Vanderveer. "He used to take his box out and stay for quite a long time, I suppose going over his investments."

They took the box into a cubicle and opened it. Inside there was five thousand dollars in cash, the bankbooks for the extra account, half a dozen pornographic books, and a receipt for fifty dollars from a *James Toomey, Private Investigations,* an address on Melrose. It was dated six weeks ago.

CHAPTER 7

James Toomey looked at the receipt and said, "Yeah, that's mine. What about it?" He looked again at Jesse's card.

"The man you gave it to is dead," said Jesse, "and I'm the lawyer settling the estate. I'd like to know what you did for him."

Toomey sighed. Some private investigators were ex-cops, or, even if they weren't, smooth and experienced operators, on the ball. Toomey didn't look like one of those. This was a cheap little office in a run-down old building far out on Melrose past Highland. There wasn't even a typist doubling as receptionist out in front: just Toomey; and he didn't look very prepossessing. He was a discouraged-looking middle-aged man with a bald head, prominent ears, and an habitual nervous tic in his left eyelid.

He said mournfully, "Oh, well. He was quite an elderly man, wasn't he?"

"What did he come to you for?" asked Jesse.

Toomey smoothed a hand over his bald head. "Well, he wanted me to look up records for him. The record of a divorce, a long time back. A divorce from his wife. She'd got it, and he'd lost the papers, and he wanted a record of it. It was 1936, a hell of a time back, but of course if she'd gotten it here the record would be on file at the courthouse, and he said he thought she'd gotten it here. So I went and looked, but I couldn't find any trace of it. So of course the next place I thought of was Reno, and I got a contact up there to look, and it wasn't there either. So then I got somebody to look in Vegas, and that was N.G. Well, I called and told him if I didn't know where to look, it was a waste of time. She could have gotten it anywhere, after all."

"Well, this is something new," said Jesse. "I wonder what's behind it—talk about ancient history. Did he say why he was anxious for this record? He wasn't a man who enjoyed handing out money, Mr. Toomey."

"Oh, I gathered that, he bitched like hell about the bill—that," said Toomey, nodding at the receipt, "was just a first retainer. I had to pay the operators in Nevada. I charged him a hundred and fifty all told. Well, he said he'd lost the papers on it and wanted a legal record. But like I say, and like I told him, she could have gotten it anywhere and when he didn't remember where—" Toomey shrugged sadly.

"I'll be damned," said Jesse. "That was it?"

"That was it. I reported to him last over a month ago."

"So, thanks very much."

"No trouble," said Toomey dispiritedly.

Jesse got back to his office about three o'clock, and as he came in Jean said, "Mrs. Gorman called for an appointment. She wants—"

"Oh, no," said Jesse. "To make a new will." Mrs. Gorman made a hobby of making wills; this would be at least the tenth he had made for her.

"What else?" said Jean. "She's worried about her dogs now, wants to make a definite provision for them. I gave her an appointment next Monday afternoon, if that's all right."

"Yes, yes," said Jesse. He went into his office and sat down, thought for a couple of minutes, and called Florence Griffin. She sounded surprised to hear from him, and even more surprised at his question.

"Aline?" she said. "Johnny's first wife? Why, yes, it was her that divorced him. Why? I told you—"

"Do you have any idea where she got the divorce, and when?"

"Why, I suppose right here. I should think. She was a local girl, I think her family lived in Santa Monica. That's funny, that you should be asking about her, Mr. Falkenstein, because after we were talking the other day I got to thinking about Aline—she was quite a nice girl, I liked her the little while I knew her—and all of a sudden I remembered that I did see her once after she divorced Johnny. It must have been three or four years afterward, the nearest I can pin it down, it was just before the war anyway. I remembered that I ran into her unexpectedly in the public waiting room at Bullock's, on the seventh floor just outside the ladies' room, you know. We were both shopping—I remember we had lunch together, and that was the last time I ever saw her."

"Remember anything she said about herself then? Did she mention the divorce?"

"Why, yes. She'd just gotten married again, she told me. She was looking quite smart—she was a pretty girl, with a lot of curly black hair—and she looked happy. She told me her new name, but do you think I can remember it now? It was an ordinary name, but not as ordinary as Smith or Brown, of course I hadn't any reason to remember it, and all those years ago—but why do you want to know about Aline?"

"Well, it doesn't matter, but they were definitely divorced then, if she was married again."

"Oh, yes, of course. Aline was rather straitlaced, I know Johnny's swearing bothered her, and off-color jokes and things like that."

"Do you know if there was any alimony, a settlement?"

"Oh, there wasn't anything like that, or Johnny would have mentioned it to Howie. They'd only been married about a year, and none of us had any money then—Johnny and Howie had just started the business about that time. What's this all about, Mr. Falkenstein?"

"Were they married here?"

"Yes, of course. What—"

"Well, it's just a little something that came up," said Jesse vaguely. "Thanks very much."

He put the phone down and ruminated about this. Why all these years later had Vanderveer been concerned about that? There wasn't anything funny about the divorce, when the first wife had remarried—evidently a respectable conventional girl. It didn't seem to make much sense, laying out money to get the record of that— Well, suppose for once that he'd been telling the plain truth? He had told Toomey he'd lost the papers. He would have been served divorce papers, of course. And it was a long time ago —in all the years of piling up the capital, of using different bank accounts for the partnership and business, of shuffling accounts around and possibly changing safe-deposit boxes, he could have misplaced the papers. An uneducated man, he might have thought them necessary to make the will valid, something like that. But it was a little funny all the same.

Still, in connection with another line of thought—could the old man have been going a little senile? Or beginning to go that way—Evidently he'd been something of a chaser in his young virile days, and here he was just lately developing a prurient interest in pornography, patronizing a place like The Red Knight. Well, that retired teacher at the rest home saying, a very quick mind—but it might have started to go just along that one line.

The phone buzzed at him and Jean said tersely, "It's Sergeant Clock."

"I did predict it," said Clock. "That house on Kingsley's been broken into—the man on the beat just discovered it. I thought you'd want to know about it. Pete and I are just going over to have a look."

Jesse swore and said he'd meet them there.

It was the usual unholy mess, which Clock and Petrovsky were more used to looking at. It was adding insult to injury to leave the wanton mess behind, on top of theft. In fact there probably wasn't much gone; there hadn't been much here of any small portable value. The one item like that, the TV, was missing. But every drawer had been yanked out and dumped on the floor, the carpet slashed in every room, the pictures smashed, in the kitchen dishes from the cupboards thrown onto the floor. The drawers of the old rolltop desk were on the floor in the den—Jesse had been through those, of course, and there'd been nothing of any value there. Not much here in the way of loot, but the old woman might have had some jewelry—"I'd better ask Marcia Coleman," said Jesse on that thought.

There were clothes from all the wardrobes underfoot, and in Dulcie's room the mirror over the dressing table was smashed.

The uniformed man, Ramirez, who had noticed the open front door and gone in to check, said, "Juveniles. What it smells like."

The back door had been forced with something like a jimmy.

"Oh, every time," said Clock. "Well, we have to work it like any burglary. The lab will be out. Not a chance in hell they'll give us anything, but we have to go through the motions."

"And somebody will eventually have to clean up the mess,"

said Jesse. He went back to the office and called Marcia Coleman.

She was distressed and angry. "Oh, I was coming up tomorrow to pack all Dulcie's clothes. This is all we needed! Yes, Mama had a few things, her wedding ring was buried with her, but there was her mother's big cameo pin, and a couple of garnet rings, and one of those old-fashioned wide gold bracelets, she hadn't worn them in years, but they were there in a box on the chest of drawers."

"Could you identify any of them?"

"I could the rings, one has three triangular stones and one, just a big one, they're set in yellow gold— Oh, Lord, I'd better come and salvage what I can, I suppose. Tomorrow morning—"

"The police are there now anyway."

"Fee—kitt'ns," murmured Davy drowsily, and slept. Nell looked fondly at him and tiptoed out of the nursery. It was just after one o'clock. She slipped lightly downstairs to the kitchen and looked out the window. Athelstane was out there at the rear of the lawn where the grove of trees ended, and the cat was sitting composedly beside him; they looked as if they were meditating together.

This was the fourth day she had been feeding the cat, and yesterday it had emerged from the bushes as soon as she got into the house, to clean up the plate. She would try an experiment today.

She called Athelstane in and prepared the plate of canned cat food. Athelstane had a water bowl outside as well as on the service porch; she had wondered if that was what had attracted the cat in the first place—where would an animal find water in California's long dry summer?—and she had left dry cat food out each night. She remembered that most Siamese didn't like milk. Now she went out quietly, talking soothingly to the cat, and put the plate down at the edge of the lawn, but this time she didn't go back in the house. She went into the garage by the side door and watched.

The cat came out to the plate at once; it was now taking more time to eat, not as frightened of possible interruption. When the plate was half empty, Nell slipped out the side door and knelt down in the flower bed there as if she was weeding; she could see the cat out of the corner of her eye. It froze, but stayed crouched over the plate; when she came no nearer it went on to finish the meal, and then retreated to the edge of the lawn and began to wash its face. It was a good-sized cat for a Siamese; by the size and shape of its head she thought it was a tom. Nell talked to it from where she was, softly and coaxingly, and the cat looked up several times as if it was listening. She felt sure by now that the cat had at some time lived with people who cared for it, had been used to human voices and stroking hands. She wondered how long it had been on its own—and why.

Jesse left the office early and got home just before dark. As he came in and bent to kiss Nell, she said, "You know, I think that cat had a good home once, it's a lot tamer already."

"Good," said Jesse absently, and then Davy ran up to be greeted, and Athelstane. He went upstairs to the bedroom to take off his jacket, and as he emptied his pockets on the tray on the chest, out with a handful of loose change and his cigarettes came the little old address book. And the third time around a bell rang in his head about it, and it struck him forcibly just how queer it was that the old man had been carrying it. He picked it up and looked at it. The thing was years out of date—he could see how it might still have been lying around at the back of a drawer some-where—but an old man at home on a rainy day, as he had thought before, wouldn't be carrying much on him. His billfold had been on the desk; all he'd had on him had been keys, a handkerchief—and this thing.

He took it downstairs with him and went carefully over it again. Nell was busy in the kitchen, and Davy was playing a game of his own on the floor, Athelstane patient about being crawled over.

The only other queer thing about the address book was that set of cryptic notes: A—Archer—1459. BC—Brown—480. C—Canning —1240. He pored over them and still couldn't make head or tail of them. But could you deduce that they were the important thing about the address book, the reason it had been preserved, the reason the old man was carrying it? That there was something significant about those letters and numbers? It really seemed to be the only logical conclusion.

Nell came to take the baby upstairs; usually he didn't raise a fuss, but he did tonight and it took her a little while to get him set-tled down. Jesse built himself a drink while he waited for her, and went on staring at his little puzzle. She came back presently and got herself a glass of sherry while he renewed his drink, and he told her about the burglary.

"And you're pretty good at crossword puzzles, are you any good at cryptograms?" He went into the study for a sheet off his memo pad and wrote down the three mysterious lines and handed it over. "What does this say to you?"

"B.C., Before Christ," said Nell. "It doesn't say anything else to me. What is it?"

He explained, and Nell was intrigued. "It's funny. That old man, all you've said about him, a real character."

"Oh, in spades," said Jesse.

"All that occurs to me offhand is that whatever it means, it has something to do with money."

"Now that I would lay a bet on."

But the thing wouldn't go out of his mind. What in hell could those lines mean? The innocent-looking combinations were so meager and yet so mysterious. They couldn't refer to the combination to a safe. They weren't long enough to constitute a real cryptogram. They ran through his head monotonously, insistently. A for Archer 1459. BC for Brown 480. C for Canning 1240. It made a weird pattern of a sort, A B C. But what were the figures meant for?

After dinner he went to his desk and played around with it a little. He tried adding up the figures, which gave him 3179, which didn't seem to mean anything either. He tried turning that back to its component parts, as in numerology, and got 20 or 2, which didn't mean any more. Finally he stacked some Bach on the stereo and tried to forget it, but the three little lines kept running through his head.

On Thursday morning as he came into the office there was a *Times* on Jimmy's desk, and she said, "There's a little in the paper about it, maybe they're short of news, impossible as it seems."

It was one paragraph on an inside page, about the burglary at the house, residence of the Vanderveers, murdered October twentieth, and one line about the daughter accused and awaiting indictment. Jesse grunted at it. He hadn't any appointments today or tomorrow. He wrote out the three lines on Jean's memo pad and thrust it at her. "What do you think this means?"

"B.C., Before Christ," she said. "I can't make anything of the rest of it. What's it supposed to mean?" Jimmy just shook her head at it.

"Dammit, it's got to mean something," said Jesse morosely. He went into his office and sat down at his empty desk, swiveling around to stare out the window.

Twenty minutes later Jean buzzed him and said he had a call. It was somebody from the Mexican Consulate. "What?" said Jesse. "What now? All right, put it through. . . . Yes. Yes, this is Mr. Falkenstein. What can I do for you?"

"Ah, Mr. Falkenstein. This is Eduardo Rivera, of the staff of the Mexican Consulate here." It was a pleasant masculine voice with scarcely any accent. "Over breakfast this morning I was reading the paper, and I noticed a small article which interested me. I thought perhaps the police would be interested, as it is a criminal case, and so I called headquarters—I am told I must call the Hollywood Precinct—I call there, and talked with one Sergeant Clock. And he tells me that you will be interested, and so I call you."

"Yes? What's it about?"

"This little article in the paper, about a burglary—a husband and wife murdered, their daughter accused—such terrible things that happen these days—the name, as you put it, rings a bell in my head. A Dutch name, Vanderveer. Mr. Falkenstein, that gentleman had an appointment, to come to our office here, to consult one of the staff, myself or whoever should be available. It was for the date of October twenty-fourth."

"The hell you—" Jesse caught himself and said, "That's very interesting, Mr. Rivera. And also very surprising. Why did he want to see somebody there?"

"Now that I'm afraid I could not tell you, Mr. Falkenstein. He telephoned, I remember, and asked to speak to the consul. Of course"— Rivera coughed gently—"that was not possible, the consul is provided with a staff to take care of the casual visitors, those who may simply want travel information or such. I happened to take the call. I asked him if I might answer any questions on the telephone, what were the nature of his inquiries, and he simply said that he must speak to someone who could give him special information. Well!" Jesse could nearly see Rivera's massive shrug over the phone. "What to do? I gave him an appointment at three o'clock on the twenty-fourth. Naturally he did not keep it. You find this interesting?"

"Very much so," said Jesse. "I'm very obliged to you for telling me. But what the hell it could mean I'd like to know. He didn't give you any hint at all?"

"None," said Rivera. "It may not mean anything, of course. We have people calling here for the most trivial reasons, you understand—asking all sorts of questions. We hand them the standard little brochures and are very polite, and they go away satisfied."

"Somehow I don't think he wanted to ask about rare orchids or the best nightclub in Mexico City," said Jesse. "But thanks very much."

And now what was that all about? Something new to think about. Why in hell should Vanderveer have been interested in Mexico? The wild thought crossed Jesse's mind that he had gotten fed up paying United States income taxes and was thinking of becoming a Mexican citizen, but, for God's sake, that was ridiculous. He swiveled around to the window again, and again the three little lines arranged themselves before his mind's eye, teasingly. Once in a while they seemed to be just on the verge of meaning something, and then the meaning slid away into mystery.

For want of anything better to do, he went out about eleven o'clock and drove down to the local post office to collect the Vanderveers' mail. The postal clerk behind the counter was a consciously efficient young man with an infectious grin. Jesse took the package of mail and handed him the slip of paper from his breast pocket. "What does this mean to you?"

The clerk took it and read it. "B.C., Before Christ. Is it a puzzle? Hey, it's a sort of catch, isn't it? Ross MacDonald."

"Come again," said Jesse.

"Guy writes detective stories about a detective named Archer. And come to think, there's a Somebody Canning who's a writer too, adventure stuff. And then there's Father Brown. You know, the priest who's a detective. Not that I ever went for those much, that Chesterton guy's quite a one for preaching at you."

"Yes," said Jesse, regarding him with some fascination. "Yes, he is, isn't he? I'd forgotten that Archer. That's very funny. Coincidences."

"What about 'em?"

"Just that they exist," said Jesse. He took back the slip.

There were no bank statements in the mail, and no personal letters. He looked at it, a few catalogs and throw-away ads, and tossed it into the back of the car. But he sat for a while thinking about the coincidences.

It didn't, in one sense, mean a damned thing, of course, but it was very funny because old Vanderveer had probably never read a book of fiction in his life. Lew Archer and Father Brown. Jesse laughed. But on the other hand, the fact that a queer, tenuous connection of sorts could emerge from such a meaningless set of figures and numbers—

Coincidences did happen. And with that idle little thought in his mind, he reached to turn the ignition key and started back for the office. At the next intersection he caught the light, and as he sat waiting for it to change, a delivery truck crossing in front of him stopped to wait for oncoming traffic before making a left turn. He never knew then or later what it was carrying or advertising, but it bore a large panel sign in red and blue letters, and the sign said, DON'T LET YOUR WIFE KILL HERSELF!

It made the left, the light changed, and the car behind him blew its horn angrily. Jesse took his foot off the brake automatically. "But my God, my God," he said aloud, "why not?"

Coincidences!

Yes, that had been a forced story—the old man deciding in earnest that they were better out of it, and lacing the midmorning drinks. Vanderveer all his life had been too materially concerned with life in this plane—the very conception of self-destruction would have been unthinkable to him. The earthy, greedy old man with his mind still running on sex and money— And he had never had any love for his wife; her illness and misery were nothing to him. He wouldn't have cared if she lived or died, and on the whole he would probably have preferred her to die and save him all the money it cost to care for her—and was going to cost in the future.

But, the wife! But, Mama! She had been a nonentity to Jesse all along—the passive invalid creature in the background. Now his mind raced busily, building her up as a person; and he thought, why not? Why not, indeed? It made a great deal more sense, in any terms of human nature.

He had never laid eyes on her, didn't know whether she'd been pretty, or homely, or in-between in her youth; he didn't know anything (except her maiden name on that marriage certificate) about her background. But from the meager mentionings that he had heard, from Dulcie, from Marcia, from Flo Griffin, he thought about her.

A nonentity. She would already have been labeled a spinster, nearly forty when Jan Vanderveer married her. Just to have a cook and housekeeper. He could buy the sex—but would prefer it free, from the willing good-time girls. But Myra—Myra putting up with that, with his grouches and penny-pinching all those years, bearing him two daughters in her middle life, living that mean restricted life in that poor little house (while the Griffins enjoyed the fruits of success)—and at the end, crippled with arthritis, fast becoming helpless, knowing what a burden she was to her home-staying daughter— Mama! They had all discounted Mama, just a name in the case, but she could be the important figure.

If anyone had a good motive for suicide, it was Mama. She had said she wanted to die and be at rest. And nonentity though she might have been, wasn't it all too likely that over those long years she had come to hate Jan Vanderveer deeply, for what he had been and had not been to her?

Not feeling well that day, said Dulcie. But there was a strength born of desperation. She could have done what was done. The old man used to her hobbling about the house; she could have gotten that cup of coffee for him. She had once worked in an office; she could have typed those six words. And then—and then—even as he had planned to build the story in court, someone coming, and the old man excitable under the overdose—someone like the gardener, or Renaldo, or the evicted tenant—almost anybody—

Back at the office, he paced, seeing that happen in his mind's eye. In terms of human nature—

It could indeed have happened that way.

He forgot to go out for lunch, and he was again brooding over the slip of paper when Marcia Coleman called. "All I needed was to see that house. My God. Of course there wasn't much of any value there, but what a mess. Mama's jewelry is gone, and the TV, that's all I can tell is missing. I saw the police and gave them a description of the jewelry."

"I don't suppose there was a record of the serial number of the TV? Well, never mind."

He did remember lunch then, and went down to the coffee shop on the ground floor of the building. The front tables were all occupied and he had to go to one at the back, near the door to the kitchen; instead of his usual waitress, the pert blond May, he got a thin-faced girl with glasses. He ordered at random, and was sitting staring at the hieroglyphics on the slip of paper when she came up and twitched it away and set his plate before him.

"Hey," said Jesse.

She handed it back. "Afraid you'd drop it in your gravy."

"What does it look like to you?" he asked curiously.

She took it again and studied it. "Doesn't look like anything. A, B, C. I'll bet it's one of those crypt things. A secret message, like. Where some naval plans are hidden or something like that. Or it could be a clue to buried treasure."

"You're a romantic."

"You bet. Nothing I like better than a good story about buried treasure, with duels and a sinister villain trying to seduce the heroine. What is this thing, anyway?"

"I wish I knew."

The only diversion he had in the early afternoon was a telephone conversation with Lenhoff's attorney, who was now in a storm of activity getting out legal evaluations of the property. It didn't look as if Lenhoff was going to miss the settlement for his wife.

At three-thirty Jean put through a call from Clock. "One of the reasons," said Clock, "that this job can be boring is that the punks are so damn stupid. The patrolman on the beat just spotted a couple of juveniles on the front porch of the Vanderveer house, and when they tried to get away he grabbed them, and found the loot in the back of their car. One TV, a handful of jewelry the Coleman woman described. They hadn't gotten around to pawning it yet."

"Congratulations," said Jesse. "Why did they go back there?"

"You never know what the stupid punks will do," said Clock.

But forty minutes later he called back. "I think you'd better come up here and listen to a story. It's an interesting one."

Jesse rather doubted that, but he was tired of sitting in the office. He drove up to the Hollywood Precinct station, parked, and went down past the desk sergeant into the big communal detective office. Clock was leaning back at his desk, Petrovsky lounging at the window. Planted on two straight chairs before the desk were a couple of sullen-looking teen-age boys.

"Not enough space in an interrogation room," said Clock. "Meet Marco Ruiz and Pedro Sanchez. Pedro has something interesting to tell you. Go on, Pedro. Let's have it all over again, just the way you told it before."

They would both conform to roughly the same description: sixteen or seventeen, dark, thin, shabbily dressed. "Both of them have little records," said Petrovsky dispassionately to Jesse. "Petty theft, purse-snatching."

"I said he was crazy—it was Pedro's idea," said Ruiz. "I didn't think there'd be nothing there, and there wasn't. Why the hell should anybody got a million bucks live in such a crummy neighborhood? Hell, I heard all the talk, but that's just what it was—I was crazy to tag along—and then him saying we must've missed something—"

"I got eyes, ain't I?" said the other one angrily. They both spoke unaccented English. He looked at Jesse. "Why we got to tell it to every cop in the precinct? Think we'd robbed a bank or something. Look, like I told you, all my life I heard how rich that old guy is—we lived there since I was a kid, everybody on that block heard that! He's got money hid all over the house maybe. I was always hearin' that. And I don't give no damn what you say, Marco, I know it's so, see? After they got murdered, I thought we'd prob'ly get in the house easy, it bein' empty like that, and we did. So O.K., we took a couple things—"

"All there was to take," said Ruiz. "What a big deal. Maybe twenty bucks at a hock shop, if we hadn't got picked up."

"All I said is, there's got to be more loot hid away! I saw it myself, only nobody believed me—me and Bill saw it."

"What did you see, and when?" Jesse pulled up a chair from an empty dsk.

"It was when I was just a kid, maybe four-five years back," said Pedro. "Me and Bill Perez saw it, only nobody believed us when we told about it. We was playing in Bill's yard, his house sorta backs up to old Vanderveer's, it's on the next street, see, and we

was at the back end of the yard and we see old Vanderveer diggin'
behind his garage. We was under the bushes at the back on account we'd been playin' jungle fightin', I said we was just kids
then, and Bill called him a name because he's their landlord and
always raisin' the rent—and he said, I bet he's buryin' money in his
yard, Ma says he's a miser—so we watched. But he wasn't buryin'
no money, he was diggin' some up! We saw it. He puts down the
spade, and kneels down—he never reached into his pocket or
nothin', but when he gets up he turns around with a great big hunk
of folding money in his hands—we saw it! So he did have money
buried—I wanted to go look there, Marco said it was crazy and besides there was a guy out in the next yard—"

Clock grinned at Jesse. "By bits and pieces you seem to be
finding this estate you're supposed to be settling, Jesse."

Petrovsky tapped Ruiz on the shoulder. "Come on, *hermanos*,
we've just got time to book you into jail before they serve supper."
He led them out. Of course they'd only stay in overnight, and get
probation from a judge.

"How in hell did I get into this?" asked Jesse plaintively. "Now
I have to go digging up his whole backyard? Nobody buries
money in the backyard. And I'm not a manual laborer—supposed
to be a brain worker." He laid his slip on Clock's desk. "What
does that say to you?"

"B.C., Before Christ," said Clock. "What's it supposed to
mean? My grandmother's maiden name was Archer, and I went to
the academy with a fellow named Canning."

"More coincidences," said Jesse. "Very funny. You wouldn't be
inclined to come and help me dig, would you?"

"My part of the case is over," Clock pointed out. "The estate is
your business."

"Oh, hell," said Jesse. "And it's nearly dark now. It'll have to
wait until morning. Why your officious patrolman had to spot that
pair—"

The only thing in his favor was that the weather wasn't hot.
And after this, he was sure to have nightmares about this house.

He found a spade in the tidy garage, and went around behind it.
Postponing work, he walked down to the end of the yard to see
where the boys might have been when they saw Vanderveer. He
hadn't realized that the house on Winona backed up to this one.

There was a picket fence at the end of this lot, and some tall hibiscus bushes at the rear of the adjoining yard. Here, there had once been a patch of lawn, as there still was in front, but it had died from lack of water, and there wasn't any attempt at shrubs or flowers. It looked as mean and shabby as the house itself.

Behind the garage, Pedro said. Jesse was thankful that it was a small garage; but it must be at least twelve feet wide, and just where behind the garage did X mark the spot? He had put on an old pair of slacks and a sports shirt; he eyed the spade with dislike, and drove it into the ground a foot behind the garage in the middle of the wall.

Luckily the ground was not packed hard, but already loosened with those two early rains, and it could have been harder digging; but as he had said, he was no manual laborer, and after half an hour he was grateful that Nell had made him take her loose gardening gloves. Without them, he'd already have had a fine crop of blisters. He dug a trench straight along the garage wall, going down about a foot and a half, out to the driveway, and of course turned up nothing at all but a few earthworms. Breathing hard, he went into the garage and sat in Dulcie's car to smoke a cigarette.

Next he started in the other direction, and muttered to himself, "Out of condition, sitting in an office all day." He felt as if he had dug out half a ton of dirt; it looked like a young trench, and he was drenched with sweat.

When he thrust the spade down and put his heel on it for about the seven thousandth time, it wouldn't go. It hit something solid— more solid than earth, about a foot down. He tilted it at a sharper angle and scraped earth away.

What he uncovered looked like a lid: a solid wooden lid with a handle on it. He uncovered it quickly, at the last kneeling to use his hands. "I will be damned—even that fanatical old fool—burying it in the backyard, for God's sake—" When it was clear of earth he tugged at the handle, and the lid came off in one piece; it wasn't fastened down. It revealed a little vault cemented on all sides; the lid had fit solidly over it. The man had been a carpenter, after all.

And it was absolutely empty.

Jesse sat back and used a number of regrettable words. All that damned work for nothing! Well, the workout probably hadn't done him any harm, but it was a damned nuisance, and he was filthy. Looking at the vault, the lid, he judged that it had been built years ago, and the old man had had second thoughts about its vulnerability. Or maybe when it got to be a little difficult for him to use the spade—

Jesse was dripping sweat, his hands were filthy even under the gloves; he was hot, dirty, and very tired. Even in that wreck of a house there would be hot water, and he had the keys on him. He went in, and among the tumbled mess in the hall found a clean towel, one of those pulled out of the linen closet. When he had taken off his shirt and washed the worst of the sweat and grime off, he felt better. Still wiping his face, he went down to the den, where he had left his saucer-ashtray, to rest awhile before he went home to change into civilized clothes.

There was litter all over the floor where the punks had ransacked the place, and he had forgotten about the slashed carpet. Halfway across the room his toe caught in a tear and, being off balance, he took a header, nearly knocked himself out against the opposite wall, and sprawled his length on the floor.

Before he picked himself up to feel for any broken bones he relieved his feelings with a few more regrettable words. "Not my day," he said bitterly, bracing himself on his hands; and then he just stayed there, frozen, looking at the piece of carpet under his nose there in the corner.

Carpeting all snugly wall-to-wall, fastened down, solid, so of course nobody had looked at it. But this piece in the corner wasn't. It was turned back in a V, and the inside edges didn't have the little tape that held fitted carpet flat. It had a few tiny tacks, that was all.

He bent closer and peered. Tiny holes in the hardwood floor where this corner of carpet had been tacked down; and now he could see where the carpet tape had been cut away. He got up to his knees and pulled the corner of carpet back with a mighty tug, and about two feet of it obediently folded over and revealed, against the dark-varnish finish of the old hardwood floor, a square of raw new wood. It was completely level with the rest of the floor, there was only a sliver of crack around all four edges to reveal that it was a separate piece. The man had started out as a carpenter.

"No fool like an old fool!" said Jesse savagely. He stood up and looked around for the steel letter opener, found it in the corner by the door, inserted it into one crack and pushed down. A little reluctantly the square of unfinished wood tilted and he got it up far enough to get two fingers in and a grip on it. It slid out without much trouble.

Underneath it were two steel cash boxes resting on the studs of the low foundation.

"Oh, my dear God," said Jesse wearily. He lifted them out and carried them over to the studio couch. Both of them had a stack of folding money inside. The first held twenty thousand dollars in fifties and hundreds; the second, twenty-five thousand, mostly in hundreds.

What in the name of all that was holy that ancient lunatic had thought he was doing— Nobody knowing. Nobody having even a hint.

He looked helplessly at all the money. He really didn't want to put it into the office safe, and in fact, of course, he was bound by law to deposit any loose funds which would be transferred by a will into an interest-bearing account, pending the end of probate. When they had come across that cash in the other safe-deposit box on Wednesday, he had opened an account at that Security-Pacific branch, a savings account labeled J. W. Vanderveer Estate. That was where this had to go.

He said a few more things. He was starving, it was after noon, and a respectable lawyer didn't go around in dirty slacks and sweat-stained shirt on a weekday; but he didn't feel much like driving all the way home with forty-five thousand dollars of some-body else's money on him. The crime rate was up, even in broad daylight.

He took the cash boxes out to the car and drove up to the bank —the one where Vanderveer's working account was lodged. He was going to cause some stir, walking in with all this cash, and he made for the New Accounts desk, recognizing the efficient gray-haired woman who had filled out forms for him on Wednesday. He groped for her name—Mrs. Lorenzo.

He planked the cash boxes down and explained frankly. "Good heavens," she said, amused, "the things people do. Well, we'll have to get a mutual count on it—several of us checking it, you know—the chief teller's out to lunch but he should be back shortly. Meanwhile you can make out a deposit slip." She slid one across to him.

He had just written the date and *J. W. Vanderveer Estate* when a pretty dark girl came up to the desk with a check in her hand. "Oh, excuse me, Mrs. Lorenzo, but it's this new account, the one just transferred from UCB—is it still on hold? I couldn't make out the date—"

Jesse started violently and dropped the pen. "Bank of California!" he said loudly. "Bank of California!"

They stared at him. "Why, yes, that's what it used to be before," said Mrs. Lorenzo.

He rushed into the precinct station at ten past one, found Clock just going out on a new call, and said frenziedly, "Battle stations! I need your official help, the damn banks won't give out information over the phone to me—we'll have to get the IRS on it too, that'll help—" He thrust the paper under Clock's nose. "Don't you *see* it? It's plain as the nose on your face! But it only hit me when that teller used the abbreviation—UCB, United California Bank—it used to be the Bank of California before it amalgamated with some others—B.C., Bank of California, so you can see what this has got to mean, can't you? Oh, my sweet God in heaven, that crafty old twister—didn't he get one hell of a kick out of planning all the secrets, and no good goddamned reason for it at all— You see what this has got to be?"

"No," said Clock. "I'm busy, I've got work to do. What are you talking about?"

Jesse was shaking the old address book at him. "This was a reminder, so he wouldn't forget names and numbers! And he must have had one of them at least since before that merger—he wouldn't notice the name change. BC Brown 480. It says he's got a safe-deposit box under the name of Brown at a California bank, box 480. And another one at a Bank of America under the name of Archer, box 1459. And another one at a Crocker bank under the name of Canning, box 1240. It just came to me when that teller said—"

Clock began to laugh. "And none of them any banks where he was known as Vanderveer," said Jesse, "and how the hell to pin them down—we'll need official help, and Dobson— Uncle so powerful these days—"

"I can't help thinking," said Clock, "what beautiful legal fun you'll have with Uncle!"

CHAPTER 8

Dobson came up at once—Uncle was always so quick on the trail of anybody suspected of trying to hide untaxed money away. He pointed out the major difficulty fretfully. "Dammit, the man's dead!" he said. "If this is true, Falkenstein, how the hell are we going to connect him legally with these safe-deposit boxes? I'll have to look up the ruling—these are all common names, and if he didn't visit the boxes frequently it may pose an identification problem. But we'll certainly look into it—"

"And the damn banks closing for the weekend in four hours," said Jesse.

"Well, of course the only place to start is to locate the individual banks, and our office can do that by phone—there's really no need to bring the police into it," said Dobson, looking disdainfully around the detective office. "It isn't very likely that he'd have used branches at a great distance, as he didn't drive—"

"But we don't know how long he'd had these boxes, dammit, that one at the California bank for nine or ten years at least! And the keys!" said Jesse in something like a wail of agony. "Where in the name of holy Almighty God are the keys? There's no crevice in that house where they could be—I know that goddamned house better than my own, and I swear those keys aren't there!"

"Nonsense," said Dobson coldly. "They've got to be somewhere. You simply haven't come across them—he probably had some rudimentary hiding place, taped to the inside of a drawer or somewhere like that." Jesse groaned. "But the identification has to be definite, it would be extremely awkward if any mistake were made."

Yes, indeed, if by chance there should be an honest citizen named Archer who rented safe-deposit box 1459 at a Bank of America branch, and found out that Uncle Busybody had unwarrantably examined the contents, there would be a howl: there might be a lawsuit. The citizen still had rights, if fewer every day, and sometimes even Uncle had to walk like Agag.

In the end, Dobson went back to his office to start hunting for the right banks, and Jesse called Marcia on Clock's phone. "Do you have any photographs of your father? Recent ones?"

"For heaven's sake, there wouldn't be many anywhere, we never went in for snapshots much. But Dulcie has a camera, she got it in high school, she used to take snapshots sometimes. Oh, I remember she took one of Mama and Papa on their fortieth anniversary, that was nearly two years ago— I've got a copy of it somewhere, and Dulcie would have too. You do ask for the queerest things, Mr. Falkenstein—why do you want that?"

He explained, and she said angrily, "Oh, just like him, of course—*just* like him! I suppose this lets us in for a fine from the government, and if I know the government it'll be a whopping big one."

"Well, we'll have to sort that out later. Right now we need this picture."

"All right, I'll look for it and bring it to you on Monday morning, if that's all right."

"Fine," said Jesse, remembering that Dulcie was due to be indicted on Tuesday; he'd had the official notice from the D.A.'s office in the morning mail yesterday.

He went up to his office, still in the dirty old clothes, and the Gordons were astonished. "What on earth have you been doing, Mr. Falkenstein?" asked Jean.

"Digging," said Jesse, and went on into the inner office and hauled out everything he had taken from Vanderveer's desk and file cabinet. He sorted through it. He gathered together a lot of canceled checks for specimen signatures, all the writing he could find. The account book would be useful if there was any question of identity.

He called Dobson before he left the office. "No, we haven't pinned one down yet, they could only let me have one man, but we're working on it. It's a pity the weekend has to intervene, of course, but it can't be helped. I'll be in touch with you on Monday, then."

*　　*　　*

Nell thought the whole thing was hilarious—except for the family, of course. "But really, Jesse, don't these people realize that they're going to die sometime? And whatever they leave will have to be sorted out?"

"They don't have that much imagination," he said bitterly. "In fact, if they can't take it with them they'd just as soon keep anyone else from laying their paws on it." He sounded annoyed.

Nell realized that he was upset about the situation, and she knew he was worried about that poor woman in jail—wondering how to handle the case. Occasionally he got involved with clients he liked.

Wisely she left him alone, and after dinner he went into the den and stacked some Bach on the stereo.

That afternoon the cat had let her come within ten feet of him and gone on placidly eating, though keeping an eye on her.

On Saturday morning the predicted rain didn't materialize; it was overcast, but in midmorning a watery sun came out. The dry cat food she had left on the back porch was gone, and that Athelstane wouldn't touch. After lunch, with Davy bedded down for his nap, she went out with a plate of food and put it down at the side of the lawn where the cat often sat these days crouched under the bushes. She thought it was spending most of the time in their yard now. She sat down on the grass six feet away from the plate and waited hopefully. In a few minutes the cat came out from under the bushes, approached slowly, sniffed the plate over fastidiously, and began to eat. She talked to the cat in a soft voice. Now, with a close look, she could see that it was a neutered tom, and normally would be a big cat for a Siamese. He looked a little fatter already. This time, after cleaning the plate, he didn't go away; he sat looking at her thoughtfully, and his eyes were a vivid brilliant blue in the thin sunlight.

"You're a very handsome boy," Nell told him. "You have gorgeous eyes, do you know that?" The cat answered her conversationally, in a raucous bass voice. "Will you let me pat you? Do you remember when people used to stroke you and tell you what a lovely pussin you are?" She began to edge nearer, cautiously, and the cat didn't move. He spoke again questioningly, and didn't stir when she laid a hand on his head. She moved the hand down his back, and felt the automatic arching of his spine to her stroke. His coat looked smoother, and his back felt warm in the sun. She went on stroking him, and presently was aware of another feeling under her hand, a slow throbbing just beginning. The cat was purring. It was a rusty purr at first, as if long unused, but it grew louder.

On Sunday morning, when she looked out the kitchen window after breakfast, the cat was drinking daintily from Athelstane's water bowl on the back porch. Nell went out—she could load the dishwasher anytime—and he didn't move away, just looked up at her. She sat down on the back step and talked to him, stroked him again. Athelstane, observing this, was delighted. He came up and pushed his large wet black nose at the cat, who patted it with a black velvet paw and uttered a comment in the raucous bass. Nell laughed at the pair of them, and the cat gave her a long deliberate stare and climbed into her lap.

"Well, aren't you a one," said Nell, highly pleased. "You were just waiting for a lap to be offered? You're a beautiful boy. What happened to you, pussin, and how did you get up here?" The cat gave a little contented sigh as she went on stroking him, and she felt his drowsy purrs coming up under her hand. Athelstane gave a huge noisy yawn and flopped down at her feet. Fifteen minutes later Jesse came looking for her.

"I wondered where you'd got to—oh, I see." He eyed the cat amusedly. The cat sat up and looked at him consideringly.

Nell said, "I think we've got a cat. Isn't he a beauty?"

"Very handsome," said Jesse. The cat got up and stretched in slow dignity, jumped off the side of the porch, and stalked across the lawn.

On Monday morning Dobson called ten minutes after Jesse got to the office. "Well, we've just located the United California Bank where a Brown has a safe-deposit box, and it's the right number. It's a branch on Sunset. What have you got in the way of identification?"

"I should have a photograph this morning, and I've got handwriting samples if we need them."

"That should do," said Dobson. "What we have to do, and it's a damned nuisance but it all has to be according to Hoyle, when we're sure that this is the right man, we have to get notarized affidavits from the bank personnel, from the family in regard to the photograph, and then we can proceed with the usual IRS authorization to examine the box."

"I see," said Jesse. "I never ran into this situation before, but I can see the reason for that. But how in hell, will you tell me, are we going to get into the boxes without keys? I swear there's not a place in that damned house I haven't looked—"

"Well, you'll simply have to find them," said Dobson. "They must be somewhere, after all. I should think you'd have been through the personal effects by now."

Jesse said bitterly, "If I have to search that damned house again, I'll put a match to it afterward."

"It's imperative that you locate them," said Dobson, sounding impatient. "I'll let you know when we've identified the other banks."

Jesse hung up and looked at the phone. If Dobson only knew, he thought. And for all they did know, these safe-deposit boxes might have been permanent caches, he might not have gone near any of them in a blue moon, and those damned keys could be somewhere quite inaccessible. But, for God's sake, where?

Marcia Coleman came in at eleven-thirty. She was looking drawn and tired; she would, of course, be worrying about Dulcie. "I had a hunt for it, but here it is," and she handed him the picture. Jesse studied it with interest. It was a five-by-seven enlargement from a colored snapshot, in a cardboard folder. It had been taken inside by flash, and the old couple was sitting at the dining table with plates in front of them. He remembered Vanderveer from the time he had seen him over six years ago—tall and gaunt, with thinning gray hair and a longish nose with a little hook at the end; he looked older here, and thinner. And she—it was impossible to say whether she'd ever been an attractive young woman or not. She was just an old lady, a rather plump old lady, with a round wrinkled face and gray hair worn in an outmoded style, curls around her face and little bangs. She was wearing a black dress with a big cameo pin at the neckline. But she had the same square little chin as Dulcie. It was a gentle face in a way, he thought, but not without character. Mama could indeed have been the X factor.

He told Marcia about the affidavit. "Well, I've got plenty of time, I asked Mrs. Burke to pick up Bobby. I'm going on to see Dulcie. What do I have to do?"

He dictated the affidavit to Jean, a short paragraph testifying that Marcia identified the accompanying photograph as that of Jan Willem Vanderveer, made at such and such a date. Jean typed it up, Marcia signed it, and Jimmy as an accredited notary public signed and sealed it. "So far so good," said Jesse.

She left at twelve-thirty, and Jesse looked at his Gordons and said, "All right, come on, we're going to close the office for the day. I'll buy us all lunch, and then you two can have the fun of searching that damned house again. I've run out of energy and imagination."

They were pleased at a little adventure, a change in routine. And he looked at them rather fondly across the table in the coffee shop downstairs. Quite a credit to be seen with, the Gordons: brown-eyed blondes and identically pretty.

When they got to the house on Kingsley, he said as he unlocked the front door, "Maybe female intuition will lead you straight to those keys, but I'd better tell you all the places I've already looked, hunting other things, so you won't waste time." They went in.

Both the Gordons said simultaneously, "What a mess!" and Jean added, "I'd hate to be the one who had to clean it up. But, Mr. Falkenstein, are you absolutely sure the keys are here somewhere?"

"They've got to be," said Jesse. "It's the only place they could be—the only place he had to keep them. Unless he buried them in the backyard, in which case we'll never find them—I refuse to do any more digging."

They began to poke around the living room, and he went to sit on the couch in the den. "Take your time," he called to them. "Just remember the old adage—if you were a horse—"

Jean said from the hall, "Uncle Foster used to hide things in shoes. He nearly lost a diamond ring once when Aunt Betty gave some stuff to the salvage."

"I've already looked there," said Jesse.

But, he suddenly remembered, he hadn't looked among the old man's underwear and so forth— He went into the front bedroom. Everything out of the old double dresser had been dumped onto the floor; it was impossible to say which drawer had held what. Her clothes and his were mixed up: shabby brassieres, panties, cotton stockings, worn little handkerchiefs, along with his under-wear, socks, ties. There was nothing but the clothes among that heap. There was nothing taped to the bottoms of drawers, or any sign that anything had been. The window in the den was the only one in the house with a box valance; all the others had curtains on plain rods.

The girls presently progressed to the kitchen. He finished his fifth cigarette and strolled out there. Jimmy was on top of a fold-ing step stool with her head inside a top cupboard; Jean was emp-tying the stove drawer.

He said doubtfully, "I don't think he'd have hidden anything here—the women coming and going. No luck yet, I see. No bright ideas?"

"This was an impossible house even before the burglary," said Jean. "What do you *do* with only a single sink?" She took the last iron skillet out of the drawer and began to feel inside.

"Well, as I said, take your time—it's only two-thirty," said Jesse idly.

"And no light over the stove," said Jimmy, descending from the stool and moving it under the middle cupboard.

Jean let out a loud scream. They both swung on her eagerly, ex-pecting revelation. "Oh, how perfectly terrible!" she exclaimed. "Oh, Mr. Falkenstein, I never did such an awful thing before—I can't imagine how we came to forget—"

Twins often communicated without speech, and Jimmy said, "Oh! Oh, Jeanie, how *could* we? Supposed to be top-notch legal secretaries—it's perfectly terrible, Mr. Falkenstein—"

"What are you talking about?"

"Mrs. G-G-Gorman," wailed Jean. "She had an appointment at two o'clock—we'd never get back in time to catch her with all the traffic—"

Jesse leaned on the doorjamb and laughed. "Well, that makes three of us—I forgot all about her too. Let's be philosophical about it, girls—either she'll be so annoyed she'll find another law-yer, or she'll forgive us—and it's past praying for now, she'll have been there and left. I really don't think he'd have hidden the keys here."

"If you're going to do something, do it right," said Jimmy. "Oh,

I do feel awful about Mrs. Gorman, but of course you're right—spilled milk."

They spent another twenty minutes in the kitchen, and of course found nothing. The refrigerator, he noticed, had been cleaned out and unplugged; that would be the efficient Marcia.

"I wonder—" said Jean suddenly. "You know those little magnetic boxes to hide keys in—some people have them to hide a house key, or an extra ignition key, in case of getting locked out—"

Galvanized by this inspiration, they examined everything made of metal in the house, and Jesse pulled the stove and refrigerator out to examine the backs; Jimmy ran an arm behind the washer. Nothing.

"They can't be here, Mr. Falkenstein," said Jean at last. "We've simply looked everywhere, even places you'd looked before. Do you suppose they could have been in something the burglars took?"

"But they got the loot back—it hadn't been pawned yet."

"Well, unless it's like *The Purloined Letter,* I give up," said Jimmy. "And if those keys are out in plain sight, we're all going blind."

"*The Purloined Letter,*" said Jesse thoughtfully.

"Yes, you know, the Poe story. Everybody was looking for it up the chimney, and it was in the letter rack all the—"

Jesse clapped a hand to his head. "Misdirection! Have I been just a little bit too clever? Oh, glory be—I wonder—" He plunged out the back door and made for the garage. They trailed him interestedly. At the neat workbench, he seized the box of drill bits and upended it: nothing but drill bits. He wrenched the lid off a tin box that had once held chocolate mints, and a collection of used washers fell out. The next box held screws of all shapes and sizes, and that was all. But when he turned the third box of sixpenny nails upside down over the bench, together with all the nails there fell out three keys, the long slender steel keys for safe-deposit boxes; and they were respectively stamped 1459, 480, and 1240.

"Eureka," said Jesse feebly.

"But I really feel awful about Mrs. Gorman," said Jean.

They went back to the office and Jesse called Dobson. "Dammit, the banks are all closed now," said Dobson, annoyed. "Well, I'll meet you there at ten."

"No, you won't," said Jesse. "I've got a client being indicted. It'll be more like eleven."

"Oh, hell," said Dobson. "No, we haven't located the other two yet. There are a lot of banks in this town, you know."

Jesse said he was aware of it, and called Mrs. Gorman to apologize. "Well, I was a little surprised," she said in her amiable woolly voice. "But if it was an emergency—oh, I quite understand —things do come up, I know—it's just that I'm rather anxious to include these provisions in my will, I mean we never know, do we, in the midst of life as they say, and while I'm only sixty-one, well, who knows?"

"Who indeed?" said Jesse. "Suppose you come in at two o'clock tomorrow."

"Oh, that'll be fine."

On Tuesday morning Nell went out and sat on the back porch; in about five minutes the cat appeared from the grove of trees, and Athelstane went to meet him happily. They touched noses. Nell called to the cat, and he came to her directly and pushed his head under her hand. "Now what happened to you, boy? You're used to people, you like people—somebody took good care of you once, didn't they?" They would never know where he'd come from. Could he have gotten loose from a car, she wondered. Some Siamese liked to ride in cars. Somewhere, perhaps, someone had been frantic, missing him. She wondered how he had gotten all the way up here.

Presently she said, "If you're going to be our cat, you'd better explore your new home," and she got up and opened the back door. "Come on—do you want to come in?"

The cat's vivid blue eyes fixed hers, and he uttered a long Siamese comment; and then he walked in ahead of her, tail straight up in the air. Nell left him to his own devices and hurried into the living room to pick Davy out of his playpen.

"Now we're going to have our own kitten, darling, but we've got to be nice to him, and not hurt him or scare him, see? We—"

"Kitt'n!"

"That's right, but we mustn't ever grab his tail—" He was really too little to understand yet, but he was a good baby; and if she knew cats, the cat would simply elude those fat reaching fingers and ignore him.

The cat came right into the living room and made for the corner of the hearth where the log box was. He looked from the logs to Nell and made a loud bass comment. Then he turned and started for the stairs.

"Just make yourself at home," said Nell, and Davy squirmed in her arms.

The indictment didn't take long: automatic legal process. Dulcie was dressed up for it, in one of her plain shirtmaker dresses; she had bright lipstick on, and looked a little more sophisticated. He talked to her for ten minutes afterward, the wardress waiting stolidly in the background.

"Mr. Falkenstein," she said worriedly, "Marcia was telling me—all the trouble about the money. He was always so queer about money. But if there's going to be trouble with the government—if there isn't going to be much left—there'll be your fee, and—"

"Needn't worry about that. There'll be more than enough left," he said, thinking about those fat packets of blue-chip stock. "There's just a lot of red tape. Don't fuss about it." And he wished he could formulate clearly in his mind just what tale he was going to spin to a judge and jury.

She sighed. "Mr. Klein's been to see me. He said if there wasn't enough money he'd see you got paid."

"I know. He's a nice fellow."

"He's been awfully good to me. I didn't know much when I first went to work for him. You wouldn't think so, he's always cheerful and telling jokes, but he's had a lot of sadness in his life. His wife died of cancer when she was only forty, and they never had any children."

He would probably never mention Dan Wolfe to her. He said lightly, "You just sit tight. I want to have a talk with you soon—plan exactly what we're going to say at the trial. You've got everything you need?"

"Oh, yes, I'm fine. Marcia's been coming every day."

"I'll see you soon."

He got up to the bank on Sunset at eleven-thirty. Dobson was waiting for him, pointedly under the clock at the entrance. "Sorry," said Jesse. "The judge was a little late."

"You did find the keys, I trust."

"Finally."

"I said it would just take a little looking. Well, I've seen the manager here, and there's a public stenographer and notary available."

They proceeded downstairs to the vault. There was a man and a woman in attendance. Dobson produced his credentials and said, "Someone called you from my office yesterday morning, about a Mr. Brown who had—has—a safe-deposit box here."

"Oh, yes," said the man. "Yes, that's right."

Jesse produced the photograph. "Is that Brown?"

They both looked at it. "That's him," said the man. They were looking at Dobson with disfavor, but curiously. "What's this all about?" Jesse launched into an explanation. "Well, I'm damned," said the man. "We never had such a thing happen before. He's dead, you say? Well, he didn't come in just so often, I think the last time we saw him would be about five, six weeks ago or more— but that's him all right, isn't it, Marion?"

The woman nodded. "All right," said Dobson. "Now I want you to compare some handwriting—may we see the card, please, with Brown's specimen signature—"

But both of them were positive, and of course when they'd seen him so recently— Dobson got hold of the public stenographer and had her type up the affidavits, got the two upstairs one by one to sign them before the notary. By then Jesse was starving, and Dobson probably was too, but he had blood in his eye and was anxious to get on with the job. They went back to the vault and he laid out his IRS authorization. The woman led them past the massive steel doors, Jesse handed over the key, and she slid out a medium-sized steel box and handed it over. They took it into one of the cubicles.

"*Just* as we suspected," said Dobson in quiet satisfaction. There was a small stack of cash in the box, and lying on top of it a ragged slip of paper with something written on it. Jesse picked that up and Dobson sat down and began to count the money. It amounted to five thousand dollars in twenties. "I'll give you a receipt for this, of course. There'll certainly be a full audit, I can promise you that. And I'll let you know when we spot the other banks."

"You do that." Jesse was looking at the paper. The scrawl across it wasn't Vanderveer's writing: a bolder hand. *Ray Holst,* and a telephone number, and an address on Lomita Street in Glendale.

He very nearly missed another appointment with Mrs. Gorman, but he had to snatch a sandwich before going back to the office. And she took up time as usual, burbling gently away about her garden, her dogs. The new will was on account of the dogs; she had realized she ought to make provision for their care if she should die suddenly, they were only three years old and you never knew. "I don't know if you're fond of animals, Mr. Falkenstein, but those of us who are get so attached—they're like my children really, Chico's a Chihuahua, you know, such a darling, and Beau's a miniature poodle, I've always adored—"

"We have a mastiff," said Jesse.

"A mastiff! In town!"

"And we've now got a Siamese cat. But we can take care of all this without a new will, you know, we can just make a codicil." He got rid of her finally, and thought she was still a little bemused by the mastiff as she went out.

It was four o'clock. He considered the slip of paper, pulled the phone nearer, and dialed. It rang four times at the other end before a woman answered. "Mr. Ray Holst?" asked Jesse.

"Oh, he's not here, he's at work." It was a neutral kind of voice, but sounded amiable. "Could I take a message?"

"When do you expect him in?"

"Oh, he'll be home after work, about ten-fifteen."

"If I call him at ten-thirty, you're sure he'll be in?"

"Oh, he'll be home then, yes. The last show starts about nine-forty and he gets away then."

"Thanks very much." He put the phone down. He wondered what he was going to hear from Ray Holst. This was all the damndest rigmarole he'd ever run into. And Dulcie—

He was thinking so hard and deep about that forthcoming trial that Jean had to prod him to show it was time to go home. "And it's started to rain again."

"Going to be a wet winter all right." It was coming down in earnest; he turned up his collar and made a sprint for the Mercedes in the lot. It was a slow drive home, up the twisting canyon road; but once he turned into their street, the twin gate lamps were faithfully beckoning him, and the gate was open. He got wetter getting out to shut it; but once he was in the house, the steady roar of the rain on the roof was rather pleasant, and Nell said she'd built a fire. There was a welcoming smell of pot roast in the kitchen.

Too lazy to go upstairs, he shed his jacket and made himself a drink, carried it into the living room, while Nell finished setting the table. Athelstane's huge brindle bulk was stretched out in front of the fire, with his stomach blissfully exposed to the heat. The cat was lying on the mantel beside the clock, paws well tucked in.

"Well," said Jesse, "you've decided we're satisfactory people to live with, have you?" The cat gave him a thoughtful blue stare. Davy had gone sound asleep in his playpen across the room.

Nell came trotting in with a glass of sherry. "Davy's worn himself out trying to get at that cat all day, but he'll calm down when the novelty wears off. Yes, it was the funniest thing, Jesse—it was just as if he'd been waiting for an invitation—first he came in here, and then he went right up to our room and smelled all around for ages, and got up on the bed and talked a blue streak to me. I wish I understood Siamese."

"We ought to think of a name for him. He looks like royalty on a throne up there. Caesar—Pharaoh—Sophocles."

"I don't like any of those. We'll live with him awhile and something will come to us. He's obviously been a house cat. I got him a litter pan—lucky you don't have to housebreak cats—and he'll have to be fed on the kitchen table, I suppose, or Athelstane would steal everything. He is a beauty, isn't he? Oh, Fran called, and she's feeling fine. Whatever it was went away and the doctor's pleased with her."

"Good. Wonder how little sister'll do at being a mother."

"Oh, Fran's good at anything she does," said Nell confidently.

She had already gone upstairs to read in bed when Jesse tried that number again at ten-thirty. This time a man answered.

"Mr. Ray Holst?"

"Yeah, that's me."

"I think," said Jesse cautiously, "you know the name of Vanderveer?"

"Yeah, that's right, who is this?"

"I'm Mr. Venderveer's lawyer—"

"Well, you took your time getting back to me," said Holst roughly. "Oh, excuse me, I know these things take a hell of a time, all the red tape—what have you found out?"

"I think," said Jesse, "I'd rather talk to you personally, Mr. Holst. I really don't have too much information, but—"

"Well, O.K.," said Holst. "I could come to see you in the morning, I don't go to work till one. Where do I come?"

Jesse told him. Cross questions and crooked answers, he thought. Well, see what Holst looked like. At least he seemed willing to talk. Whatever he had to talk about.

He showed up at the office at ten-thirty on Wednesday morning, and he turned out to be a rather rugged-looking young man in his early thirties; he was medium height, stocky, with dark curly hair. He wasn't exactly handsome, with a slightly pug nose and a large mouth, but he had a frank, ingenuous expression and very blue eyes.

"Well, I'm pleased to meet you, Mr. Falkenstein," he said. He sat down beside the desk and got out a cigarette. "Haven't you found out anything?"

Jesse said, "Suppose you tell me your end of this first, Mr. Holst. I'm not really too clear on the whole—" He let that trail off.

"Oh," said Holst. "Well, for God's sake, I thought he'd tell you about that, but I guess he's a pretty close-mouthed old geezer, maybe not quite all there, his age and all. Haven't you—well, excuse me, don't mean to tell you your business." He shrugged. "But Ma's kind of curious, and"—he laughed—"so am I! See, it was funny—I knew Ma had been married before, she'd said this and that about her first husband, but it wasn't till after Dad died that she told me *that*. She said it was a long time ago, and she guessed once she'd have felt terrible about it, but now it didn't seem to matter much—anyway, she wasn't sure if they were really divorced. Legally, see. It was in the Depression, she didn't have a job or much money, so she went down to Mexico to get a divorce because it was cheaper, and it wasn't till years later she heard that wasn't always legal. Well, she was married to Dad by then, she just didn't say anything about it—well, I tell you, it shook me a little, think I might be a bastard!" He laughed easily. "But hell, it is a long time ago—they were married nearly ten years before I came along—it sort of seemed like water under the bridge."

Jesse said, "But later on it got more important to you?"

"Well, it did," said Holst, very frank and earnest. "When I heard about the money. Ma always said her first husband had the makings of a miser, saved every penny, but I never thought much about it, why should I, until the house next door got put up for sale. See, some real estate guys came to look it over, this was back like maybe August sometime, and they were out in the side yard there, and I was in our yard because Ma'd asked me to weed the rose bed. I couldn't help hearing them talk, and pretty soon one of them said you'll never believe who I ran into the other day, old Johnny Vanderveer, and the other one said my God, I thought he was dead, and the first one said no, he looked about a hundred but he was still shuffling around, and he says, I'll bet he's got a pile laid away, very warm man as the British say, and the other one said yeah, he and Griffin had made a fortune apiece, real bundle of loot, in that building boom. Well—" Holst gestured graphically. "Maybe you can see that sort of made me think. It isn't an ordinary sort of name—so I asked Ma again and she said that'd be him, he was in construction work. I looked up the address— See, I'm a projectionist at the Glendale Theater, I don't make the hell of a lot of money, and Dad didn't leave much, he was a bus driver for the city. If Ma never was really divorced from this guy—why, they were still legally married and—well, hell, all she's got is the Social Security. We own the house, but it's tough to get along these days. You can see what I'm driving at."

"Clearly," said Jesse. "You're not married, Mr. Holst?"

"Who, me? No, Ma and I get along just fine, I never met a girl I felt like settling down with. Well, frankly, Mr. Falkenstein, I thought Vanderveer ought to know about this situation, see, I thought he might be interested to know about it—we didn't know if he'd ever got married again or not, but see, if he had and there were any kids—well, maybe he'd want to do something about it."

A little blackmail on the side, thought Jesse, whether the mother knew about that or not. Thinking Vanderveer would slip them a little something to keep quiet about the possibility. But pieces were falling into place. "So what did you do?" he asked. And at the back of his mind he was thinking what an unholy mess this was going to be if there hadn't been a legal divorce. God in heaven. All that money—whatever and wherever it was, however it had come—the second marriage invalid, the girls illegitimate, that will worth absolutely nothing. It would, of course, be a very simple matter, legally speaking. The legitimate widow would get a third, and the state would probably get the rest, when there wasn't a valid will. God.

"Well, I went to see him, on my day off. That house sure as hell didn't look like money, but what those guys said—well, you never know till you try. So I rang the bell, and he answered the door—I mean, it had to be him, way Ma had described him—and I'd just said my piece about the divorce when he lost his hair and threw me out—I mean, for real, gave me the bum's rush and calling me a goddamn liar and don't dare ever come back—"

So that was what that had been all about. And of course the old man would have realized the legal aspect of the thing— With a flash of insight Jesse saw that the old man hadn't been so much concerned about the effect on his will as the possibility that the first wife would have some claim on him here and now. And so first he had gone to Toomey, to check on the divorce. He'd never had any divorce papers; possibly she'd just told him she was going to get one. And then, when Toomey couldn't turn up any records, he'd intended to try to check with Mexico, hence the call to the consulate. And his third thought, of course, had been legitimate legal advice, and he had made the appointment with Jesse. It all followed as the night the day.

"So?" he said.

"Well, hell, I had to make him listen to me—get at him about maybe owing something to Ma, make things easier for her. She's never had much," said Holst emotionally. "If they were still married—I figured he'd stand still to read a letter from her, and I got her to write one. I went back there one morning, I was trying to think of some way to calm him down until I could hand him the letter, I was just going up the walk when I saw him come out the back door with a wastebasket—he was going to the garage to empty it, see, and when he got in there I nipped up the drive and got in the door quick before he could see— I figured—"

"Oh, you did? Suppose there was somebody else in the house?"

"Why, I thought he lives alone," said Holst. "I didn't see anybody else there the first time—" Holst's eyes narrowed on Jesse. "Anyway, I just waited on the service porch and he came back in a minute, he started to yell when he saw me, but I just handed over the letter—and he *did* read it. He read it right there. He just sort of grunted at it, and then he said we'd have to find out for sure about the divorce, if it was legal or not. He said even if it wasn't he didn't figure he owed Ma anything, and I said I thought he did, and he said to get the hell out, he'd let Ma know about it when he found out one way or the other. And that was that. We've been waiting to hear, see?"

"Do you remember what day that was?"

"Hell, I don't know. Five, six, seven weeks back. So when you called, I naturally thought—"

And Jesse, looking at him coldly, thought—possibilities here? The careful old man, going out to empty the wastebasket, the back door unlocked for two minutes. If Holst got in once he could get in twice. Yes? Or anybody else?

Holst the type for petty blackmail. Who could say whether the old man had slipped him fifty or a hundred to keep quiet, and then when he thought about it—and then decided to go the legitimate route, disappointing Holst?

The coincidences. He could be quite right that it was Mama who had arranged the overdose—and it could very well have been Holst who walked in on Vanderveer ten minutes or half an hour later.

He put out his cigarette. Holst was looking at his watch and saying he had to get going, pick up lunch and get to work. "You don't seem to be aware," said Jesse very gently, "that Mr. Vanderveer is dead, Mr. Holst."

Holst subsided back into the desk chair as if he'd been shot. "Dead?" he said. "Dead!" He licked his lips. He looked at Jesse in silence. Then he said slowly, "He was a damned old man. But— you'll have to find out about the divorce, won't you? If he had anything to leave—and they weren't divorced—will Ma get anything? Maybe?"

Jesse was just leaving the office when Jean said, "Mr. Dobson's on the phone—they've found the other banks."

"I've just left, have him call me back."

The house on Lomita Street in Glendale, oddly enough, was almost a replica of the house on Kingsley Drive, an old California bungalow painted white with green trim, on a shabby residential street in an old part of town. Aline Holst welcomed him in amiably. Again, it was impossible to say if she'd been pretty as a young woman, all those years ago. She was a little dumpy now, dowdy in a printed cotton housedress, low-heeled slippers. She had gentle, vague blue eyes and a soft girlish voice.

"Well," she said, "I always thought Johnny'd be one to end up with some money. But it never occurred to me I might be due any from him, till Ray said—and then it came to both of us, if that wasn't a real legal divorce—I was sort of a green girl back then, I just knew I wanted to get shut of Johnny Vanderveer, and a girl friend of mine said it was quick and cheap over the border, so that's where I went."

"Where exactly?" he asked. Tijuana, and the divorce was almost certainly not legal. God.

"Oh, Mexicali," she said. "It was only nine dollars on the bus, I remember."

He breathed a little easier. A fairly big town even then—quite a big town now—a better chance that records would be straight, crooked lawyers at a minimum. "What was the date?"

"Oh, I couldn't say exactly, it being so long ago. It was the spring of 1936, about then. When I got back I just phoned Johnny and told him we were divorced. But when Ray found out just a while ago that Johnny probably had some money, he said we ought to go into it, find out, and maybe I'd be due something. Ray's pretty smart, now that Chuck's gone I usually take Ray's advice about things."

CHAPTER 9

Twenty minutes after Jesse got back to the office Dobson called. "I thought you were supposed to keep regular office hours, Falkenstein," he said coldly. "Really I would think you'd be concerned to get on with this matter, as it's a question of settling the estate—of course I realize that can't be resolved finally until after the trial, but that's your side of the business. As far as my own office is concerned, we're anxious to find out all we can about this as soon as possible, and after all your cooperation—"

Jesse apologized. "Things come up," he said vaguely. "Where have we gotten to now?"

"We know the other two banks. A Bank of America in Atwater, a Crocker bank on Third Street. It's too late today to get into them, but I'd be obliged if you'll meet me at the Crocker bank at ten tomorrow morning, if that's not too much trouble." Jesse hastily agreed that he'd be there.

The client with the four o'clock appointment was a woman who had a divorce in mind. Taking notes on that, listening to her ramblings about her delinquent husband's drinking and playing around, he was abstracted. He left a little early; Fran and Clock were coming for dinner.

He looked at his little sister across the table—Fran looking quite herself again, despite the bulge in the middle—a very pretty girl, Fran, with her pert gamine face and smartly cut black hair—and Clock said amusedly from beside him, "I hope to God it looks like her."

Athelstane, of course, came around the table begging for handouts, and Fran said disapprovingly that they ought to cure him of that, it was an obnoxious bad habit. "Sally never does, she's good as gold, never comes near the table."

"That hairy floor mop," said Jesse.

They heard about the cat, and Fran said how funny for Athelstane to make friends with him, it showed that the big bumble-headed idiot had some finer instincts after all. The cat made a studied regal entrance after dinner, coming down the stairs; he now condescended to let Jesse stroke him, but obviously preferred women. After making a token visit to each of them in turn he leaped lightly up to the mantel from the log box and settled down with paws well tucked in.

"He really is a beauty," said Fran. "You'll have to think of a special name for him."

But, with the girls talking babies at the other end of the room, Jesse brought Clock up to date on Vanderveer. "This is the damndest rigmarole I ever came across."

"Well, I'm bound to say," said Clock, "if you're right that the girl didn't do it, I think you may have something about the old lady. She really did have some reason for suicide, and with all you've turned up, she'd probably hated that old devil for years, the life he led her."

"Yes, what belatedly occurred to me too. But you know, Andrew, he'd never have remotely realized it—realized why most people didn't like him—he didn't know they didn't—he didn't miss the social contacts, the affection—he just didn't know any better. I can see him as a rather pathetic character really, not an ogre—the narrow, selfish, greedy old man completely ignorant of the realities of life, the real importances."

"Yes, in a way," said Clock doubtfully. "How are you going to play it at the trial?"

Jesse tossed his cigarette stub into the low fire. "Dulcie won't like it, or Marcia, but it is the likeliest answer, isn't it? Mama. Mama arranged the overdose, and somebody walked in on the old man. There are possibilities to suggest—I'd better look up those evicted tenants—there were plenty of people who had reason to have a row with him—and it mightn't have taken much to provoke him into a physical attack."

"That's very funny, about the initial effect of the overdose—there wasn't anything in the autopsy report about that."

"Technically speaking, it might have been no more than self-defense," said Jesse. "There's Schultz, and now Holst—there are, when you think, quite a few people—it could have been anyone."

"What about the divorce?"

Jesse groaned. "Oh, my God, that's another thing. Write the courthouse in Mexicali, see if there's any record on it. At least there she was more likely to pick up a legitimate attorney, instead of some fly-by-night who'd take her money and assure her the divorce was legal. Yes. Even in 1936. When Vanderveer went to Toomey he hadn't received her letter, he probably thought she'd gotten the divorce here and Holst was just trying to slip something over on him for the little payoff—and then he found out it was a Mexican divorce from her letter. And at the last, he'd evidently intended to hand the whole thing over to me. Hell, I don't know, Andrew. About the trial. Dulcie will put up a good appearance in court, and if I play on the sympathy of the jury, emphasize the home situation, even if they think she did it they might let her off."

"I suppose so," said Clock, massaging his jaw. "There but for the grace of God."

"And I don't know that I'd worry about any circumvention of justice," said Jesse morosely. "The old man had had a longer share of life than a lot of people, to grab what he could on this physical plane, toil and moil away piling up the money. And the old woman's life was no pleasure to her, God knows."

He met Dobson at the Crocker bank on Third Street on Thursday morning, and here again they hadn't much difficulty. The supposed James Canning hadn't come in often to visit his safety box; the latest time had been eight months ago; but Vanderveer was a distinctive old fellow, and all three vault attendants identified the photograph without hesitation. They swore to the affidavits, so Dobson and Jesse didn't have to consider the handwriting samples. By eleven-thirty they had the box handed over and were opening it in one of the cubicles.

There was a little stack of cash in it, a folded sheet of typewriter-size paper, and a business card. Dobson sat down and before he began to count the cash he said, "Why in God's name do people do such ridiculous things, Falkenstein? If you hadn't figured out what those jottings meant, all this would never have come to light—when the rent was up on these boxes they'd have been opened and examined and the money turned over to the state as untraceable. What the hell did the old boy think he was doing, not telling a soul about where this was? He'd have known that too."

Jesse said absently, "He was just following a pattern. The habit of secrecy had grown on him." He had unfolded the sheet of paper and was reading what was on it.

It purported to be a partnership agreement, and it had been composed by someone who had very hazy ideas about legal terms. It was amateurishly typed on an old machine with elite type and several letters out of alignment.

This is to certify that an agreement is made this day—it was a date about a year in the past—*between Richard Bugotti and J. W. Vanderveer in partnership with J. W. Vanderveer to put up whole cost of establishing a business at the below address in return for 50% of all gross profits.* It was an address on Hollywood Boulevard. *Richard Bugotti contracts to take all responsibility to establish the business and operate.* There were signatures and witnesses to signatures: Henry Dudenhoff and Antonio Vasquez.

The business card simply said *Kevin Anderson, Investment Specialties,* and bore an address and phone number in San Marino. The bits and pieces the old man had left behind— He wondered what that agreement was all about.

Dobson gave him a receipt for another five thousand dollars, and they stopped for a sandwich before proceeding on to the Bank of America in Atwater. Here they ran into trouble: nobody there had any vague recollection of Robert Archer, or recognized the photograph. Dobson said resignedly that he'd see the manager, follow it up, and see what showed; Jesse had an appointment at four o'clock and left him to it.

But he had some time on hand, and instead of going upstairs he got into the Mercedes and drove up to Hollywood Boulevard. The address on that peculiar agreement was spang in the central part of town, and it had a sign on the double glass doors, The Blue Room. He parked a block up and walked back. It was a fairly big and classy porn shop: books, pictures, and no doubt other things under the counter; as the fellow at that other place had said, catering to all tastes. With the relaxed laws, there wasn't much the police could do about these places. At this hour, there was quite a little crowd in, all young men. There was a counter with a cash register on it at the rear of the store, and a man lounging behind it. The atmosphere was strangely quiet and peaceful; the men stood around browsing at the tables as if they were in trances.

Jesse went up to the counter. "I'm looking for a Richard Bugotti."

The man looked him over. "That's me. What can I do for you?" He was about twenty-six, with a widow's peak of black hair and handsome sharp features; his eyes were dark and cynical.

Jesse handed him a card. He looked at it and said, "A lawyer. That's sinister, man. What do you want with me?"

Jesse produced the funny little typed agreement and said, "Did you know that Vanderveer's dead? I'm responsible for getting his estate settled."

Bugotti looked at the paper, looked back at him, and said expressionlessly, "Yeah, I read it in the paper. So you found that stashed away." He was silent a moment, and then went to a door leading into the rear of the store. "Hey, Henry, come out and take over awhile, will you?"

A sandy beefy-shouldered young man about the same age appeared. "Sure, Rick."

"Come back here," said Bugotti, and led Jesse into a cluttered tiny office with a scarred old desk and a couple of straight chairs crowded together. He flung himself into the chair behind the desk. "That thing!" he said. "I've been worrying about that damn thing so bad I can't sleep. I guess it's true, you sure got to learn by experience. I was the biggest goddamn fool on the face of the earth to sign that thing. What I'd like to know is—you a lawyer, you can tell me—what position am I in now the old bastard is dead? Do I still have to go on paying, like to his heirs?" He looked angry and anxious.

"Suppose you tell me how you came to sign it," said Jesse. "It's an odd enough little document, Mr. Bugotti."

"Is it? I don't know much about the law, but I tried to make it sound, you know, businesslike—he told me what I should put down more or less. Hell, I even typed it, on that old thing." There was an ancient Olivetti on the desk. "Talk about goddamned fools! I'll tell you how it was, Mr."—he glanced at the card—"Mr. Falkenstain. I had a hole-in-the-wall porn store way out Vermont, making peanuts because I hadn't any capital to buy really good stock, rent a bigger place in a better location. Look, I don't happen to go for this crap myself, but there's a big demand, there's a market for it, and you supply what the public wants, you build up business and make money, no? It's simple. But you got to have capital. This old buzzard used to come in sometimes, bought a couple of things—surprised the hell out of me, see a guy his age still interested, you know? Well, about the third time he came in, Henry out there had dropped by to see me, and I was bitching about the way things were going, said if I just had the capital to stock a bigger store some place better, I could make some real money—and the old guy sort of pricked up his ears, know what I mean, and right out of the blue he said, sounds like an interesting proposition, what do you say if I put up the capital? I was flabbergasted, I nearly laughed in his face—he looked like an old bum, ragged old clothes. But then I saw he was serious. He asked all sorts of questions, how much it'd cost to rent a place and stock it, and in the end he offered me twenty thousand to get started. I didn't believe the luck—then! I was the original eager beaver, rarin' to go and make a million— I started to look around, I found this place at a pretty good price, up for lease. Well, I expected I'd sign a note for the bread at so much interest, but the old man says he's interested to keep an eye on the business, we make it like a silent partnership, and he suggested what we should put in that agreement. Hell, I can add and subtract, but I'd never been in big business before, and being a damn fool it sounded O.K. to me, I typed it up and we signed it. Then he gave me a cashier's check and I went to the bank—signed the lease that day. This place was a mess, needed painting and cleaning, and I got a couple of pals, the same ones witnessed that thing, to help—we really did a job, slicked it up good, and I ordered a lot of stock and we opened with a bang."

"How's business?" asked Jesse. "This was about a year ago, by this date."

"For God's sake!" said Bugotti. "You should ask? I just hadn't thought the thing through! We started to do business hand over fist—right on the boulevard, all the walk-by traffic, it was great! I went on thinking of that old bastard as a kind of fairy godfather for a few months, and then I woke up. With another bang."

"Yes," said Jesse. "You were doing all the work, and he was taking half the gross profit as the silent partner."

"You're goddamned right. Hell, I knew about net and gross, it was him said to put that in, but it wasn't until I was keeping the books it hit me between the eyes. Here I was paying the rent, paying the utilities, paying Henry to help wait on trade, and that old s.o.b. is taking fifty percent of all the profits! He'd taken me like some hick in from the country the first time, and the more I thought about it the madder I got. I told him so next time I saw him—he used to come in the first of the month to get his cut—and he just grinned like an old snake and said I could put it down to getting business experience, there was our agreement all nice and legal. I couldn't weasel out of it, he said, and I'd know better next time. I told him what I thought, but he didn't give a damn if I called him every name in the book. When I'd run out of things to say, he just said, how much did we make this month?"

Jesse asked curiously, "And how much have you been making, if you don't mind telling me?"

"It's been running about ten thousand a month gross—"

"Oh, ouch," said Jesse.

"Yeah, you see what I mean! And another thing, God, how could I be so innocent? Me! I mean, I knew what he was doing, but I was so grateful to the old bastard then I agreed to it—he wanted to be paid in cash—he wasn't reporting that to Uncle Sam. Along last April, I woke up to the trouble I could get into there, and I told him that was a no-no from now on. He bitched about it, but I wouldn't play. After that I gave him cashier's checks."

"Very wise of you," said Jesse dryly.

"My God, when I saw in the paper he was dead—I'm not surprised somebody murdered him—I was never so thankful in my life! But listen, what's the legal position? Do I have to go on paying his heirs?" Bugotti ran a nervous hand through his black hair.

"This contract or whatever it's supposed to be isn't legal, you know—and it was just between the two of you, and he's dead. You'd paid him back his capital plus whatever interest he'd have gotten on a loan."

"That I had."

"Why don't you just tear this up and forget it?" said Jesse casually, and laid the sheet on the desk.

"Do you mean it?" asked Bugotti incredulously. "Well, thank God! But I guess the old bastard taught me something, at that— and maybe he was right, the business experience was worth it."

Jesse just made his appointment, with a new client who wanted a legal separation from his wife, but as he took notes and answered questions, at the back of his mind he was thinking, another one with cause to hate the old man—another possible enemy who could have dropped in on Vanderveer to argue about money that rainy morning. When the client had left, he folded his notes together and sat staring out the window, thinking about it.

Whoever might have come by ending up committing a homicide, all too likely in self-defense. The picture was taking clearer shape for him, what might have happened that morning. He could see the old woman—not feeling well that morning, said Dulcie—lying in her bed wishing she could be rid of life and at rest. Thinking of the crabbed, unloving old husband, and how they were a burden on Dulcie—why shouldn't he be removed too? And painfully getting herself out of bed, onto the walker, hobbling into the kitchen—warming up the coffee, making the eggnog. Such a dark gloomy morning it had been, raining and cold, just the day for suicide and murder. He could see her getting the codeine capsules from the bathroom, adding them to the drinks, putting the bottle back. Taking the coffee to the old man sitting in the living room, or calling him to come and get it. Getting herself back to the bedroom, to lie and wait for the blessed unconsciousness— And then? Who had come to the door and played a part in the final scene?

Marcia—no, she belonged to another story. If Marcia was guilty, she had done all of it. But he could see Holst, coming back to argue that Aline was owed money—saying they knew the divorce wasn't legal, he didn't have to investigate, and he'd better pay to keep them quiet. Or Schultz, coming to beg for more time on that IOU. Or the evicted tenants to argue about the damages. Or Bugotti, swearing about how he'd been conned. Or even Bill Perez, learning of the indignities the landlord inflicted on his mother. Or—or Gloria Worth, futilely pleading to be let off the blackmail?

What a grubbing, grasping, mean-minded old bastard he had

been. And the one or the other of them losing his temper, reaching for the poker.

He could suggest all that to judge and jury. There were enough witnesses to testify to his character. And it was an academic question—they'd never know who had last handled that poker and struck the old man down.

The cat was already choosing his own places in the house, his own routines. Like all animals who tended to be creatures of habit, and turning into a properly respected house cat again, he was developing new habits for the new house. He spent the mornings outside with Athelstane, unless it was raining; about eleven o'clock he came in and went immediately to the log box to curl up for a nap there. In the afternoon he would be folded neatly together on Jesse's desk in the study, and the evenings he spent largely on Nell's lap; but promptly at ten he went upstairs to the master bedroom, where he spent the night at the foot of the bed.

"I wish I could think of an appropriate name for you," Nell told him as she got out his lunch. "You're quite an addition to the household."

The cat answered her at length in Siamese.

Before he drove down to Sybil Brand Institute on Friday morning, Jesse dialed the phone number on that business card. An obviously efficient secretary answered the phone: "Investment Specialties, good morning." Jesse asked for Mr. Anderson. "I'm sorry, Mr. Anderson is in Phoenix on business. He's not expected back until Monday. Could someone else on our staff help you?"

"No, I'd like to speak to Anderson."

"Whom shall I say called? Is there a message?"

"Never mind, I'll call back."

When the wardress brought Dulcie into the bare little room, and stationed herself outside, Jesse said, "Now I'm going to say a few things you're not going to like hearing, Miss Vanderveer, but they've got to be said." He began to sketch the story to her, watching to see how she took it.

"No!" she said in distress. "No—not Mama! Mama was brought up to believe that suicide's a sin."

"Well, you know," said Jesse quietly, "sometimes people get to thinking different about things as they get older—and in different situations. She'd said to you that she wanted to die and be at rest, hadn't she?"

"Yes, but she didn't mean it—like that."

"She'd been suffering a good deal of physical pain, hadn't she? And she was getting more helpless."

"Yes," whispered Dulcie.

"And she knew what a burden she was being, and was sorry about that, sorry for the trouble she was to you—"

"She was a good woman, Mr. Falkenstein," said Dulcie unsteadily. "Every time I did something for her she always thanked me. She was so sorry she had to get me up so much at night—she couldn't help it."

"No," said Jesse. "And it's not a very kind or nice thing to say to you, but—looking back—do you think she'd really had a very happy life with your father? Even if she'd loved him when they were married, or even just liked and respected him—even if she'd just married him to have a husband—do you think she could still have had any positive feeling for him now, all those years later?"

Dulcie's mouth set in a firm line. "I don't know—if anybody could judge that." And she was silent, and then suddenly she sat up straight and met his eyes, and her little jaw was set and her voice harder than he had ever heard it. "I never knew him to speak an affectionate word to any of us. He was a mean, cantankerous, selfish, horrible old man, and he couldn't have been much different when he was young. I hope I didn't hate him, because hating just comes back on you, it's hurting yourself really—but I don't think anybody could ever have felt the least affection for him anytime. Oh, I know what you'll say—Uncle Howie—but it's different with men, and he didn't see Papa at home—just in business—he didn't realize how he was to us. Aunt Flo did, of course. Oh, I can remember things—the things Mama wanted and never had—that cheap little house, when Uncle Howie bought that beautiful, beautiful place—I was just fourteen, and I thought it was the loveliest house I'd ever seen, and all the beautiful new furniture— and I couldn't understand—if they were partners, why didn't Papa have enough for a house like that—and Mama just saying, your father thinks it's extravagant— Extravagant! She liked the movies when they used to make good ones, but he always grudged the money—gave her twenty dollars a week for the groceries, he always had to see the bills—a little more later on but—oh, I remember so much, when I was starting to grow up and realize things—understand things." Her hands were twisting together convulsively. "Just ordinary things!" she said a little wildly. "Permanent waves—it sounds silly, but it's important to a woman to look right—and Mama liked nice things, liked to look right—it wasn't as if they cost much back then, you could get a permanent for ten dollars, but he—but he— And shoes, she had trouble getting fitted, and the only ones really comfortable for her were those Enna Jetticks, and they cost more than most shoes and he said the ones at Sears were just as good, she could go there— Dishes!" said Dulcie incoherently. "It wasn't as if she wanted Haviland. They hadn't a thing when they got married, she'd been living in a furnished apartment—and I know it was still the Depression then, and not much money—but later on, when I was noticing, all we had were odds and ends of things that didn't match, and she wanted nice dishes to look nice on the table, the set she wanted was forty dollars at Ward's, and he wouldn't let her—she saved it up from the housekeeping money, it took her ages. After I was working—he never gave Marcia and me any money at all, like an allowance, you know—I tried to get her things she wanted, take her places— oh, you mustn't think Marcia didn't care, but she was living away from home, and then she was married— Catalina!" said Dulcie, and began to cry bitterly.

"Catalina," said Jesse cautiously.

She cried for just a minute, and sat up and groped for a handkerchief. "I'm sorry. It was just—about the first time I noticed— how things were—I guess I was about seven or eight. Her friend Mrs. Wayland wanted her to go to Catalina with her for the weekend, just a little vacation, it would only cost about thirty dollars— and he was furious, he wouldn't let her go. I'm sorry, it was just that it all—sort of came back at once. How everything was. She was a good, kind woman, Mr. Falkenstein—and of course she was miserable with him, how could she help being miserable? Oh, I hope not hating him— But what could she do? She wasn't young— when Marcia and I were born—she couldn't get away, because of us. And he never gave anybody anything, not even a kind word—

he just took and took, all her work and all her youth and all her happiness—and forty-two years—*forty-two years*—the meanest kind of living, that old-fashioned house in an old street, never any money for decent clothes, never going out anywhere, never any fun, never having *anything*—"

"You should have let all that out before," said Jesse.

"Oh, don't you think Marcia and I have said it a thousand times? Haven't thought about it?" She was silent, still mopping her eyes, and then she said very quietly, "I've got to say—I think it's possible, Mr. Falkenstein. It's clever of you to see that—it never entered my mind—it could have been Mama. But it could have been."

"We'd never prove it, you know. But I think I can make a good case to put to the jury. It's not going to be pleasant for you and your sister to hear all this in court, about your father and mother—but you're more important than two people who are—out of it."

"That's one way to look at it," said Dulcie. "You're the one to say. You know what ought to be done at the trial. You do what you think is right." She looked exhausted now, and went off down the corridor with the wardress, walking slowly.

Dobson called at three-thirty on Friday afternoon. "I don't know how we're going to get over this one," he said grimly. "That box at the Bank of America—I was chasing all around that damn bank yesterday, and then over hell's half acre trying to get current addresses. He rented that box sometime in 1960, and he'd never been near it since as far as we can make out."

"Oh, for the love of—"

"Yes," said Dobson. "I know. Nearly twenty-two years, and practically all the bank personnel has changed. Also, they had a fire that destroyed some records in 1965, and there's no record of who rented him the box. There were four people who worked in the vault—that is, three regulars and one posting clerk who substituted during lunch hours, and any one of them might have waited on Vanderveer that day. One of them is now dead."

"Fine," said Jesse. "But they must have had an address, to send him the yearly bill?"

"That's right. General Delivery, the Hollywood post office. He paid in cashier's checks."

"Very helpful. What do we do about it?"

"Well, we'll have to try. If you'll meet me at my office in the morning, we can use my car." He didn't sound hopeful.

Still, a picture was supposed to be worth a thousand words.

Jesse went home to find Nell poring over a dictionary of names. "Oh, I didn't realize it was that late," she said, looking up in surprise as he came in. "I'm sorry, darling, I forgot the gate."

"I know you did, it's all right. What are you doing, naming the baby?"

"Now, Jesse—you know that's been decided months ago. It's Amanda Elaine for a girl and Geoffrey Andrew for a boy. No, I'm looking for an appropriate name for the new member of the family, and I can't find one. Nothing seems really to fit him." Davy was prattling to himself in his playpen, Athelstane was sound asleep in front of the fireplace, and the cat was curled up on the mantel watching them with his brilliant blue eyes. He looked much fatter and sleeker now.

"Have you thought," asked Jesse, "of doing anything about dinner?"

"Heavens, the meat loaf!" Nell dropped the book and fled.

But over drinks before dinner, she reverted to the topic. "Nothing seems to fit him, but there's something queer about it too."

"Always something queer about cats. The ultimate independent entities," said Jesse lazily. "Reason some simian human beings don't like them—they just can't understand anybody who's completely indifferent to somebody else's opinion."

Nell laughed. "Quite true, but there is something funny about it." She sipped sherry. "I very nearly christened him Solomon this morning—he looks so wise, after all—and when he came in with Athelstane for lunch I asked him if he'd like to be called Solomon, and he stopped short and looked at me, and honestly, Jesse, I could nearly hear him saying, no, that's not my name."

"Imagination."

"It was not. And I thought of a few others, like Graymalkin and Chang and Domino and Thibault. And Tobermory, only he didn't speak Siamese. And Webster."

"That's a new one on me."

"The cat in the Wodehouse story."

"Oh. Yes."

"But they don't fit."

"Something will occur to you."

"Well, I hope so. We can't go on calling him Puss. He's going to the vet for immunization shots on Monday, I hope he won't mind. And how are you coming with your little puzzle? Found any more wads of cash stuffed into old chairs?"

"Don't remind me. We seem," said Jesse, "to have run into a little snag."

"I don't expect," said Dobson, "that we'll get a single reaction, but of course we have to try." They had started out at the bank in Atwater.

It had been there a long time, and it was a big bank. Only three of the personnel who had been there in 1960 were still there: the manager, the chief teller, and a security guard. None of them, of course, had anything to do with the vault, but Jesse showed them the photograph and they all looked and shook their heads at it.

"I couldn't say I never had seen him," said the chief teller, "maybe coming in once—but nobody'd remember just once. And that long ago—"

At least the manager had been able to supply Dobson with the names of the employees who were on duty at the vault then. "How do you know it was 1960 if the records were destroyed, by the way?" asked Jesse.

"They were only partly destroyed. Up to 1959 that box was rented by somebody else, there's a listing on that, and it's never been on the free list since. I had a hell of a time tracing down addresses for these people, they'd all moved since leaving the bank. These post office people are getting more inefficient every day."

"Look who's talking."

"Two of these people retired—Mrs. Willey and John Partridge—and another one was fired, James Lukens. In 1970."

"What did he do, try to embezzle funds?"

"He was found drunk on the job. Mrs. Willey went to live with her sister when her husband died, the people next door gave me that. It's Altadena."

Mrs. Willey, who was small and neat and obviously conscientious, pored over the photograph for some time before she said, "Oh, dear, I wish I could help you, but I don't recall ever seeing this man in my life. You say he rented a box? Well, you know, the vault's open the same hours as the bank, and it could have been any one of us who waited on him. I might have been out to lunch when he came in, or waiting on someone else so I didn't notice him. And of course Mr. Lukens came down from upstairs on different lunch hours, or if we were busy. And Mr. Brandon—oh, dear, that was such a dreadful thing—he had the heart attack right in the bank, you know, he dropped dead right in front of the New Accounts desk—he was only fifty-nine and such a nice man—" She handed back the photograph. "I wish I could help you, but I can't say I'd seen him when I never did."

Mr. John Partridge lived in Hawthorne. He had moved in with his daughter's family when his wife died. And it was obviously a nice family: the daughter, Mrs. Pickering, was friendly and attractive, and there was an enticing smell of fresh-baked bread in the house. "Something about the bank? Well, Daddy's out in back planting bulbs—he always was a gardener, he's made a difference to this place, I don't have the time and my husband can't abide yard work." She showed them out the kitchen door into a green and pleasant backyard.

Partridge was a perky thin little man in his seventies, with a thin halo of white hair around a large bald spot. He sat back on his heels and dropped his trowel and said, "I was late getting the new ones in this fall, but looks as though we'll have a wet winter, I hope they'll do well. You from the bank, you say? What can I do for you?"

"IRS," said Dobson curtly, and Partridge's smile faded. Jesse hastened into the conversation and explained what they were after.

"Well, now, isn't that a thing," said Partridge. "False name, hah? On a lockbox? I don't know that I ever ran into a thing like that before. We better go in, I've got to wash my hands before I look at your picture." They went in and sat in a comfortable, homey living room while Partridge washed his hands.

He came back and sat down and Jesse handed him the photograph. He studied it carefully. "I've never laid eyes on him," he said regretfully. "I've got a good memory for faces—dealing with the public, it makes a difference if you take the trouble to re-member people, call them by name. In a bank, of course, it's not the same thing as your own business—people have to deal with banks—but it makes things more friendly. I knew all our regulars, of course. But this"—he tapped the photograph—"I think I'd have remembered him, if I'd ever seen him. He's not just ordinary-look-ing. But I never did. Rented a box from us, did he? Well, it could have been Mary Willey or Bill Brandon or even Lukens rented it to him. When I was out to lunch or busy with somebody else. You know that Brandon's dead? Died of a heart attack, right at the bank."

"We heard," said Dobson sourly.

"Well, I'm sorry I can't help you," said Partridge. "Renting a box in a fake name—you know, come to think, people might be doing that all the time, all we ask is a name and address and the rent."

James Lukens, Dobson had located in Huntington Park. On the way, Jesse said, "The handwriting analysts can come up with some hard facts these days. Think I might get Sergeant Clock to turn Questioned Documents onto it."

"Onto what?" asked Dobson briefly. "We've got plenty of sam-ples of Vanderveer's writing, but the form he filled out, renting the box, is gone. They've got nothing to show us but cashier's checks—that is, the latest one."

"Oh, Lord, of course."

The address in Huntington Park was one side of an old frame duplex. The woman who opened the door was about forty, with hennaed hair and a bad-tempered mouth. Inside the living room, immediately inside the door, a TV was on loudly.

She went over and turned it off with a snap. "Somebody to see you. I didn't get who, you run that damn thing so loud."

"From the bank," said Jesse. "That is, going back to your job at the bank, Mr. Lukens—"

"If you only had that bank job back," said the woman bitterly. "Good steady money—but you had to get drunk on the job—"

"Shut up," he said. He was a middle-aged man, too fat and pasty-faced, in slacks and a T-shirt. "I got a job, haven't I?"

"Oh, you got a job! A lousy part-time job at a liquor store, not enough to pay the rent, I got to wait on tables at that Mex restaurant to put groceries on the table—"

"Knock it off. What are you guys after?"

Dobson told him. He said, "Dammit, that's a hell of a long time ago. I couldn't tell you." He looked at the photograph again. "He doesn't look like anybody I ever saw before."

"You wouldn't recognize him if he was your best pal," she said. "You half drunk alla time—"

"Shut up, you bitch," he said tersely.

Dobson turned the ignition key in expressive silence. On the way back to Hollywood, he said, "So there's absolutely no way we can prove any connection! We know Archer had to be Vanderveer, but there's no way to prove it legally. The box rent is paid up to January. All we can do is wait until then to get a look at it—our office has the authorization, but of course you haven't anything legally to connect it with the estate—"

"Not one damned thing," said Jesse. Maybe just because he couldn't get at it, he was damned curious about what was in that safe-deposit box.

CHAPTER 10

It occurred to Jesse that he should at least get the names of those evicted tenants to add to the list of people with reason to dislike Vanderveer, and on Sunday morning he went up to that apartment on Fountain. It was the kind of place called, for some unfathomable reason, a garden apartment, built the long way of the lot with some landscaping and open carports at the side; the building was two-storied. He started with the ground-floor front; the name slot beside the door held a slip with a typed name: R. RYAN. The woman who opened the door was a young, fairly good-looking blonde. She listened to his self-introduction and question and said, oh, the Sidneys. They had moved out a couple of months ago.

"I understand," said Jesse, "that there was some trouble with Mr. Vanderveer—the landlord."

"That's right," said Mrs. Ryan, "but a lot of people in this place had trouble with him. You're the lawyer seeing about the will and so on? I wonder if we could get that money back—it was only forty dollars but it was the principle of the thing—come in and I'll tell you about it." She introduced him to her husband, who looked like a sub-junior executive type; they were both in their mid-twenties. "It's the lawyer arranging all that old man's affairs, Rex. It's awful about his daughter, we didn't know he had one, but she probably had a reason. Sit down, Mr. what did you say?—oh, Falkenstein." The little apartment was bright and neat, built on an open plan and furnished in Danish modern. "Listen," she said, "this is the kind of thing he'd do. He always came the first of the month to get the rent checks—if it was a weekday he'd come in the evening. He was a real old creep, like a mummy come to life. But after all, he owned the place, he was supposed to keep it up. And the dishwasher went on the fritz—"

Rex Ryan said mildly, "Not a plumber. Like Vera says, he was supposed to keep up the place." He had pale blue eyes and a prominent Adam's apple, and was wearing a red plaid robe over pajamas. "The old man came and worked on it, said it was fixed. It wasn't. Finally, after he'd fooled around with it a couple of times, I had to call a plumber, and the bill was forty bucks. I sent it to him, and he hit the ceiling. I had a hell of a row with him, he wouldn't pay, and of course I was the one who got dunned. I paid it—didn't have any choice—and never got him to fork over."

"Well," said Jesse. "Did you know the Sidneys?"

"Now there," said Vera Ryan judicially, "I have to admit he had a case. You're not supposed to have children or pets here, but she had her sister's two little boys this summer, the sister was sick, and they were real brats, threw stuff down the toilet and ruined the plumbing and crayoned all over the walls and carved up the kitchen counter—I saw the place when they moved out."

"Do you know where they moved?" Neither of them did.

"They were riffraff anyway," he said.

"Who's going to own this place now?" she asked. "We had notice to pay rent to some other address—"

"There's some question about that, it may not be settled for a while." And that was just more grist to the mill.

On Monday morning Marcia Coleman came into the office about eleven o'clock. She was looking rather fine-drawn and haggard. "I don't want to take up your time, Mr. Falkenstein—I know I haven't got an appointment, and you're probably busy—but Dulcie told me on Saturday—what you think. What—well, what line you'll take at the trial. I just wanted to put in my opinion—for what it's worth."

"As I said to your sister, not very pleasant hearing in court—for either of you. But—"

She made an impatient gesture. She sat down in the chair beside his desk, accepted a cigarette and a light. "It doesn't matter. It's queer, but it never remotely occurred to either of us that *that* was the answer, Mama was always so gentle, never complaining, putting up with things and making do—never any arguments, everything just the way he ordered it—but now you bring up the possibility, both of us can *see* it. There must have been just one last straw. After forty-two years. I wonder if it was the washing machine."

"What about the washing machine?" asked Jesse.

"Well, there was the usual fit about that when we got it—and when was that?—Charles and I have been married fifteen years, and it was about three years before that, so it must have been 1962 or 1963. Mama had an old wringer washer, and it finally gave out—of course she should have had an automatic years before. But equally of course he said they cost too much. But Dulcie stood up to him for once and kept after him until he finally went to Sears and bought one. It was fine for quite a long time, but they don't last forever and the last couple of years it needed repairs and parts a few times, and of course he kicked about that. And the week before—before they died, it went out again and the repairman said it couldn't be fixed, they'd need a new one. And Papa said no, Dulcie could take everything to the Laundromat. On top of everything else she had to do. You wouldn't wonder but what it was the last straw. For Mama. She knew what a lot of work she made for Dulcie, and that was going to be too much. And maybe, after forty-two years, she finally hit back at him."

Marcia was silent, smoking, and then said with a little laugh, "I nearly didn't marry Charles—on account of Mama and Papa. Kids —they take their attitudes to life, and to marriage, from their parents. It's an irrational thing, by then I was an adult, and I'd had some experience with people, different kinds of people. But when I thought about marriage, all I could see was Mama, forever shortchanged and going without and making do, putting up with that damned old tyrant—my God, Charles as different from Papa as night from day—but you see what I mean."

"I do indeed," said Jesse thoughtfully.

"And I knew I wasn't like Mama either—if I'd been in that situation, hard as it was, not young and with two kids to raise, I'd have spit in his eye and gotten out, if I had to scrub other people's floors or whatever to support myself. I never could see why Dulcie didn't get out long ago. After Mama had the arthritis and strokes, of course she was stuck, and she was over thirty then, knew she'd probably never marry. I couldn't have stood it—but Dulcie's a pretty strong character in her own way. Well—" She stood up. "I just wanted to let you know that I'm quite willing to cooperate, whatever you want me to do at the trial, whatever you want me to say. No, it's not a very nice story, is it? But if it's the way to get Dulcie off, we'll have to play it that way. Just tell me what you want me to say—the unpalatable truth as it were."

"Thanks very much, Mrs. Coleman. I'm glad to know that, and I appreciate your coming in."

As he ushered her out past the Gordons' desks, Roberto Renaldo was sitting in the outer office, handsome and phlegmatic. He stood up and gave Jesse a correct little bow. "I have come to give you the key of the house, sir. We have found another house, near to Lucia's sister, and have moved yesterday. You understand, we want a house because we hope to have sons and daughters, and in all these apartments it is forbidden to have the children. It is very strange—American landlords would perhaps like to see the race of man die out entirely?"

Jesse grinned. "I can see it might look like that."

"So, we have moved. The rent is paid to the end of the month, but Lucia was impatient to move, she says she can see the terrible old man in every corner as if spying on her—women have fancies, but I love her, what am I to do?" He shrugged cheerfully and went out. Jean reminded Jesse that Mr. Hausman was due to come in to sign his will, and there was a new client at two o'clock.

The new client turned out to be a Mrs. Ringrose, breathing vengeance at the Griffith Park Observatory, on whose too-polished floor she had broken an ankle and sustained other injuries. Jesse listened to her, soothed her by saying they'd get her medical expenses with no difficulty: a routine claim against the city. She went away mollified, and he suddenly remembered Kevin Anderson.

He sat back and lit a cigarette and got out that business card from the second safe-deposit box and dialed the San Marino number. On the second ring the phone was lifted at the other end, "Investment Specialties, may I help you?"

"I'd like to speak to Mr. Anderson."

"Thank you." And a moment later a deep masculine voice said, "Anderson here."

"I think," said Jesse, "that you knew a Mr. Jan Vanderveer."

"Knew? Is he gone? Well—who is this?"

Jesse introduced himself. "Oh, I see," said Anderson. "Well, he was getting up in years, of course. I hadn't seen him in some time, as a matter of fact."

"Do you mind telling me the nature of your, er, connection with him, Mr. Anderson?"

"Why, no," said Anderson, sounding a little puzzled, "but since you knew my name I assumed— He'd been buying gold from me for about fifteen years. That's what we deal in—silver, gold, investment diamonds."

Jesse said gently, "Mr. Anderson, will you please stay right in your office and I'll be with you in half an hour. I think we've got things to talk about."

It was a small office building on a secondary main street in that exclusive community. There were several smartly groomed secretaries flitting about a communal office. Individual executive offices were along a side corridor; Anderson's was at the front. Everything was very top quality and quietly elegant. Anderson was no exception; a stocky fair man in an expensively tailored silver-gray suit. He looked at Jesse across his wide oak desk, smiling. "He was a very shrewd man, Mr. Falkenstein, as you probably know. He saw which way the economy is headed. When a government is operating on fiat money, the unbacked paper, it's in deep trouble— there's bound to be a crash of some magnitude sooner or later. And at a time like that, the only assets of any immediate value are the actual specie, gold and silver. Vanderveer had been in the stock market all his life, and he was holding a lot of top-grade paper. He thought—and I won't say whether I agree with him—he thought that the biggies would be shored up, some value still there, and after some bank failures some of those would come back too, but in the meantime he was sinking some large investments into the hard stuff."

"My God, my God, I might have known!" said Jesse. "Why didn't I guess it? But what the hell was he doing with it? Where did he keep it?"

Anderson's confident smile vanished. "You don't mean to tell me you haven't *found*— Well, he took it away with him, of course. You buy gold, you make your own arrangements to store it. You don't mean you didn't know about it? That nobody—"

"Oh, no, no, no," said Jesse, "do I have to get a bulldozer to dig up his whole damned backyard? There is no place left to look for anything in that damned house—"

"He didn't leave any record of where he stored it?" Anderson was appalled. "Good God—at current prices he must have been holding half a million in double eagles and Krugerrands—"

"Oh, my God, that safe-deposit box!" said Jesse. "There's one we haven't been able to get into—" He explained, and Anderson just shut his eyes in brief comment.

"These secretive souls—how big is it?"

"One of the medium-sized ones, why?"

"Then you can forget it," said Anderson. "It wouldn't be big enough to hold it all. I thought the old man had better sense—my God."

"He didn't even give you a hint as to where he was keeping it?"

Anderson gave him a wintry smile. "You don't ask clients loaded questions, Mr. Falkenstein. It's people's own business. Good God, this is a hell of a situation. I can give you a list of exactly what he held, and I can tell you that he told me he was sitting tight on it, the gold he'd never sell. He got a lot at bottom prices before it started up so fast a few years back, and of course there's been fluctuation—he hadn't been buying for a couple of years, but I had a standing order to let him know if it went below a certain price. I—"

"You sent him a postcard the other day." Jesse had just remembered it.

"Right. Gold took a little dive, but I knew it wouldn't stay down long. I couldn't get him on the phone—of course I had no idea he was dead."

"My God, would he have kept it in the house? That's impossible, for God's sake, I've been through everything—"

"People do," said Anderson. "In safes. He never would have a safe in the house, he said somebody always knew and it was just advertising that you had valuables in the place."

"Oh, my dear God," said Jesse, "not another lockbox in the name of Fred Zilch, no, please God—there's no record of another one, of course—"

"I had just mentioned to him that he might find it practical to rent one of these private storage boxes—it's rather a new firm, but the idea is catching on. There are branches all over the county and

up the Coast. You can rent boxes of any size, and unlike the ones
at the bank, you get the only key."

Jesse uttered a heartfelt groan. "Don't ask me to believe there
is another key hidden in that house! Besides, there'd be some
record— Oh, God, would there? We'd better ask at those places—
can you give me the company's address?"

Anderson nodded wordlessly. "I don't know what else to tell
you. He didn't inform anybody?—he didn't leave any—my God.
And I thought he was a shrewd man."

"How did he take delivery?"

"Well, the actual gold comes in here, he'd come to pick it up
and hand over payment—he'd know the exact figure from phone
confirmation, and he always used cashier's checks. The last few
times I saw him, the D.M.V. had stopped him driving, and he
came in a cab—he was in a hurry to pick up his gold and leave."

"How's it packaged?"

"In plastic tubes the diameter of the coins. Oh, my God, when I
think what he was holding!" said Anderson almost in agony. "I
can make you an exact list—but at least three quarters of it is in
double eagles—uncirculated twenty-dollar gold coins—and a good
many rolls of Krugerrands and British sovereigns—at the current
price, sweet Jesus, when I think—"

"How much space might it take up?"

Anderson was holding his head. "Call it two feet by one,
stacked close. That's another reason to hold gold, you know. This
is a hell of a situation for you—my good God, I hope you can
locate it. I really thought the old man had better sense—these
damned secretive lunatics—well, let me know, will you?"

"Just make me up that list, as soon as you can."

"I'll get right on it."

Jesse sat outside the elegant office, behind the wheel of the
Mercedes, and considered this new problem. That forever-foxy
old man playing both ends against the middle!—and he should
have expected this, he really should. But what in the name of God
and all the angels had he done with the lovely shiny gold?

On Tuesday morning Nell was just about to leave for the market when the doorbell rang. She went to answer it, and on the
front porch was a nice-looking elderly woman in a rather old-

fashioned navy-blue tailored suit. She wore rimless glasses and her white hair was done up in an untidy bun very unlike Nell's own neat fat chignon. She began talking as soon as the door opened.

"This is a quite unwarrantable intrusion and I do apologize. But I've just got home, you see, oh, dear, I should introduce myself, I'm Mrs. Frances Lucas. I just got back to California. I've been worried about it for months, ever since I knew she had died, and I just had to come and ask. And I don't even know your name, I'm sorry—"

Nell told her. "But what—"

"You see, I'd gone back to Indianapolis to spend Christmas with my daughter, and I fell on the ice and broke my hip," said Mrs. Lucas earnestly. "I was in the hospital quite a long time, they couldn't get that pin to stay in, you see, and then I had pneumonia, and altogether it was nearly April before I was sitting up and taking notice again—"

"Yes, but what—well, won't you come in?" said Nell with reluctant hospitality.

Mrs. Lucas followed her into the living room, and got out a minute handkerchief to dab her eyes. "Oh, dear, it all looks so *different*—oh, excuse me, it's all very nice, of course, but all Bertha's things gone—you see, Bertha Spicer was one of my oldest friends—"

"Oh, I see," said Nell, enlightened.

"And I never knew when she died! My daughter was worried about me, I'd really been very low, and when Bertha died—it was very sudden, a heart attack, just after Christmas—a mutual friend wrote my daughter, but she was afraid to tell me, that it would be too great a shock. Oh, it was April before she told me Bertha was gone—and I was just heartsick. Well, about Bertha *too,* of course— And that friend, Mary Thompson, can't drive and she lives in Long Beach, so there was no way—and nobody knew the lawyer's name or I'd have written to him—I knew I had it written down somewhere at home, Bertha had told me in case—she was quite alone, you see, no relatives here— And my daughter said I wasn't to come home and live by myself again until I was perfectly well— I've been there all summer—and I just got back on Saturday. And I found the lawyer's name and called him, and he said the estate was settled and the house had been sold—"

"Yes, we bought it in June."

"Oh, Mrs. Falkenstein—" Her faded blue eyes filled with tears. "I just had to come and ask—if anybody had seen—oh, dear, it's Bertha's cat! He was only two years old and just like her child, he ruled the household—his little bed just at the right of the hearth, and—and the house was shut up right away, and the lawyer didn't know about him so he never looked—"

"What kind of a cat, Mrs. Lucas?"

"Oh, he was a beautiful big seal point Siamese with the bluest eyes—"

Nell smiled at her. "Come here and look." She shepherded Mrs. Lucas out to the service porch and opened the back door. On the back porch Athelstane's huge bulk was stretched out comfortably in the pale sun, and the cat was curled between his front paws.

"Why, *there he is!*" cried Mrs. Lucas joyfully. "Oh, and he looks fine! Oh, how could he have—"

"He's been here all the time," said Nell, with awe in her voice. "Only we didn't know. She went away and left him, but he stayed —because it's his house. He must have nearly starved, living on what he could hunt up here—I don't know how he survived. Mrs. Lucas—what's his name?"

"Why, his name is Murteza—it means the lion of God in Arabic —some of the pictures Bertha was painting just before she got him were for a children's book about Sinbad—oh, Mrs. Falkenstein, I'm so thankful to know he's all right! I'm so thankful! You know, I put up a prayer to St. Francis for him every single night."

"And maybe that helped," said Nell. "Maybe it did, Mrs. Lucas. I'm thankful too."

"But he always hated dogs—and that enormous creature out there—"

"Well, it was really Athelstane who found him," said Nell. "Let's have some coffee and I'll tell you all about it."

On Tuesday, Wednesday, and Thursday, Jesse spent all the spare time he had chasing down all the branches of that private storage firm. He had called Dobson to tell him about this latest development, and Dobson said viciously that he was sorry he'd ever heard the name of Vanderveer. It was, of course, necessary to visit all the various depositories, armed with the photograph, in case Vanderveer had used another alias.

But at three o'clock on Thursday afternoon Jesse knew definitely that he hadn't rented space in any of these places; all the various attendants had denied the photograph. There weren't that many of these private depositories, and he wasn't known at any of them.

What the hell had he done with it? What the hell? Jesse would take seven Bible oaths that that gold was nowhere in the house. The backyard—impossible. Even Vanderveer—even if he had been losing his wits, and the experience of Rick Bugotti gave no evidence of that—

He sat in the Mercedes outside the last place he had checked, which was in South Pasadena, and wondered just where to go on this now. And suddenly he thought, I'll bet Howie knew—I'll bet he told Howie. Howard Griffin must have been the one man Vanderveer had trusted absolutely. But—Howie enough like him that he wouldn't trust a woman with a secret? Not his own secret—no reason to tell her, every reason not to. She didn't know anything, obviously, or she'd have spoken up. But she might, just possibly, hold some sort of tenuous clue.

He got to the house in West Hollywood forty minutes later, and Flo Griffin was surprised to see him. "I was just going to have a cup of coffee in front of the fire—such a cold dreary day—it'll be nice to have some company."

And when he told her about this latest hunt, she said incredulously, "*Gold?* My good heavens. My good *heavens.* Could that have been what— Was it something real, then? I thought it might be just cash—Johnny was always a miser—if there was anything to it at all— Could that have been what Howie was talking about?"

"Did he tell you something?" asked Jesse. "About what?"

"Yes—no—I really don't know, Mr. Falkenstein." She stirred dairy creamer into her coffee. "Of course Johnny told him things—and usually he'd never have dreamed of telling me—confidential things between partners, you know the sort of thing. But you see, Howie wasn't really himself—that last couple of weeks. He'd ramble on about something that happened years ago, and then in a minute he'd be talking quite sensibly. You just didn't know. But—I remember now—just a few days before he died, I was with him one afternoon, in his room, and he was going on, just rambling talk, about how Johnny always said, the only safe place for whatever valuables you had was right under your own hand—and how he had a pretty cute hiding place in the house, a place nobody would ever think to look. He said Johnny had fixed it himself years ago, and he was the only one who knew about it. All the same, he was worried, he said, because there were smart burglars around, he'd told Johnny he ought to move it, didn't know if he had—"

"Well," said Jesse.

"But, Mr. Falkenstein, I never thought it really meant anything —I just didn't mention it, because the way Howie was—he could have been talking about something that happened years back, you see? And to tell the truth, even if that were so, I thought Johnny might have been spinning him a tale, Johnny always liked to boast about how clever he was."

"Yes, I see," said Jesse thoughtfully. That house. Again. A pretty cute hiding place. His imagination had deserted him. He simply didn't see how there could be another hiding place in that house. Well, they hadn't taken all the floors up, of course. Or looked up the chimney. Or there was the crawl space above the ceiling. Or—

He yawned and apologized. He'd been doing a lot of driving in the last three days and he was tired. And he was very tired of the house on Kingsley Drive. In any case he couldn't do anything about it tomorrow; he'd be in court most of the day, and there was paper work at the office.

On Saturday night there was a movie being rerun on TV that Nell wanted to see. It began at nine-thirty; but the newest member of the family did not approve late hours and could tell time as well as anybody. Promptly at ten o'clock Murteza proceeded up to bed. When they came up at eleven-thirty he was asleep on the foot of the bed.

"The lion of God—I do like that," said Nell. "Murteza just fits him, of course, because it's his name. I'll bet Miss Spicer always went to bed at ten o'clock every night. I do hope she knows he's all right and happy again."

"I can only say it's lucky we decided to get a king-size bed,"

said Jesse. "Being aware that any cat always runs the house." He
scratched Murteza's ears in passing and the lion of God uttered a
sound of disapproval at being wakened. Athelstane had followed
them up, and now subsided onto his rug at Nell's side of the bed
with a noisy yawn.

"I'll just go check on Davy."

But they were all wakened by the shrill summons of the telephone an unspecified time later. Jesse sat up sleepily and peered at
the bedside clock. It was three-thirty. "What the hell?" he muttered, thrusting the covers back. The phone in here was across the
room. He staggered over there in the dark and got it on the seventh ring. "Yes?"

"I thought you'd want to know," said Clock tersely. "Pete went
on night watch on Monday, and he called me ten minutes ago—the
beat man suspected arson right away and called in. That house on
Kingsley—there are two companies out now, and it looks as if the
whole thing's going to go up."

"Oh, my God."

"It evidently got a good hold inside before anything showed,
and in the middle of the night—I needn't have waked you up, I
suppose, but I thought you'd want to know. You thought there
might still be something there that you missed, didn't you?"

"I don't know," said Jesse. "I really don't know. But if there
was—"

"Past praying for now. I thought you'd be interested."

At 8 A.M., when Jesse parked in front of the place, Clock's
Pontiac was parked just ahead, and Clock was standing in what
had been the drive of the old house. The house was gone, and the
garage; there was nothing but a blackened waterlogged mass of
crumbled charred wood fallen in on itself. All Dulcie's and Marcia's bitter memories, the few possessions Dulcie had had here, the
portable typewriter and the cheap furniture, the old rolltop desk
with its secret drawer, the dishes Mama had saved up for—it was
all gone. He walked up to where Clock was standing. There were
a few people out from the apartment house next door; he saw
Eberhart at the rear of the drive, peering over at the black rubble.

"Probably juveniles out for a Saturday night kick," said Clock
sadly.

"Kind of thing they'd do. I wonder if there was any insurance. I don't think so—I haven't come across any policies."

The nearest door up the apartment-house driveway opened and a man came out, came over to look next door. That would be the kitchen door of the downstairs apartment there; those people, Jesse remembered, had been away somewhere. Somebody had said the name—Lutz.

The man turned and looked at them. He was a nondescript medium-sized man in his forties, with horn-rimmed glasses. "That's quite a mess," he said. They agreed. "You know there was a murder in that place the other day."

"Yes," said Clock, and Jesse introduced himself.

"I was around here asking questions—I was Vanderveer's lawyer. I understand you'd left the day before on a trip."

"No, it was that same day," said Lutz. "Of course we never heard about it till we got back. Is that so? Don't think I ever heard those people's name. Hell of a thing, we got back at five o'clock yesterday, and then get hauled out in the middle of the night, but thank God there wasn't any wind, and it didn't spread. Yeah, we were sure interested to hear that—imagine, right next door. But any city these days—" He left the thought there. "We've been in Florida visiting the wife's mother." After a minute he went on, "Funny sort of people lived there, I guess. The place was usually quiet, you hardly ever saw any comings or goings. This drive right across from our back door, we noticed. Yeah, we left that morning about ten, the plane didn't leave till noon but the wife always likes to be early. It was raining like hell that morning, you know. Reason I happened to notice, somebody came next door then to see those people."

"Oh?" said Jesse.

"That's right. I just happened to notice. The cab came into the drive, easier to load the suitcases from the back door, and I was helping the driver get them into the trunk when this car drove in next door."

"Have you heard much about the murder?" asked Clock.

He shrugged. "Heard the daughter put poison in the coffee at dinner, wasn't it? Just from the lady upstairs—like I say, we just got back yesterday."

"But you saw a car drive in here that morning? On October twentieth?"

"Yeah, and the reason I remember is that I happened to notice the tag—it was funny—one of these vanity license plates, and it was the same name as our best friends—vanity plate with a name on it, you know."

Jesse asked gently, "And what was it?"

"Why, it was Seager. Spelled the same way as Bob and Emmy spell it, too, and I—"

Clock and Jesse looked at each other. "But who the hell—" said Clock.

"Oh, Howie knew," said Jesse. "Howie the only one who did know—and there's a possible witness, and what the hell was the name—Dickey, Adam Dickey."

Clock could ask for a search warrant, because they had an exact description of what they expected to find—Anderson had sent Jesse a list of all those uncirculated coins. But it was Sunday, and it took a while to rout out a judge. It was three-thirty when Clock, Jesse, and Petrovsky—who said he wanted to see the finish of the thing—stood waiting outside an apartment door. It was an old apartment building on Romaine Street, and well-built; the hall was very quiet.

She opened the door, and Clock and Petrovsky held out their badges. She looked at them, the rather tall thin woman with too-golden tinted curls, and her expression didn't change at all. Her skin had a grayish tinge in the harsh cold light of the hall window; it was dark and raining again today.

"Mrs. Patricia Seager?" said Clock formally. "We have a search warrant which allows us to search this apartment. I think you know what we're looking for."

Her eyes moved over his rough-hewn face incuriously, and passed on to Jesse with no sign of recognition. After a long dragging moment she said, "But how could you possibly know? How did you?"

"There was an unexpected witness next door, Mrs. Seager," said Jesse, "who noticed your license plate. He only mentioned it this morning."

She threw her head back and laughed, high and sharp. "The

millionth chance!" she said. "That's funny. That's really very funny. But it's all funny. A comedy of errors."

"And there may be another witness—Mr. Dickey, the temporary patient sharing Mr. Griffin's room just before he died. He might be able to tell us that you spent a lot of time with Mr. Griffin, talking to him—and listening to him."

She looked at him with complete indifference. "Oh, I'll tell you all about it," she said casually. She turned to Clock. "It's all at the back of the wardrobe in the bedroom. I was going to sell it but I thought I'd better wait awhile. It doesn't matter now. Now that I won't get to enjoy it. I was just diagnosed yesterday, the final results came back from the lab—terminal cancer of the liver. So I suppose I can do a last good deed and let that other woman off. Yes, Griffin told me about it. He was getting a little childish, and the effect of so much analgesic medication—after he'd first mentioned something about Johnny's gold, and a secret hiding place, it didn't take much persuasion to get it all out of him when he was half under. All that gold. And the hiding place—a very good hiding place, too. It was a false wall at the back of the shelf in the front hall closet. Just a piece of plyboard cut the right size and wedged in, painted the same color as the wall—about six inches out from the real wall. With things stacked against it, you'd never notice."

"Oh, by God," said Jesse. "Yes, I see—so very simple."

"It wasn't any trouble—I knew it wouldn't be. It just went wrong at the end." She sat down on the couch and lit a cigarette. "I've never had much," she said dreamily. "Worked hard all my life, and nursing can be damned hard work. I had a husband and a boy once, but they were both drowned—on a camping vacation up north, a freak accident. That was ten years ago. And I thought, that old man, with all that gold—what good was he ever going to get out of it? I thought—I'd have something—while I could still enjoy it. That old man had had his life, and I'd heard from Mrs. Griffin that his wife was a hopeless invalid. In my job, you know, death isn't that important. It's a great relief and a release sometimes." A little spasm passed over her face: other deaths than mine, she meant.

"No trouble?" said Clock. He sat down beside her.

"No. I knew what medication his wife was on because once

when I brought Mr. Griffin his capsule, Vanderveer said that was the stuff his wife took. I brought an extra supply along in case there wasn't enough there, but the bottle was nearly full. And of course Vanderveer was always saying that, you're better out of it when you get to be old—not that he meant it—so I thought that would do for the note." She put out her cigarette. "I just called the house and said I was checking on their visiting nurse, I knew there was one coming in because Mrs. Griffin had asked Vanderveer about it once when I was in the room. I know all about that service, of course, and how it works. So I knew what days the woman was coming. I just drove in that morning, thought I'd better leave the car in the garage, and it looked natural because of the rain. I went to the door and explained that I was their new visiting nurse, the schedule had been changed, and I'd come today instead of tomorrow. I was in uniform, and I'd gotten a black wig and used a black pencil on my eyebrows. Vanderveer didn't look twice at me."

Jesse didn't interrupt her to ask what car she drove; it would be a medium-sized tan car like Dulcie's, like Marcia's.

"Neither of them paid any attention to what I was doing, of course. I was just the nurse, coming and going in the house. I warmed up the coffee and made the eggnog—the old woman was pleased at that, a little extra attention—I went to the bathroom for the codeine capsules and dissolved them in the drinks and took them in. The old lady was in bed, I helped her to sit up to drink it. I had a cup of coffee myself, waiting. For them to settle down, pass out. It might take half an hour, forty minutes, before they were unconscious. But I didn't wait quite long enough—that was what made it go wrong. I found the typewriter—I was going to do the note by hand and I was looking for some paper—you see," she explained. "I thought nobody would look into it very thoroughly, they were just two useless old people nobody cared about. But I thought the typewriter would be better, just in case. And I did the note, and brought it out to the living room—too soon. I didn't realize the old man was still conscious—he saw me put it on the mantel, and he managed to stagger up and look at it, and he called me a bitch and grabbed the poker, hit out at me—and before I thought about it I got it away and hit him. I had to stop him then."

"What about the old woman?" asked Jesse.

"Oh, I suppose she heard the noise, I couldn't bother with her—I wanted to finish it and get out, then. Seeing the suicide plan wouldn't work, I threw the note in the fire. I found where the false wall was wedged in, and I got all that gold—it took three trips with my nurse's bag to get it out to the car. I took the piece of plywood too so nobody would find it and know there'd been anything there—and I put all the boxes back on the shelf, so it all looked ordinary. The old woman had knocked herself out falling. I just left her. And that's all, isn't it?" She looked at Clock, and there was an attempt at cool cynicism in her eyes. "It doesn't matter now, I don't suppose you'll have time to bring me to trial. I've got about three months. But it doesn't seem fair—when I nearly got away with it."

And Petrovsky came in from the bedroom with his hands full of round plastic tubes and began to arrange them on the coffee table; through the clear plastic the deep yellow shining color of the heavy gold coins drew all their eyes automatically.

And Jesse said in a remote voice, "Old Jeshu ben Sirah said it a while ago, Mrs. Seager—*Gold hath destroyed many, and perverted the hearts of kings.*"

"Well, at least," said Nell, "that poor woman is out of jail. She sounds like rather a nice woman. Andrew should have listened to you in the first place."

Jesse laughed. They were relaxed in front of the fire, Athelstane asleep at their feet and Murteza dozing on the mantel. "You know, I had a little thought about it. It would be funny if she and Klein got married. I think it'd be a damned good idea. Think they'd get along just fine. As old Jeshu says, *Forsake not a wise and good woman, for her grace is above gold.*"

The lion of God sat up and yawned, leaped lightly down to the arm of the couch, and made for the stairs. "There, it's ten o'clock exactly," said Nell. "I'm going up to read in bed."

Jesse, getting up to follow her, yawned too and thought, but it would be funny—and somehow he had the little hunch that that was exactly what was going to happen.

DeWitt came into the office on the first day of the month with the account book. "And how is your latest client doing—the one who's hung up on telepathy?" asked Jesse idly.

"Who? Oh, the Finch woman. Oh, she's abandoned us—we're all a bunch of frauds. But we got some very evidential material through her, at that. It's funny how things work out," said DeWitt.

And one day in early December, with another rainstorm predicted, and the baby imminently due, Fran and Clock came to dinner. Afterward, with the girls talking obstetrics, Clock said to Jesse, "That indictment got postponed again. The Seager woman. I gather they don't expect her to last long, and the D.A.'s going to save the county the expense of a trial."

"Oh, really. Simplest thing to do in the long run."

"That was a very damned funny business," said Clock. "A complicated business."

"Oh, no, it wasn't so complicated, Andrew," said Jesse soberly. "Not complicated at all when you sort it out. Matter of the workings of human nature. And it had a very simple moral for us, too. *Every man shall be put to his death for his own sins.*"

Lesley Egan is a pseudonym for a popular, very prolific author of mysteries. Her most recent novels are A CHOICE OF CRIMES, MOTIVE IN SHADOW, and LOOK BACK ON DEATH.